Ruthless

Somerset University

Ruby Vincent

Published by Ruby Vincent, 2020.

Chapter One

"Are you really okay with this? This isn't what you planned."

Sofia didn't pause in putting away her makeup. "I have no regrets, Val. This was the right choice."

I eyed her as she whirled around the room, packing up her things.

She certainly looks happy.

"But you turned down your acceptance to Princeton," I said. "You and Zane broke up because you didn't want to do long distance. Somerset is a great school, but it wasn't your first choice."

She threw up her hands, smiling away. "What can you do? Life doesn't follow the perfect plans we make. You learn to adjust and accept what is."

I cracked a smile. Sofia had been spouting a lot of positive sayings at me lately.

"Well, if you're happy, I'm happy," I said.

She stopped throwing things in her suitcase long enough to join me on the bed. "Is it weird that I am? I mean, Dad's heart attack was awful. I was so angry with him for missing my graduation, I called his hotel intending to curse him out, only for the staff to tell us he was in the hospital."

I grabbed her hand, squeezing tightly. That had been a hard day. It was the first time I'd ever seen Madeline cry.

"I couldn't leave while Daddy was recovering," Sofia continued. "It wasn't a hard choice for me. Actually, it wasn't a choice at all. I needed to be here for him, and ever since he came home from the hospital, things have been so different."

"I know." I laughed. "I caught you and Madeline dancing in the kitchen last week to old nineties songs. Your mom has some serious moves. She could give me a run for my money."

"She was hiding a few talents," Sofia said with a chuckle. "We've been working on a scrapbook and it looks amazing because of her. But that's what I'm talking about. Dad's heart attack woke us all up. He got sick alone in a hotel room miles away from his family, and it had been four months since we'd seen each other.

"Now that he's taking it easy, he's home every day. We watch movies in bed and play board games. And Mom and I cook and dance and talk—really talk about stuff. I may have lost Zane and Princeton, but I have my family." She smiled at me. "And I have you. Honestly, I'm excited about starting at Somerset tomorrow. Aren't you?"

I flopped onto my back. "I'm feeling so many things that they bunched up into one twisty ball of emotions. I'm crazy excited about my first day of university. I'm bummed that Jaxson won't be there with us. I'm nervous about Adam's first day of preschool. And there's the ever-constant worry about how I'll manage being a mom, having four boyfriends, living together, and going to college."

Sofia patted my arm. "If anyone can handle all of those things, it's you. Plus, one thing that makes it easier is that Somerset is nothing like Evergreen. If we can survive that place, we can survive anything."

Masquerades, midnight battles, secret societies, and twisted killers flashed through my mind.

"Can't argue with that."

"Good." Sofia shot off the bed. "Now get up, you lazy bum, and help me pack."

She moved back to the vanity to finish clearing it up.

I groaned. "Why are you moving into the dorms again? Somerset is like thirty minutes away."

She gave me a look. "At some point, I will start dating. Not in the near future, but there will come a day when the pieces of my smashed heart put themselves back together. When that happens, your girl will need some privacy to make up for this three-months-and-counting dry spell."

A smirk curled my lips. "I don't have that problem. My longest spell was three days, and it was only that long because Mom and I went away for her birthday."

Sofia held up a finger. "One second." She crossed to the bed, picked up a pillow, and promptly threw it in my face. I tipped off the bed, howling.

"Rubbing your ridiculously hot sex life in my face is beneath you, Valentina Moon."

I peeked over the mattress, grinning. "Nothing is beneath me. Although I am beneath Ryder, Maverick, Ezra, or Jaxson almost every night."

"That's it!" She jumped over the bed.

I took off shrieking.

I didn't like the circumstances that caused Sofia to stay, but I couldn't have been happier about having my best friend with me at Somerset University. A whole new chapter in our lives would begin the next day, and we'd do it together.

EZRA

"How many do you have, Adam?" I plucked his sudsy foot out of the water. "How many toes?"

The toddler pointed at his big toe. "One, two, fwee, four, five!" he cried.

"Only five?" I lifted his right leg. "What about these toes?"

Adam gaped at his other foot like he'd never seen it before. I fell against the tub laughing.

"You're good at this."

I jerked.

Ryder strode into the bathroom and sat on the edge of the tub. "The whole dad thing," he finished.

"I don't know about that," I mumbled. I picked up Adam's towel and held it up. He stood and presented his arms for me to lift him. "The kid is adorable. I like taking care of and playing with him, but it takes more than that to be a dad."

"Does it? What would you and I know about what makes a good dad?"

Ryder couldn't have said that to anyone else without pissing them off. But we were brothers—no, we were closer than brothers. We understood each other.

"Nothing," I replied. "We'd better ask Maverick and Jaxson."

"Ask me what?" Jaxson poked his head into the bathroom. "If you need to do something about those clothes, hair, and shoes? I've only been telling you that every day since I met you, Ezra."

"Fudge off."

Adam giggled. "Fudge off, Jaxson!"

Jaxson shook his head. "Our lady isn't going to be happy that you taught him that."

I tensed. *Shit, he's right.*

"Adam," I began, "don't—"

"Hello? Where's my baby?"

Adam bounced in my hold. Just hearing her voice had that effect on him. It had that effect on all of us. "Mommy!"

Valentina slipped past Jaxson and held her hands out for Adam. He tumbled into them happily.

"There he is." Val snuggled him to her chest and a sweet smile lit her face.

My breath caught. I thought after two years together that the day would come when I'd see this girl and her beauty wouldn't knock me on my back. Thankfully, I was wrong. I'd never get used to Valentina, like I would never get used to staring directly at the sun. I'd love her until it burned me away.

"I hope he wasn't any trouble," she said to us. "And you didn't have to give him his bath. I would've done it."

"Stop saying stuff like that," Ryder replied. "We're not babysitters or roommates. Adam is just as much our responsibility as he is yours."

Ryder's gift for that comment was a soft, lingering kiss from Val.

Now to get me one of those.

Jaxson, Ryder, and I followed her out of the bath and into Adam's room. It still struck me how different this space was. Ryder's old, bland, colorless bedroom had been transformed into Adam's playland. He had everything a kid could want and more: an over-sized toy chest, a drawing corner, colorful furniture, and a huge race-car bed big enough to fit him and Val.

The guys and I had argued about who would share a bedroom with Val for weeks until we decided she wouldn't get her own room at all. Between Jaxson's, Ryder's, Maverick's, Adam's, and my bed, she wasn't hurting for a place to sleep. She loved our idea.

Val placed Adam on his bed and began toweling him off.

"How is Sofia?" I asked. "And her dad?"

"She's great. Super excited about orientation tomorrow. It helps that her dad is doing much better, although he won't be jetting out of the country anytime soon. He's semi-retired and sticking close to home."

"That's good," I said. "What about you? Excited for orientation?"

"Excitement is one of the things I'm feeling." Val held up Adam's shirt. "Arms up."

Adam pouted. "I don't like that one, Mommy."

"We're going to lunch with Grandma Caroline. You have to wear your nice shirt."

"Fudge off!"

"Wha—" Val spun on us, eyes bugged. "What did he just say to me?"

"It was Ezra!"

"Ezra did it!"

Ryder and Jaxson beat it out of the room, ditching me in the line of fire. So much for brothers.

VALENTINA

"You're lucky I forgive you."

"I'm lucky in more ways than one," Ezra returned, slightly out of breath.

I hid my smirk in his neck. I got no small amount of pleasure out of wearing him out. Tonight, I was in Ezra's bed and we'd given the mattress a workout. We didn't have a schedule or anything in terms of whose bed I shared on what night, but if I was with anyone the most, it was Adam. He was at that stage where he wouldn't fall asleep without me, and if he woke up and I wasn't there, he'd call for me.

I didn't mind. Boarding at Evergreen took so many nights away from us, I was happy to fall asleep snuggling with my son. But it did mean I had to work harder to get times like this with my guys.

"What were you saying before you ripped me a new asshole?" Ezra asked. "About excitement being one of the things you're feeling?"

I told him what I talked about with Sofia.

"You don't have to worry, Val," he said. "Caroline, Olivia, and all four of us are here for Adam. We won't let you get overwhelmed juggling school and being a mom."

"I know you won't. You've all been amazing." I shifted and propped my chin on his chest. "I'm mostly excited, though. I'm majoring in psych and minoring in dance. You'll do journalism. Ryder's getting his MBA. Maverick is majoring in computer science. We'll get to learn what we love at a *normal* school with *normal* people. The first day of the rest of our lives starts tomorrow."

He chuckled. "Glad you're not putting too much pressure on it."

I poked him in the side. "Did your dad call today?"

"Yeah. He said good luck and congratulations on getting into Somerset. He also said my gift is in the mail and I should get it this week."

I glanced away.

Ezra cupped my cheek and turned me back. "It's written all over your face, so you might as well say it."

"It's been nineteen years and you two haven't met in person," I blurted. "I don't get why he doesn't quit sending gifts and just put himself on a plane instead."

"You'd have to ask him."

"You should ask him," I replied, softening my tone. "He's your dad. It's not wrong to expect more from him."

"I don't need more from him. I've got you, Adam, those three assholes, and Mom. What else do I need?"

I ran my fingers through his hair, saying nothing. Ezra's dad was a difficult topic. I had to know when to push and when to back away.

I backed off. "I know what you need." I rose up and straddled him. "To make love to me one more time."

A wolfish grin spread across his face. "Not one."

"EZRA, PUT THAT IN THE bathroom. Jaxson, that goes in the kitchen."

"Yes, ma'am."

Sofia laughed. "I appreciate you guys helping me move into my dorm."

"They call this a dorm room?" I spoke up.

Sofia skipped freshman housing and requested a single room in Klein Hall. The space boasted a bedroom, living room, full kitchen, and a walk-in closet. Maverick, Ezra, Ryder, Jaxson, and I came early to help her move in. Her parents were around, but Sofia didn't want her dad to even think of lifting a box.

"Where are the cinderblock walls, dungeon bed, smelly carpet, and furniture they found on the side of the road?" I raised my brows at her. "Are you sure about this, Sof? This isn't the full college experience."

She swatted my arm. "Like you'd know. We are having the full college experience. I'll just be sleeping on silk sheets at night."

"We?"

"Yep. Clubs, parties, and late-night study sessions. We're doing it all." Sofia reached into her purse and pulled out a checklist. An actual checklist. "First, we'll do the meet and greet. Then, register for classes." Her head snapped up. "We're taking the same classes, right?"

"Not the same math or science classes, Miss Chemistry Major, but we could snag English Lit and history together."

She squealed. "This is going to be great—oh, hold on. Put that in the bathroom, Maverick."

Sofia went off after my boyfriend. I dropped my smile. Her checklist filled up the page and I bet there was more on the back. Sofia was throwing herself into activities to take her mind off the breakup and if she needed me to take World History with her or tailgate some game I didn't care about, I'd do it.

We finished putting away her things, said goodbye to Jaxson, and then headed over to the meet and greet. We had a full two days of presentations, touring, and handling little details like getting our pictures taken and setting up our email accounts.

Day one, we mingled with the other incoming freshmen and registered for classes, and after lunch we would check out what the school's clubs and organizations had to offer.

I hooked my arm through Maverick's as we crossed the quad. Somerset's campus was even more gorgeous than I remembered. Red brick buildings surrounded the quad. The green space dipped in the middle and we strode up a gentle incline to get to class. It made the spot feel tucked away amongst the hundreds of students streaming about.

Signs easily led the way to the student union. We walked inside and a girl seated at a table just before the entrance jumped to her feet.

"Freshmen," she called. She waved us over, beaming. "I can always tell. You have that wide-eyed hopeful look."

"I've never had that look in my fucking life," Ryder said under his breath.

Giggling, I shoved his shoulder. He caught my hand and pulled me away from Maverick. I burrowed into his side. The only thing that would have made this better was Jaxson being here too. But higher education wasn't in the cards for my goofball.

"My name is Dior."

Dior was as pretty and unique as her name. She had five studs in each ear and the ends of her brown hair looked like they had been dipped in bright blue ink. It paired well with her blue-framed glasses. "You sign in here, grab your orientation bags, and then head on over to the mixer. We've got plenty of treats for those who were too hyped up on first-day jitters to eat."

If she smiles any wider, I'll see her wisdom teeth.

We signed in and accepted our bags. Sofia tugged me away from Ryder and linked our arms. The student union was the perfect setup. I could see myself dropping in between classes, grabbing a bite from the restaurants, and enjoying it at one of the tables throughout.

We walked into the meet and greet and took in the buffet, high-top tables, and people dressed in blazers and slacks—instead of tanks and move-in jeans.

Sofia tugged on her shorts. "I didn't know we were supposed to dress up," she hissed.

"The email didn't say we had to."

"Don't stress about it. You look cute in that tank top." Maverick kissed my forehead. "Some of the guys from our old football team are here. I've been meaning to hit them up about weekend pickup games."

"Okay."

"I'm going to grab some food," Ryder and Ezra said at the same time. They loped off, leaving me and Sofia alone.

"Look." Sofia pointed at the other side of the room. "Evergreen girls. Want to go over and say hi?"

"Depends. Did they torture me for four years?"

She cringed. "Everyone tortured you, so... yes."

"Pass."

"That's okay," she replied, rebounding fast. "We're here to start over and make new friends. How about those girls over there? They look friendly."

Sofia pointed out a table with three girls dressed in t-shirts and shorts. We made a beeline for them.

"I guess we're not the only ones who didn't get the memo," I said.

The girls glanced up, took one look at us, and burst out laughing.

"Oh my gosh, are we happy to see you," one of them said. "We felt like the biggest idiots for not being in on the secret email that went around."

Another girl rolled her eyes. "Apparently, we should have known to dress our best. This is Somerset University, not my Hicksville state school. Or at least that's what the charming girl kissing up to the dean said."

"We know the type," I replied. "Nice to meet you. I'm Valentina."

"I'm Keily," said eyeroll girl. She kind of resembled Sofia with her auburn hair and delicate features. I'd have to make a joke about her dad spreading his seed worldwide—when he was better, of course.

"I'm Mai," said a girl with short, thick black hair and braces. She reached out to shake our hands.

"Palmer," greeted the girl who first spoke. "The three of us are from Jersey. Where are you guys from?"

"Locals," Sofia replied.

Palmer pulled a face. "Bummer. I was going to say you guys should hang out in our dorm tonight. We're throwing a little let's-avoid-unpacking party."

"I can come. I live on campus."

"I can't come," I confirmed. "My kid's bedtime is nine o'clock, which means it's my bedtime too."

"Oh, you have a baby?" Keily cooed. "How old?"

"He's four."

Her smile twitched. I could practically hear her doing the math in her head.

Sofia came to my rescue as always. "What are you guys majoring in? Maybe we'll have the same classes."

"Pre-med," said Mai.

"Graphic design," Keily added.

"Chemical engineering," Palmer said.

Sofia perked up. "I'm chemistry. I bet our classes overlap."

"Oooh. We should sit together during class registration. Make sure we get the same ones."

Just like that, the five of us hooked up. We got to know each other during the meet and greet and then moved to the building next door to register for classes. Dior and her band of volunteers were helpful, going around the room showing people how to organize their schedules.

"I'm so glad we got the same English class, Val. Did you think about what clubs you want to join? They have dance teams."

Our group followed the crowd going to the quad. The last event of the day was checking out the club booths.

"I don't know if I'll have time," I said. "I read somewhere that it's better to join clubs in your sophomore year after you've learned how to handle your course load."

She shook her head. "That doesn't apply to us. After Evergreen, we can handle anything."

"We couldn't do that anyway," said Palmer. "If we want to be Sallys, we have to pledge as freshmen."

"Sallys?" I repeated.

"It's a sorority."

"No, it's the best sorority," Mai corrected. "The Somerset Sallys go on to be senators, CEOs, pro athletes, and more. They all say they wouldn't have gotten where they are if not for this sorority. Can you imagine the internship opportunities in that alumni network?"

Keily rolled her eyes, but she did it with a smile. "I'm sure the alumni network is awesome. Though I hear it's their parties that are legendary. Girls try to get in just to be sure they'll score an invite."

Palmer raised her hand. "And I'm pledging because these two swore up, down, and sideways I'd regret it if I didn't."

"Of course you would," Keily said. "Being in a sorority is a huge part of the typical college experience."

"Do you hear that, Val?" Sofia asked out of the corner of her mouth. "Typical college experience."

My eyes flared. "No. Oh, no. If I don't have time for a club that is three hours a week, I definitely can't join a sorority."

"Please, Val." She clapped her hands together. "Please, please, please."

The next thing I knew, they were all on me.

"Please," said Palmer. "Think how much fun we'll have."

"Can I at least check out their booth before I decide?"

"Yes!" The four of them jumped up and down like they'd already won.

Keily grabbed my hand. "Come on, we'll find it. The Greek Row booths are near the fountain."

It wasn't hard to find the right one. The sign reading "Are You A Future Sally?" gave it away.

Girls in hot pink tops sporting Greek letters handed out flyers, cookies, and a cup of something that looked perfect on a hot day. Needless to say, they had the largest crowd in front of their booth.

"Val."

I turned as Ryder came up to us. He grabbed my chin and kissed me. "I'm heading out."

"So soon? Did you get a chance to sign up for a club?"

"I'm not joining any of these clubs."

I shot him a teasing smile. "You know, you don't have to be a loner."

"Yes, I do." He kissed me again. "I'm going to pick up Adam from school."

"You are? I thought Caroline wanted to get him."

He shook his head. "She does, but she needs to rest. I'll bring Adam home and she can read to him in bed. She'll like that."

"He will too," I whispered against his lips. "Thank you. I love you."

Caroline and Ryder had been amazing with Adam since the first moment they invited us into their home. Caroline doted on my son. Ninety-nine percent of the toys in his room were items she bought over my protests. Whenever she was well, she surprised us with picnics, shopping trips, you name it. It warmed my heart that she treated him like family.

It also touched me that Caroline was finally comfortable enough to talk to me about what she'd been going through. The bouts of depression didn't shock me. The cancer did. Suddenly her fatigue, loss of appetite, weight loss, and Ryder's protectiveness made sense. I was the dense one who didn't see it sooner.

"Love you." Ryder backed away. "Maverick and Ezra are around here somewhere. Tell them I left."

"I will."

He waved and disappeared around a booth. A hot breath ghosted over my ear.

"*That* is your boyfriend?" asked Keily. "Good job."

"One of them."

"What?"

I clapped. "Why are we all standing around here? Let's meet these Sallys. Their cookies look good if nothing else."

The girls didn't need more prompting. We weaved through the crowd to the front of the booth. A girl in a hot pink top materialized at my side as I reached for a pamphlet.

"Afternoon, ladies. Interested in the Sallys?"

"Yes." Sofia stepped up next to me. "Can you tell us more about you guys?"

"Happy to," she said warmly. "My name is Teagan. I'm a sophomore and a Sally, so I can tell you everything you need to know. First, our Greek name is Zeta Rho Sigma, but around campus we're known as the Somerset Sallys. Our brother fraternity, Nu Alpha Theta, are the Somerset Sams."

Someone bumped my back. I peered behind me and found a few other people pressing in to listen.

"The Sallys and Sams are special because we're not part of the original Somerset Greek houses. We were founded and named in honor of a young heroine who saved our school. In 1984, a student brought a gun on campus."

"A gun?" I cut in. "That's awful. I never heard about it."

She nodded. "The only reason we're not in the history books is because of Sally Hollenbeck. She came out of the bathroom just as the shooter walked past with his gun, heading for a crowded auditorium. She couldn't stand by and do nothing. Sally had a few years of martial arts training under her belt and she used it. They fought, struggling over the gun, and in the midst, it accidentally went off."

The crowd was silent. We all stood spellbound by her story.

"The bullet struck Sally and the gunman took off running into the arms of the campus guards."

"What happened to Sally?" asked Sofia.

"She was rushed to the hospital, where she later died."

A collective sigh of regret passed through the crowd.

"Sally saved countless lives that day," Teagan said. "There is nothing that can truly repay her sacrifice, but every day, we Sallys strive to embody what she taught us about bravery, strength, and intelligence. Our house only accepts girls with a 3.5 GPA or higher. We believe it's our duty to help our community and ask for fifty service hours a semester despite the Greek requirement being ten.

"The Sally house is a great place to live. We have a separate healthy, high-protein meal plan. The girls have the option of sharing or having a single room. And the best part is we have almost daily house bonding activities. Sometimes, these activities take us off campus. Last year, we went horseback riding and did a ropes course.

"Our sorority is unlike any other house because our girls are unlike any other. We're a family that studies together, plays together, and grows together. I won't pretend this will be easy." Teagan's smile swept over us. "Upholding the Sally name takes hard work and commitment, but I can promise you, it pays off in the end. The next four years of your life will be like none other and I can't wait to be a part of them. Join us."

Everyone burst into applause, my crew loudest of all. I could tell they were sold. The funny thing was, Teagan sold me too.

EZRA

I spotted Valentina at the front of a group. They were all hooked on whatever that woman was saying. I pushed through, heading to Valentina.

"Would you like to join?" the woman said to her.

"I think so. What would we have to do?" Val gave her a look. I don't think she knew how fierce a punch her green eyes packed. "There isn't any hazing, is there? Because I'm good to walk away right now."

The woman laughed. "I like you already. To answer your question, first you rush to give all the Greeks a fair shot at you. After rush, if we like you, we'll give you a bid. Once you accept our bid, you'll become a pledge. You spend ten weeks proving you're fit to carry the name Sally, but there will be absolutely no hazing."

Valentina was nodding along.

Is she really interested in this? We talked just last night about all the stuff on her plate.

"Val?"

She turned around. "Hey, love. There you are." Val draped her arms around my shoulders and kissed me like no one was watching. "You guys totally ditched me," she said.

I chuckled. "Don't play. I snuck a peek and saw you with your new friends. It took you ten seconds to replace us."

Val poked my chest. "I could never replace you guys. I don't have the energy to break new boyfriends in."

"You're funny," I deadpanned. "Very funny."

"I love you too," she said with a grin.

"So, what's going on?"

"Sofia, Teagan, and my new friends have talked me into a sorority."

"Perfect," Teagan said, overhearing us. Papers were in her hand in a flash. "You can fill out the registration right now."

"I didn't know that was your thing."

"It'll be fun," a girl that looked kind of like Sofia piped up. This wasn't the place for a private conversation. "Sorority sisters make friends and memories for life."

"Well said," Teagan agreed. "And you can join too. The Somerset Sams would be happy to have you. And we'll be ecstatic to have Valentina."

"Sure. I'll take a registration form."

"Really?" Val asked.

"Why not? You can make great connections in a fraternity. It's also good on a resume."

Val came with me to pick up a registration form from the fraternity. We walked in on one of the guys giving Teagan's speech. I took in the boys wearing green Nu Alpha Theta shirts. They all strained to contain these guys' physiques.

Is this a requirement they're leaving out? You have to be ripped?

One guy crept closer to Val, a smile plastered on his face, and I snaked an arm around her waist. I didn't need these guys getting any ideas.

Val stroked my forearm. "You don't have to be so possessive, baby."

"I know what every straight guy is thinking when he sees you. I do have to be this possessive."

I couldn't see her roll her eyes, but I could sense it.

We left with our forms and went off in search of Maverick. Day one down. Four more to go.

Val and I walked hand in hand, following the curve of the fountain. Water lapped at the rim of the basin, spreading a soft, soothing sound for those listening. On the other side of the booths, a couple of guys threw the football around the quad. Maverick had no trouble sticking out amongst his slighter friends.

"Do you think that kid will ever stop growing? By next week we'll need to heighten the doorframes."

Val threw her head back laughing, revealing her smooth, slender throat. It begged to be kissed, so I did. I felt her hum against my lips.

"I'd love Maverick if he was ten feet tall or ten inches."

I licked a strip up her neck and pressed my lips to her ear. "I'm the one who is ten inches."

A thrill went through me at hearing her suck in a breath. "You don't have to tell me."

"Maverick's busy. We can go to the car and—"

"Ezra. Ezra, over here."

I whipped around. "Mom?"

My mother, Amelia Lennox, the Media Maven, the Times' most influential person, passed under a flying Frisbee and by a couple making out to get to me.

I positioned Valentina in front of me. My imagination had gotten to the car with Valentina before I did.

"Hello, sweetie." She kissed both my cheeks. "How was your first day?"

"Good, Mom, but what are you doing here?"

"I was invited, wasn't I?" She reached into her purse and pulled out an embossed envelope adorned with golden letters announcing Parents' Orientation. Somerset didn't do things by halves.

"You said you weren't going to make it."

"I didn't think I would. We finished taping earlier than expected." A soft smile graced her features as she gazed around. "I was dying to see the old alma mater. You're going to love it here, Ezra."

My human shield stood quiet between us.

"Aren't you going to say hi to Val, Mom?" I asked, jerking my head at my girlfriend.

Mom's mouth formed an "o" of surprise like she just noticed Val was there. "Valentina. Hello."

I waited for Mom to say more. Nothing came.

"Hi, Ms. Lennox," Val said. "Your blouse is cute. Where did you get it?"

Mom stuffed the envelope back in her purse and hitched it up her shoulder. "I don't have time to talk. I just wanted to catch you before you left and remind you about dinner tonight."

"You've called, texted, and messaged me. I haven't forgotten. Why are you being so intense about dinner?"

She winked. "It's because I have a surprise for you. Obviously." Mom leaned in for another kiss. "Bye, sweetie. See you tonight."

She strode off without another word.

"Did you see that?" asked Val. "Amelia acknowledged I exist and spoke two whole words to me. She's thawing."

I stared after Mom, shaking my head. "She might as well be an Arctic iceberg at the rate she's melting. I'll talk to her again tonight."

"Ezra, leave it. She has every right to hate me. I tricked her into thinking you bashed my face in."

"That was years ago. And you only did it because of the Parents' Day video—like I've told her over and over."

Val laid her head on my chest. "She's your mom. Amelia is hard-wired to forgive you. Me, not so much. It's okay. We'll get there eventually."

"You give my mother more understanding than she gives you."

"Because I'm a mom too. If someone let me believe about Adam what I let her think about you, I'd do a lot worse than hit them with the silent treatment."

I held her securely. Valentina Moon was rage and pain, peace and forgiveness, mercy and ruthlessness. It made no sense that she could be all things... but she was.

I was not all things. I was simply one thing.

Val loved me all the same.

Chapter Two

E*zra*   I parked in front of the garage and killed the engine.

"Why am I here again?" asked Ryder.

"Because Val refused to come."

"So, I was your second choice."

"Nope," I replied. "Fifth. Jaxson had work to do, Maverick's ordering textbooks, and Adam has a bedtime."

Ryder cracked a grin. "I can drive my ass back right now, you know."

"You could, but you wouldn't leave me without a buffer."

"Wouldn't I?"

"Get out of the car." I threw open the door to Ryder's side, laughing.

He caught up to me on the cobblestone front path.

"Why do you need a buffer? You and your mom are creepily close."

"This from you? You'd still be breastfeeding if Caroline let you."

I darted to the side and his punch hit empty air. "Watch it."

Putting my hands up in surrender, I explained, "I'm going to talk to Mom about Valentina again. She'll be pissed about it for the rest of dinner, so you can fill in the awkward silence."

"Because I'm known for my conversation."

"Like I said, fifth choice."

I unlocked the door and let us in.

"Mom? Mom, I'm here. Where's my surprise?"

"I think that would be me."

A tall man with hazel eyes and a matching sweater stepped into the front room.

I gaped at him. "Brian?"

"Miss me, little brother?"

"Nope." I ran and seized him in a hug. "Forgot you exist."

We laughed, pounding each other on the back.

"Aw, look at my boys," I heard.

Mom enfolded us in Chanel perfume. She kissed my temple. "And you say I can't keep a secret."

I untangled myself from the group hug. "What are you doing here, Brian? Are Amina and the girls here too?"

He shook his head. "They're visiting her mother in Wyoming. Just me. Hope you're not disappointed."

"You are more bearable with my nieces around."

"Ezra, behave." Mom bopped me upside the head. "We're so happy to see you, sweetie," she said to Brian. "It's been too long since Christmas. I cleared my schedule this week so the three of us can get in some quality time. Speaking of which"—she turned on Ryder—"I love seeing you, dear, but I planned for tonight to be a family dinner."

"Mom," I said. "Ryder is family."

"It's cool," Ryder cut in. "I have some stuff to take care of anyway. I'll come back and pick you up, Ezra."

"No need," said Mom. "Brian or Eddie can take him to your house later." She looked at me. "Or you could spend the night."

"Can't. All my stuff for orientation is back home."

"This is your home."

I pecked Mom on the cheek. "And it always will be."

She smiled, appearing mollified. I learned tact and diplomacy from the very best, and I knew when to use it.

Ryder snagged the keys and headed out. I followed Mom and Brian to the living room to wait for dinner.

Chef Cora was an angel sent by the heavens. Stuffed mushrooms, avocado tuna tapas, and crispy meatballs awaited us on the ottoman. I grabbed the entire tray of mushrooms and set it on my lap. Mom and Brian weren't going to eat it. Both were allergic.

One of the many things they have in common.

There was the hair, the eyes, and the allergy between them and just them. Those were two more traits I didn't share with them.

I watched the two fall into conversation about Brian's kids. His visits always felt like a special occasion for how rare they were. I didn't blame him. He was twenty-nine with a wife, two daughters, and a career as a pilot.

"Are you staying for a week?" I asked.

He reached for a tapa. "A week. Maybe more."

"You can stay for as long as you want, Brian," Mom assured him. "Ezra would love to spend time with you. He started at Somerset today. You can give him tips for navigating university life."

Brian grinned. "My baby brother isn't a baby anymore."

"We're not going to get all sentimental, are we?" I asked.

"Why shouldn't we?" Mom held out her arms for us. "All three of us together. We're going to get all Brady Bunch up in here."

I winced. "Mom, for the love of all the saints, never say 'up in here' again."

"Why?" She did a little wiggle. "I'm hip. I'm cool. I'm sexy."

"Holy hell."

"You know your old mom can still turn an eye with the flip of her skirt."

"Why would you be flipping your skirt?" I cried.

Mom tossed her head back laughing. That was one thing the three of us shared. The curve of our lip and the gleam in our eyes when our words cut someone to size.

Chef Cora saved me twenty minutes later and called us in to dinner. She laid out the food in the small dining room. The space was a little nook, decorated with family photos and a television so Mom could watch the news while we ate—which she flipped on as soon as we sat down.

Brian leaned over at the start of her segment. "Mom says you're still with that girl who has a kid."

"Her name is Valentina and her son is Adam," I corrected. "Yes, we're still together."

"Is it true you and your friends are all...?"

I looked him in the eye. "Val is dating the four of us. I love her, they're my best friends, and I don't have a problem with it. Do you?"

"Whoa, calm down, little brother. I'm not judging." He shot me a disarming smile. "I just want to know all the facts before I meet her. You are going to introduce us, right?"

"I want to. I was thinking the five of us would have dinner." I turned on Mom. Her eyes were on the screen, but her stiff jaw revealed she was listening. "You cleared your schedule this week. Why don't we do Friday?"

She flapped a hand. "We'll see, sweetie. We don't need to plan every second of the week right this minute."

"We'll see" was more than I would have gotten a month ago. Maybe Val was right about her thawing.

The three of us made small talk and kept things light through the rest of dinner. Brian filled us in on what we missed the last few months.

"They changed my route," he said. "I mostly fly to Central America now. Gorgeous, and I have more time at home to spend with the girls and Amina."

"Didn't you and Amina meet on a trip to Costa Rica?" I asked.

"It was crazy. Both of us at the same school for three years and it takes a semester abroad for us to find each other."

"I never thought I'd meet the love of my life while caked in sand and on assignment." Mom stroked my cheek. "But life has a way of putting us where we need to be when we need to be there."

Brian tore off a bite of his breadstick and busied himself chewing. It could have been to avoid having to respond, or maybe he was just hungry. I couldn't tell if it bothered him that she always referred to my father as the love of her life and never his. Not even I knew what to say when Mom spoke about my dad like this.

It was even weirder that I was certain the feeling was mutual. Not once had my father ended a call without asking how my mom was or what she was up to. I'd usually tell him to ask her himself and Mom would disappear into another room with the phone.

No wonder his wife isn't too fond of us.

"I'm thinking about joining a fraternity," I announced, changing the subject. "Bri, you ever heard of the Somerset Sams?"

He whistled. "Setting your sights high, Ezra. When I went to Somerset, they were the hardest frat to get into. Just as hard to stay in it too. The requirements to stay in got stricter every year and they'd boot anyone who didn't make the cut. Didn't stop all the guys from wishing they could be a Sam, though."

"Did you pledge?"

He shook his head. "Older friends warned me off. Somerset is rigorous enough without the added pressure. Also, washing out puts a black mark on your resume that a lot of guys dropped out to get away from. You sure you want to join?"

"I don't wash out," I said simply. "I've got nothing to be worried about."

He chuckled. "Here I was thinking you'd get humbler with age."

"Lennoxes aren't humble."

"Oh?" Mom remarked, lifting a brow. "Aren't we?"

"Weren't you the one bragging about being cool and sexy twenty minutes ago?"

Mom erupted into peals of laughter and we were a beat behind her.

After dinner, Mom's driver took me home. My feet carried me through the house and to the one place I knew she'd be.

I silently pushed open Adam's room. It was dim inside. The only light came from the carousel lamp that cast dancing animals on the walls.

Valentina's lovely voice filled the room, telling the tale of magical forests and the unicorn without a horn. She read as Adam lay spread-eagle next to her—out cold.

"Ready for bed?" I whispered.

She looked up and smiled at me. "I am now."

Val kissed Adam's forehead, whispered something to him, and then joined me in the hall.

"How was dinner?" she asked. "Ryder said the surprise was your brother."

I nodded. "Brian is going to visit for a while. He says he wants to meet you."

"I want to meet him too. If it's okay with you."

"Why wouldn't it be?"

"I don't know. You just... don't really talk about your brother. I wasn't sure if you were on good terms."

I let us into my room and shut the door. "I love the guy. He taught me how to shoot action figures with a slingshot and showed me the best hiding places on a news set. The nannies would lose their minds looking for us."

Val smiled. "But...?"

I heaved a sigh.

Why does this woman know me so well?

"But Brian grew up with his father three states away. He'd visit every summer, but for how long depended on Mom's assignments. Sometimes it was two months. Other times a whole year passed and

I only saw him two weeks out of fifty-two. Plus, he's ten years older than me. He's got his own life."

Val hopped on the bed and spread out on her stomach, kicking her feet in the air. "What's his dad like? And what happened between him and your mom?"

"I dare you to ask her."

She shuddered. "If I did, I bet she'd say more than two words to me... and I wouldn't like any of them. You tell me."

"No can do, coward."

"Ezra," she protested.

"Sorry." She yelped when I leaped on top of her. I flipped her over and pinned her arms above her head. "If you want to know about my mom's affair with her journalism professor, you'll have to ask her."

She gasped. "He was her professor? Scandalous. Now I have to know." Her smile turned wicked. "I have ways to persuade you to give me what I want."

"That's what I was going for."

I cut her giggle off with my kiss.

VALENTINA

"What's your schedule?" asked Maverick.

"English and General Psych on Monday, Wednesday, and Friday. Algebra and biology on Tuesday and Thursday."

Maverick and I cuddled on the couch, picking at bowls of blueberry oatmeal. Ryder's chef cooked extra-healthy meals for Caroline and neither one of us felt right doubling his workload by asking him to prepare separate meals for us.

"We're good people," I said, "but I still hate oatmeal."

Chuckling, Maverick saved me from myself and took the bowl away. He set it on the table and lay back down, resting his head on my stomach. "We'll grab breakfast on campus."

"We have the presentation from the financial aid office, a small group meeting, and a College 101 session. The schedule says we get out early today, so the girls want to scope out Greek Row."

"Why?"

"Rush starts tomorrow and they want to see where they'll be living."

"I like the confidence," he replied. "Ryder and I are getting the rest of the books we need from the campus bookstore. Want to give me your class list? I'll get yours for you."

"How about you come with us instead? You didn't get to hear the reps yesterday, but the Sallys and Sams were pretty impressive. You could rush with Ezra."

His coarse hair tickled my stomach as he shook his head. "I'm taking extra credits this semester and joining the intramural league. I won't have time between that and getting enough Valentina time in."

I ran my hands down his chest. "You can get some time in now."

Maverick's oatmeal was forgotten. We sank into the cushions, mouths connecting hungrily. His tongue dueled mine and claimed my soft moans as a prize.

All of my guys' kisses were different. Ryder kissed me fiercely like my affections were a war he hadn't yet won. Jaxson was teasing and playful. He could make me laugh even in the midst of a liplock. Ezra was all heat and passion. I'd sometimes touch my lips after to feel if they truly burned. And Maverick was sweet and gentle, reducing me to quivering jelly in milliseconds.

How did I get this lucky?

I drew my legs up and wrapped them around his waist. Maverick slipped a hand inside the band of my jeans.

I tore away. "Maverick," I hissed. "We're in the living room. What is with you and fingering me on couches?"

His chuckles rolled out of his chest. "They remind me of the first time I kissed you."

"Well, we'll get one for our bedroom and you can have your way with me on that." I pecked his nose. "We have a kid running around now. We have to behave ourselves."

Maverick hummed. "We have a kid. I love the way that sounds."

I had to kiss him again for that and we came dangerously close to breaking the no-sex-in-living-room rule.

At eight o'clock, Ryder and Ezra found us and we left for orientation. The remaining day of presentations passed in a blur. Reps from the financial aid office shared tips for maintaining a budget that my boys completely ignored. Sofia texted me details of the previous night's party all through the College 101 sessions.

"I can't say I got much out of orientation," I said to Sofia as we left the hall. "I blame you."

She laughed. "Forget that stuff. It was nothing we didn't know or couldn't figure out ourselves. The best thing that's come out of it is you're going to be a Sally with me."

"Don't we have to get in first?"

She didn't seem to hear me. "I can't wait for rush tomorrow. We were talking about the Sallys last night. Wouldn't it be great if all five of us got close, pledged together, and spent the next four years as sorority sisters? My mom is still friends with two of hers. They get lunch whenever they're in town."

I leaned on her shoulder. "As long as the two of us are best friends till our teeth fall out, I don't care who else joins the ride."

Sofia laid her cheek on my head. "That's a given."

"Where are Keily and the others?"

"They ran back to the dorm to change. We'll meet them there."

Sofia and I cut through the sprawling, green campus in the direction of Greek Row. Fall hung heavy in the air. The wind kicked up red and brown leaves and sent them swirling. There was something romantic about autumn. It wasn't just the couples we strolled by, lying on blankets or walking hand in hand.

The slight chill in the air made me want to snuggle. The changing colors bathed the scene in beauty and who didn't want to be with the one they loved when the world was mesmerizing them?

I told Sofia as much.

"You should have been a creative writing major," she mumbled.

I winced. *Why in the hell am I going on about snuggling with the person you love? She and Zane just broke up.*

"Sorry," I said.

Sofia squeezed my arm. We didn't say more about it.

Of course we had talked about her and Zane, and I offered my shoulder and copious amounts of chocolate as she cried over him. Since then, we hadn't gotten into it. Zane and Kai were still my friends on Facebook. Zane certainly looked happy at Princeton in his photos. And Kai and Paisley were the cutest couple NYU had ever seen. I wanted my best friend to find the same happiness here. She deserved it.

Ezra is rushing to become a Sam. I should have him check out the other guys for Sofia. If they're the brother fraternity, we'll hang out a lot. A great guy will be waiting in the wings for when she's ready to date.

"I think it's this street." Sofia pointed ahead of us. "The campus map puts the Zeta Rho Sigma house on the end."

We rounded the street corner and stopped dead.

"Wow," I breathed.

What I knew about Greeks and fraternities could fill a bottle cap, so the string of colonial-style houses up and down both sides of the street threw me. Somerset University was a top school that could afford the best and they gave it to their Greek students.

Sofia tugged my arm. "Come on."

"I thought we were waiting for the girls."

"We can take a quick peek before they get here. The Sally house is on the end. I think I see it."

I let Sofia pull me down the sidewalk.

The street wasn't quiet—far from it. Greeks spilled out of their houses and chilled on lawn chairs, tossed the ball around, or drank from red Solo cups in full display. A car passed us blasting music.

"It's pretty loud," I remarked. "Can't imagine it's any better at night when they throw parties. Do you have to live here if you get in?"

"I don't have to, but it won't be the same if I'm across campus."

"Parties aren't your thing."

"Maybe I need a new thing."

"You don't. You're perfect."

The corner of her mouth curved into a smile. "Have I mentioned lately that I love you?"

I sniffed. "No, and it really started to hurt."

We burst into giggles.

Houses adorned in all the letters of the Greek alphabet passed us by. We continued past the all-day parties to the last two houses in the cul-de-sac. Zeta Rho Sigma and Nu Alpha Theta were immaculate.

"Wow," I said for the second time in ten minutes.

There were no half-drunk students littering the lawn or forgotten Frisbees covering the roof. The Sally and Sam houses looked good enough to show.

Flower pots lined Zeta Rho Sigma's porch banister. A fresh coat of paint added to the home's charm and the mailbox had little blue birds painted on the side.

"I actually could live here," Sofia said. "Look at this place."

"Where is everyone?"

"Inside. In class. Come on. Let's get a closer look."

We walked up the path and onto the front porch. Sofia peered through the window on the left while I took the right. I squinted through the gossamer curtains.

"See anyone?" she asked.

My gaze was met with a living room. It looked cozy. There were two couches, an armchair, beanbag chairs, and popcorn machine in a corner. They all sat in front of an impressive entertainment system.

I saw all of that, but I didn't see a person.

"No one in the living room," I said.

"No one in the kitchen. Do you think they all went out together?"

"...okay..."

"Hold on." I straightened. "I think I heard something out back."

"Of course. They must be in the backyard. Let's go and say hi."

We stepped off the porch and veered around the bushes. I turned the corner.

Someone streaked across my vision. I lurched back and smacked into Sofia. We went down hard.

Teagan stood over us, panting hard. At least, I thought it was Teagan. She looked nothing like the girl I'd seen the day before. Wisps of blonde hair whipped around her face, free from their ponytail. Sweat covered her forehead and soaked her collar.

"I'm sorry, I—" She looked over her shoulder. "I-I have to go." She raced off before I could get a word out.

Sofia and I struggled to our feet. I stood and gave her an arm up.

"Where did she go?" Sofia asked.

I glanced around. That was a good question. I didn't spot Teagan anywhere among the carefree Greeks taking up the street.

"I don't know."

"We can talk to her tomorrow at rush. What's going on back there?"

We crept closer and the voices we had been listening for grew louder. A ten-foot-tall wooden fence also loomed larger.

We put our foreheads on the wood and peered through the gaps.

"Whoa," Sofia said. "I'd run away too."

"One, two, three. Count them down, ladies," said the girl I caught the largest piece of. She stood before a group of girls doing jumping jacks. They all took up the count as ordered.

"Must be exercise time or something," I mumbled. "Think that's mandatory?"

"It'll be good for us if it is."

"Speak for yourself."

My phone buzzed in my pocket.

"That's the girls or my boys. Either way, we should go. Getting caught lurking won't win us a bid."

We scurried off the lawn and returned to the top of the street. A car horn sounded minutes after we arrived.

"Hey, Val. Sofia."

Keily pulled up next to us and climbed out with Mai and Palmer.

"Wow," Palmer said. "Look at this place. Can you imagine living here?"

"I can now," Sofia replied.

EZRA

"I wanted to talk to you last night, but Brian was there. You have to ease up on Val, Mom. I got what I deserved."

"And what about what I deserved?" she shot back. "Did I deserve to cry and worry and believe I failed to raise a good man?"

I bit back a sigh. The tough thing about having a mother who questioned murderers, terrorists, and corrupt politicians for a living was that she was the master of verbal trip-ups.

I drifted farther out of the living room, phone in hand. The guys—Ryder, Maverick, Jaxson, and Adam—were watching a movie while we waited for Val to come home.

"You didn't deserve it, Mom, and Valentina has apologized. Brian is here and she wants to get to know my family. Can we put everything aside at least while he's visiting?"

"I'll think about it," she clipped.

"That's all I ask, my kind, wise, beautiful mother."

"That silver tongue doesn't work on me," she said, sounding faintly amused. "Even when it's true."

The conversation shifted to an easier discussion on what she and Brian had gotten up to that day. Mom took him out to lunch, and after, they swung by a museum. Her voice was laced with excitement like a kid describing their trip to Disneyland.

"He showed me a mountain of photos of my grandbabies," she said. "Brielle is getting so big. You should see her little buck-toothed smile."

"I've seen it. I have met her before."

"Oh, I can't wait until you have kids of your own—but there's no rush on that," she added quickly.

I laughed. "I'm not in a rush. You've got two, maybe three decades to get ready for another baby Lennox."

"Three decades?"

Val stepped in front of me. "I wouldn't bet on that."

She winked and continued on.

I gaped after her. "Mom, I have to call you back."

"Bye, sweetie."

I hung up before she finished her sentence. Surging forward, I snagged Val's arm and pulled her up short.

"What the hell did that mean?" I hissed. "Are you...?" My eyes flicked down to her stomach.

"What?" She followed my gaze. "Oh, Ezra, no," she cried. "I'm not pregnant. I'm also not waiting decades to have your baby. I want more kids, Lennox. Lots of them."

"Lots of them?" I repeated dumbly. "Like three?"

Her lips twisted into a smirk I didn't like. "No, not like three."

"Two."

"You're going down." She rose up and kissed me on the cheek. "Don't look so scared. You'll be a great dad. Look at how amazing you are with Adam."

I tossed my head. "How did we get into this conversation?"

She shrugged. "We're planning a future together, Ezra. We have to get into these conversations."

"Not right now." I slid my hand down her arm and laced our fingers. "Everyone is in the living room watching a movie. Chef made snacks to tide us over till dinner."

Val didn't appear put out by the subject change. "Perfect, I'm starved."

"How was Greek Row?" I asked as we headed to the others.

"What you'd expect from a street full of college students, except for the Sam and Sally houses. They're neat, clean, quiet. And in the back, we saw the Sallys exercising together. Teagan was right about them being different. I want to support Sofia and make the most of Somerset, but I'm not interested in screwing around. Looks like the Sallys aren't either."

"Cool. I'm looking forward to rush."

WHAT THE HELL AM I doing here?

"My father, Senator Worth, feels we need a bigger presence in foreign countries," said the kid on my right. "Ours is a global economy and we need to ensure it runs smoothly. My father, the senator, was speaking to the president about this just last week."

"Your father?" I repeated. "What does he do again?"

"He's a senator," the guy said for the twelfth time in an hour.

Years of practice kept the irritation off my face. I didn't know how it happened, but at some point, I looked up and this group had attached themselves to me.

It was open house on Greek Row. New students flitted in and out of the houses, learning about their potential future frat or sorority. Sofia dragged Val away the minute we stepped out of the car, so I walked into one frat alone and came out with five guys on my tail.

I ducked inside Kappa Lambda Mu and went straight for the bathroom. When I came out, all five were hovering outside of the door.

I keep replaying it in my head, but I still don't get how I ended up standing in a hallway with these guys.

Austin Worth, senator's son. Luca Esposito, diplomat's kid. Miles Beck, son of the CFO of Sunshine Food. Lincoln Iona, son of a hedge fund manager. Colton Trent, son of a pro-athlete-turned-businessman.

I knew who they were. I had to.

I plastered a smile on my face. I had to do that too.

Austin clapped me on the back. "My father would love to sit down with your mom sometime," he said. "Discuss some foreign policy."

"I'm sure she'd be honored," I said smoothly. "I'll let her know and they can set something up."

"If Ms. Lennox is doing a segment on foreign policy, it's my mother she wants to speak to," said Luca.

"I'm certain she'd agree. Send me her contact information and I'll pass it along to my mother."

Luca inclined his head, looking smug. Although, that could have just been his face.

"We're lucky we ran into you, Ezra," Lincoln said. "Somerset isn't what it once was. There're more scholarship students in now." He said "scholarship" like a face model says "chin warts." "Guys like us have to stick together."

I grinned at him.

Stick it in your ass, friend.

Austin's nose wrinkled. "Speaking of which, what are we doing here? The Kappa Lambdas have a 2.9 grade point average and their most famous alum is known for winning the Vegas beer pong tournament. Are you interested in this one?" he asked me.

I shook my head. "My top choice is Nu Alpha Theta."

"Of course it is." Austin shoved Colton's shoulder. "See? What did I tell you? Ezra is a Sam all the way."

Who gave you permission to call me by my first name?

"Let's get out of here, then," Colton returned. "I've heard the Sallys are their sister sorority. We'll meet the ass we'll be tapping for the next four years."

I walked off as the fist-bumping began. Mom taught me how to fake it like the best, but I didn't need to encourage that shit.

The guys caught up to me outside and trailed me to the Sam house. They decided I was their friend today and I'd let them think it. They weren't the first people to think kissing up to me would get them closer to Mom. I'd make the contacts that would help her and shake off the rest. Ezra Lennox, son of the Media Maven. I played this game better than anyone.

VALENTINA

Sofia kept a firm hold on my hand. Bodies crushed in on all sides of us and more people pushed through the door.

"Welcome, ladies," said the girl standing at the foot of the stairs. "My name is Thea, and on behalf of the Sallys, I'd like to say we're all excited to have you here." Thea swept out her hand. "Please, walk around, help yourself to some food, and chat with any Sally you meet."

She clapped and the hold on us was released. Girls streamed in every direction to do as she ordered.

Sofia, Palmer, Mai, Keily, and I followed a group headed toward the kitchen. A veritable feast opened up before us. Bread, cold cuts, salad, fruit, and a taco station covered the kitchen island.

"Nice," said Palmer. "The other houses only had cookies and juice. If I wasn't sold already, I am now."

The girls descended on the food while I veered off into the dining room. It was just as neat and cozy as the other rooms I'd seen. Sisters and hopefuls milled around with champagne flutes filled with apple cider. I knew because I spotted the bottles in the kitchen.

"That's her."

I jumped. Keily had expertly snuck up on me.

She jerked her chin at a pair of girls by the window. "The girl who said we weren't in Hicksville anymore. Why am I not surprised she's here too?"

"Everyone is here," I said. "She could just be checking out all the houses."

"I'd believe that if she wasn't talking to the president with that too-wide smile on her face."

"The president? Which one?"

"The short one."

The president of the Sallys *was* short. The other girl had a head on her at least, but what she lacked in height she made up for in everything else. Her reddish-gold hair fell in gentle waves around a cherubic face. The smile she gifted her companion wasn't too wide. It shone brighter than the chandelier and drew every eye to her.

The girl who insulted Keily flipped her hair over her shoulder. I'd seen that move plenty of times in my years at Evergreen. It packed a double punch of being flirtatious and forcing people to notice the expensive bracelet and earrings you bought with Daddy's credit card.

"Let's go say hi."

Keily moved off without waiting for me to agree.

Don't see why not.

The president's eyes slid off her face as we approached. She held up a finger. "Could you excuse me for a second, Blair? Thank you." She walked over to meet us, hand out. "Hello. Welcome to the Sally house."

Blair spun around, nostrils flaring at us.

"Hi," I said. "I'm Valentina and this is Keily."

"Nice to meet you both. I'm Leighton." She gestured around. "What do you think of us so far?"

Blair didn't leave. She stood at Leighton's back, openly staring.

"I'm impressed," I admitted. "Seems like the Sallys are about more than partying. Not that I have anything against parties, but with a son to raise, I'm all about staying focused and building a better life for him."

Blair's brows shot up at the word "son."

"I completely understand, Valentina, and you're correct. The Sallys work harder than we play. We're about building up every sister into the best version she can be. Where are you two from?"

"I grew up close by in Wakefield."

"I'm from New Jersey," said Keily. "My best friends and I got into Somerset. We're hoping to pledge your sorority."

"And I'm from New York," Blair announced. She planted herself next to Keily. "Blair Davenport of the New York Davenports." Blair looked at me as she said, "I'm a legacy. My mom was a Sally."

"Nice to meet you, Blair," I replied. "I love your earrings."

She blinked. "Uh, thanks."

I turned back to Leighton. "If you're not too busy, I wanted to ask about the requirements for becoming a sister."

"You want to know if the Sallys will take too much time away from your child," she said, hitting it right on the head. "It's true our charter requires more from the sisters than other sororities, but we try to be mindful of everyone's situation. For example, most houses ask members to do their service hours together, while we let you get them done on your own time. How old is your son?"

"Four."

She clapped. "See? You could volunteer at his preschool to complete your hours, or something along those lines. As for the other requirements, I'm sure maintaining a solid GPA is already one of your goals and we only ask that the sisters attend at least two bonding activities a week. We hold so many of those you're able to choose the ones that best fit your schedule."

"My schedule is wide open," Blair threw in. "I have no other commitments."

"That sounds doable," I said. "And it's cool if I can't live in the house?"

"Of course. Some of the sisters are locals and we don't want to force them to pay to stay in the house when they live twenty minutes away."

"I would love to live in the house," said Blair. "It's gorgeous."

Finally, I returned Leighton's smile. Every word assured me that if I had to pledge a sorority, this was the one.

"What kind of bonding activities do you guys do?" Keily asked.

"We have game nights, scavenger hunts, rope courses, and things of that nature. We also exercise together. We have morning and nightly runs that we do as a group. It's safe and a great way to keep yourself accountable."

My mind sparked with a memory. "Oh, yeah. I saw you guys exercising yesterday when we literally ran into Teagan." I peered through the sea of girls. "Is she around? I should apologize."

"Who?"

"Teagan," I repeated.

A tiny crinkle appeared in her forehead. "I'm afraid I don't know a Teagan, but I haven't met all of the potential sisters yet."

"Potential sisters? No, Teagan is a Sally."

"Yeah," Keily spoke up. "She's the one we spoke to at your booth. She told us all about the sorority."

"At our booth?" She shook her head. "I know all of my sisters and we don't have a Teagan—Wait. You must mean Reagan." She pointed over my shoulder. "She's right over there if you want to talk to her."

I looked where she was pointing and landed on a girl with short brown hair and a pierced lip.

"I have to make the rounds," Leighton said. "You keep mingling and make sure the sisters love you. I hope to give you a bid by the end of the week."

"But—" I began.

Leighton was already walking away.

"Teagan must have been a volunteer, not a sister," Keily said. "The five of us *will* be sisters."

"Don't bet on it," said Blair.

Keily pulled a face. "Are you still here?"

"I'm just reminding you that this is the most popular sorority on campus," Blair said, sounding almost nonchalant. "Every freshman girl is rushing this house and most of them have better things to say than 'I'm from Jersey' and 'I got pregnant at fourteen.'"

"I don't know about that," I said lightly. "You haven't seen how cute he is."

She sniffed. "It's friendly advice. Stop wasting your time."

Keily stepped forward until they were nose to nose. "You're the one wasting my time, Blair Bitch. Back off. No one asked for your advice."

Blair didn't flinch. "Blair Bitch? How original. This is what I'm talking about, Jersey. You're not fit to play on this level."

She whipped around and her hair slapped Keily across the face. She strode across the room to Reagan and her smile turned back on.

"Ugh," Keily spat. "And she's most likely going to get in for being a legacy. What do we do?"

"We curse my luck. Only I can make an enemy in ten minutes."

EZRA

"The two fitness sessions are mandatory, but we offer them morning, afternoon, and night."

Mandatory fitness sessions?

The brother, Easton, folded his arms and they bulged beneath his shirt. I wondered if that was on purpose.

He had been with us since we walked through the door. He peeled away from his friends and gave us a personal tour of the Sam house that ended in the backyard. There was a decent-sized pool and enough grass for the guys to toss the ball around. Overall, the house was impressive. My awe mostly stemmed from the fact it was so clean despite being filled with college guys.

"The Sallys are your sister sorority," I said. "What does that mean? How much do we do with them?"

Easton gave me a knowing look. "Your girlfriend is rushing the Sallys, isn't she?"

I nodded.

"No problem, man. Not everyone's motives for joining are pure." He gestured at the house next door. "We were formed under the same charter, so we're about the same things. We'll have sessions together, do joint bonding activities, and host parties. If you both get in, you'll see each other plenty."

"Great," I said, "but she's not my only reason. We've met before, Easton."

He cocked his head. "Have we?"

"Two summers ago. The correspondents' banquet."

Recognition lit his face. "Hold on. You're that Lennox? Good to see you, man." He pumped my hand. "Forgive me. Of course, you're serious. Never met anyone who has it as figured out as you, and the Sams put overachievers to shame."

"Oh, yeah?" Austin clapped my shoulder. "What does our boy have figured out?"

I wouldn't be your fucking boy if I sprang from your loins.

"Attend Somerset University, win one of the 'summer abroad' spots in the Middle East, intern at MMBC in junior year, graduate top of my class, take over Mother's local network to free her up for more assignments abroad, and finally, own a network of my own by thirty-five."

Austin slid off my shoulder. "Damn."

Easton nodding along, looking just as impressed as he had when I told him two years ago. "You're the kind of guy we're looking for, Lennox. Smart. Driven. Willing to do what it takes." He leveled a finger at me. "There's a bid coming your way. Accept it."

Easton strode off, leaving me with my new entourage.

"Wow," said Luca. "You're in."

"We're *all* in," Colton corrected. "These guys know we're the only brothers worth having. So, let's get out of here. I'm starved for real food."

"We can take my Jag," Miles spoke up. "You coming, Ezra?"

"Can't. My girlfriend's waiting for me."

And she was. Valentina waved from the sidewalk as I walked out of the house.

"What did you think?" she asked.

I pulled her in and pressed my lips to her temple. "I think I promised you car sex and have yet to deliver."

She hummed. "I was thinking about that too." Val untucked my shirt and snuck her hand underneath. I closed my eyes as she trailed her finger along the top of my belt.

"But this time I was asking about the frat," she continued.

"I like it. I like it even more because you'll be next door."

Val pressed in closer. "You don't need a frat to be close to me. I'm in your bed every night."

"Not every night, but you will be tonight."

"Why are we still here?"

"We're not."

I grabbed her hand and practically took off running. Val stumbled behind me, giggling her head off. We must have looked obvious to the brothers, sisters, and freshmen watching. Or maybe I just thought that, because it had to be written all over my face how much I wanted this woman.

We threw ourselves in the car and peeled out. The thirty minutes home had never seemed so long.

"It's too far."

Val put her hand on my thigh and squeezed. "So, pull over."

I didn't need to be told twice. Hills, woods, and trees were the main scenery around the university. I veered off onto a side road and drove a good distance from the passing cars. Val unbuckled her seat belt before I killed the engine. She clambered through the seats to the back and I fell on top of her, already scrabbling at her buttons.

The car rocked as we shed our clothes in a frenzy. We sank into the seat, our mouths connected in a whirlwind of clashing tongues. Val always tasted sweet—like chocolates, honey, and cinnamon rolled into one. She laughed when I told her and said those were my favorite things and I was just so loved up I associated them with her. I *was* out of my mind for her, but she was wrong about this.

"Delicious," I whispered.

She smiled, lips swollen, eyes glazed, and my pulse picked up speed.

I kissed along her jaw and continued the trail to her throat. Val arched to give me better access. I stopped and gazed down at her. Val's body was a masterpiece. Every curve and dip crafted for the sole purpose of driving me to distraction.

Val moved her legs between us and placed her feet on my hips. She pushed me back, ripping a growl from my chest. It only made her giggle.

"You'll forgive me."

Val held my gaze as she put her fingers to her collarbone. She traced soft, tiny circles on her rippling flesh, leading down.

I swallowed, trying to pull moisture into my suddenly dry mouth.

She reached her nipples and swirled around the hardened nubs. I tried to lean in, but her pressure was firm. Val pinned me to the door, that tantalizing smirk playing on her lips. She stopped teasing and took hold of the little pebble, tweaking it as soft hisses whispered between her teeth. One breast fell prey to her ministrations while she freed the other to continue her journey down.

Val passed through her light dusting of brown hair and she slipped her fingers inside. She liked to tease me, but she didn't tease herself. She set a quick pace, plunging in and out, and her head fell back as a moan tore from her lips.

I lost it.

Grabbing her ankles, I ripped them from my hips and placed them on my shoulders. Val barely got out a cry before I bent her in half. I wasn't one to watch, which is why she loved to make me. When I had Val to myself, I had to be the one making her moan, worshiping her nipples, making her surrender.

I pulled her fingers out and placed them on my lips. Val bit back a sharp exhalation as I licked every drop of her clean. I was right. Honey and cinnamon.

Chest heaving, Val reached between us and positioned me at her entrance.

I smirked. "There's usually more foreplay than this."

"Fuck foreplay— No, fuck me."

I pushed inside with no more prompting. She melted into the seat, eyes fluttering shut as she opened her body to me fully.

My feet pressed hard into the door. This was one of her favorite positions. Ankles at my ears and me on top of her. I knew that, although she never said it. I knew everything about Val, like where under her ear she liked to be kissed and that if I lifted myself a fraction, I could hit the right—

"Oh, Ezra," she exclaimed. "Yes, right there."

Once I found the spot, I hit it relentlessly. Heat radiated off of us and fogged the windows, plunging us into our own little world. Val's moans reached a crescendo, but she wasn't there yet. I moved her legs down to my waist and lay on top of her.

Tangling my hand in her hair, I brought her lips to mine and pumped faster. Val's cries were near screams. Her pants sucked the air from my lungs and I liked the connection it evoked. We were one body. One person.

All of a sudden, sharp pain blossomed in my back. Her nails dug into me as we both tipped over the edge. I jerked. Ropes of cum poured out of me, filling her up. She whispered in my ear, begging for it, and all I could do was hold on to the bits of my mind not blown apart by pleasure as my body gave into the command.

Boneless, I collapsed on top of her.

Val wrapped her arms around my shoulders and nuzzled me in the crook of her neck.

"Ezra?"

"Yeah?" I croaked.

"Wasn't it just last month that we said we wouldn't have sex in the car anymore?" she asked, sounding amused more than anything.

I rested my head between her breasts and enjoyed her heart fluttering beneath my cheek.

"Here's the thing," I said. "I lied."

Laughter shook her body and I snuggled in tighter. I could stay here like this all day. There was nowhere else I wanted to be.

She patted my arm. "We should go. We have to pick Adam up from school."

Never mind.

VALENTINA

"Pass the salt, please."

Amelia picked up the shaker and placed it in my general vicinity. I shot Ezra a smile as if to say "Progress."

Saturday night brought the dinner we all approached with differing feelings. I was hopeful, Ezra was nervous, and Adam was just happy about life.

The five of us survived hors d'oeuvres and small talk in the sitting room. Meeting Brian rattled my assumptions, because he didn't resemble Ezra. Ezra had dark, piercing eyes while Brian's were a light, soft hazel. Ezra was coiffed hair, sharp angles, polished shoes, and a polite smile that hid his true thoughts. Brian's tousled hair and wrinkled sweater proved he was the laid-back one of the family.

That said, Amelia looked at both of her boys like she couldn't have been prouder.

I sprinkled a bit of salt over my seared scallops. Adam tugged my sleeve.

"Pass the salt, please, Mommy."

I chuckled. Along with not falling asleep without me, he was also at the stage where he copied everything I did.

I pretended to put a little salt on his cheesy chicken casserole.

"I'd love to thank your chef later," I said to Amelia. "I cook for Adam at home because our chef has his hands full. It was nice of her to make something especially for him."

Amelia inclined her head. "I'm sure she'd appreciate it."

"So, Val," Brian spoke up. "You said you always had your mom to help you, but now she's away traveling and taking time for herself. How are you coping being a single mom?"

"I—"

"She's not a single mom," Ezra broke in. "She has me, Ryder, Maverick, and Jaxson."

I took his hand over the table, soothing him.

"I love it," I replied. "Of course, I'm not alone. We have so much love, help, and support, I wake up some days wondering how I got this lucky." I smiled at my baby and got a full-mouthed grin in return. "As for me and Adam, we can't get enough of all this time together. It was impossible not seeing him every day when I went to Evergreen."

"Impossible is the word, Val," said Amelia. "Having to leave Ezra with nannies while I was on assignment or at the studio crushed me. The first few months after he was born, I'd duck into my office during every break to cry."

My grip on Ezra's hand tightened. It was happening. Amelia was talking to me—bonding with me.

"It is hard," I replied. "When he was a baby, I used to come home, put him on my chest, and do nothing but hold him for at least an hour."

She laughed. "I did the same. Ezra spent the rest of the day strapped to me in his baby carrier."

"Mom, you never told me you cried," Ezra said.

"You can't be surprised I missed you."

"I wonder how much crying you did over me."

My smile melted away. Brian's comment hung over our heads, and a silence so thick it was crushing pressed down on us. Even Adam stopped eating.

Amelia set down her fork and looked her eldest in the eye. "I missed you too, Brian. I still do—every day we're apart."

I flicked between their faces. Ezra refused to tell me the whole story, but by now I knew Amelia slept with her college professor, got pregnant with Brian, and made the choice to let his father raise him because she wasn't ready to be a mother. Whatever feelings he had about that choice were valid; I just didn't expect them to leak out at the dinner table.

Mother and son gazed expressionlessly at each other for so long, I considered picking up Adam and stepping out.

A smile broke through his blank face. "I missed you too, Mom," Brian said. "I'm glad we can all be together now."

Amelia reached across the table and took his hand. "Me too."

I released the breath I'd been holding. Sparking a fight between Amelia and Brian would not have earned me points with my kind-of mother-in-law.

Amelia got to her feet. "I'm going to tell Cora we're ready for dessert. Val, come with me."

"Do you need two people to do that?" Ezra asked.

"As a matter of fact, you do."

I followed Amelia through the swinging door that led to the kitchen. Cora leaned over the island sprinkling flakes on something covered in chocolate.

"Chef Cora," I began. "Thank—"

"Come with me."

Amelia seized me and led me past Cora to the door on the opposite end of the kitchen. We stepped out into a hallway. Amelia turned on me, bearing a serious glint in her eye.

"Don't talk," she ordered when I opened my mouth. "Just listen. What you did after the game was wrong. It was dangerous, underhanded, and the slightest bit psychotic. While I acknowledge Ezra behaved no better, you put my relationship with my son in jeopardy and I will never forgive you for that."

Taking a deep breath, I held it as disappointment welled inside. Ezra desperately wanted us to be close, but there was nothing more I could do.

"But..."

I straightened. "But? But what?"

The tight lines around Amelia's eyes relaxed. "But I see how my son looks at you. And I saw how he looked at me all night, silently hoping we'd get along. The kid can hide what he's thinking to everyone but me. It's been two years and I'm willing to give you another chance if you're willing to earn it."

"I am," I said quickly. "One hundred percent, Ms. Lennox."

She flapped a hand. "None of that Ms. Lennox stuff. Now, let's go back or Ezra will come looking for us."

Amelia knew her son well. The two of us walked into the kitchen at the same time Ezra stepped in holding Adam. He checked me up and down like he was searching for bruises.

I ran up to him and kissed the worried furrows on his forehead.

"Everything okay?" he asked.

"Better than okay. Ready for dessert?"

"Actually"—Ezra glanced over his shoulder—"let's take Adam out for ice cream. We can call the guys to meet us. It's been a while since we've done something like this."

Bouncing in his hold, Adam clapped like ice cream was a rare treat instead of one my boyfriends snuck him more than they should. "Yes, Mommy. I want ice cream."

I smoothed back his curls. "I know you do, my love, but Chef Cora made us dessert."

"That's right," the cook spoke up. "It's your favorite, Ezra. Neapolitan cake."

"I'll be back for the leftovers, Cora," he said. "Bye, Mom."

"Bye, sweetie," Amelia replied.

I let him pull me away without protest, but my eyes narrowed on the back of his head.

Something happened.

EZRA

The door swung shut on Mom and Val.

"Did you have to, Brian?" I asked under my breath. "With Val sitting right there?"

"Do what?" Brian pushed his plate away and picked up his napkin. His movements were calm and reserved as he wiped the corners of his mouth.

I glanced at Adam, who was oblivious. "You know what. I wondered how long it would take you to bitch Mom out. Whether you're here for two days or two months, you never miss a chance."

He shrugged. "I was just asking a question, little brother. It was interesting to hear Mom had a problem being separated from her son."

"Look. If you have something you want to say to her, say it. Sit her down and talk about it *alone*."

He finally looked at me. "Do you ever get tired of it? Being her spokesperson, secretary, defender, and clone?"

"No," I bit out.

"Of course not," he replied. "Thanks for the advice, Ezra, but this is between me and Mom."

"Then keep it between you and Mom." I stopped and shook my head. "Or better yet? Let it go. It's been twenty-nine years and she can't go back and change it."

His reply was quick. "She *wouldn't* go back and change it," he hissed. "There's a difference. She chose her career then and she'd do it all over again. You were a victim of it too, but you don't see it."

"What the hell are you talking about?"

"Did you ever think"—Brian glanced at Adam and lowered his voice—"if Mom hadn't been wrapped up in her job, she would have noticed something was wrong when that woman was molesting you?"

My chair toppled over with a crash that startled Adam. He gaped at me, suddenly on my feet. Rage tightened around my neck like a noose. Brian knew not to speak about this to me. That door was closed, locked, and bolted. I loved Valentina more than life itself and even we didn't discuss what happened.

My clenched fist shook. Years of learning to rein in my emotions fell apart at the seams.

"Throwing this in my face to score points against Mom? What the fuck is wrong with you?"

Brian got to his feet. "I'm not blaming her, but deep down, isn't there a reason you didn't tell her sooner?"

I lurched forward.

"Ezra?" a tiny voice spoke up. "What's wrong?"

I froze, breathing hard through my nose. Val wouldn't thank me for fighting in front of Adam and that thought pulled me back. Upsetting them was the last thing I wanted to do.

Staring hard at my brother, I said, "You know you crossed the line, Brian. I'll give you a chance to apologize, but not today. Get your shit together."

I turned my back on him, picked up Adam, and went to be with the part of my family that wasn't fucked up.

Chapter Three

V*alentina*
"Can you believe we got bids?"

Sofia handed me a mug and then hopped on the couch and put her feet on my lap.

Monday had dawned and brought with it twelve new notifications. Eleven were from the girls, all gushing about getting their bids. The final one was from the Sallys, announcing mine. My first official day of university and I walked on campus as a pledge.

Sofia and I had the same general education classes that afternoon: English and General Psychology. Afterward, we were to report to our first day as pledges at six o'clock on the dot.

Meeting up in her dorm for tea, sandwiches, and chatting before the day started was one of the many things I was grateful we could do. Once again, I hated the circumstances, but I loved that she hadn't moved away.

"Honestly, I can't." I paused to blow on the steamy liquid. "That Blair girl had a point. I don't have money or connections. What's my appeal to the best sorority on campus?"

She tapped my belly with her foot. "It's cute how you conveniently forget who your boyfriends are."

"That doesn't make it better. They should want me for me. Not because of who I'm dating."

"Maybe they do, Val. I've been looking into the Sallys. A lot of them go on to do well, but it's not a rich girls' club. Let's just get through pledging. If you're not feeling it, you don't have to join."

I nodded. "You're as wise as you are beautiful, Sofia Lorraine."

"Shut up," she said, laughing.

"I also can't believe you'll have to repack all of this stuff."

Sofia's dorm was amazing. She decorated her bedroom with pictures of us, her family, and the photos of her travels. The living room was my favorite. She hung up pink lights and curtains to match the couch. The area rug was so soft and plush that I loved squidging my toes in it.

"You've seen their rooms. They're even better than this." Sighing, she dropped her head back onto the cushion. "I needed this win, Val. I know it's a small thing, but Evergreen was a nightmare. Not as bad as it was for you," she added quickly. "I can't pretend our experiences were close. It's just I didn't get the best years of my life that I was promised. It'll be different here."

Any lingering reservations about the Sallys evaporated. If my best friend wanted four years of fun, friendship, parties, and studying like regular college students, it wasn't too much to ask. She stuck by me through hell. I'd stick by her.

"Yes, it will be different," I agreed.

We finished lunch and headed out. Professor Bude's English class was on the other side of campus. During our time inside, gray clouds moved in to threaten Somerset with the promise of rain and frigid winds. We drew our coats tighter and picked up the pace. Fat droplets hit the pavement just as we rushed into Classroom Building One.

The auditorium was filling up when we stepped inside.

"Let's sit up front," Sofia said.

We went down to the second row and claimed the two seats on the end. I took out my stowaway tray and set my notebook, pencil, and textbook on top.

"Can I be unbearably cheesy right now and take a selfie of us in our first college class?" I asked.

Sofia held up her phone. "This is why we're best friends. I was literally about to ask you that. Say unbearably cheesy."

Laughing, I stuck my face next to Sofia and cried, "Unbearably cheesy!"

"Maybe a little, but it's also kind of cute."

We twisted around. A guy stood over us, grinning like he meant what he said.

"Do you mind?"

Sofia and I picked up our bags and feet to let him pass. He scooted in and plopped down next to Sofia.

"I'm Logan."

I studied him as he introduced himself to Sofia. Logan was cute. Thick, wavy hair. Blue eyes. Dimples.

He's too cute. The kind of attractive that makes you laugh when people call you ugly because in no universe would it be true.

The kind of attractive that's perfect for Sofia.

"What's your name?"

I shook his hand. "It's Valentina. You can call me Val."

"What are your majors?"

"I'm psychology and she's chemistry."

"With a focus on cosmetics," Sofia added.

Logan lit up. "No way. I'm psych too. Do you have General Psychology after this?"

"We both do," Sofia replied.

Logan leaned back, grinning away. "Guess I'm sticking with you guys."

A bang cut off my reply. A man in a blue blazer and khaki pants strode down the aisle and took his place at the desk in front of the room.

"Good morning, class, and welcome to English Literature." He leveled us with a wide smile. "I'm about to be your favorite professor.

Today, all we have on the docket is a review of the syllabus and the expectations for this class. After that, you're free to go."

"Whoo!"

The class burst into cheers and applause. Professor Bude shook his fists over his shoulders, yukking it up.

"I'm going to like this guy," I said.

"All right, all right," he called. "Let's get to it."

As promised, Bude's teaching assistant passed out the syllabus and we went through it page by page. Online quizzes, assigned reading, one paper due at midterms and another for finals. All in all, it appeared to be a pretty straightforward class. We wrapped up in thirty minutes.

"Get out of here," Bude ordered. "The torture begins on Wednesday."

"We've got an hour to kill until psych." I tossed my things in my bag and hitched it on my shoulder. "Want to grab some coffee?"

Logan grabbed Sofia's backpack as she reached for it. He held it up for her to slip on and her cheeks pinked as she did so.

"Thanks," she mumbled.

"Mind if I join you guys?" he asked. "I'm an out-of-state transplant and I don't know anyone yet."

"Sure," said Sofia.

My bag vibrated with a text. Trailing behind them, I took out my cell and checked the screen.

Jaxson: What are you doing right now?

Me: Going for coffee with Sofia and Logan.

Jaxson: No, you're not.

Me: Excuse me?

Jaxson: You're grabbing coffee with me. Look up.

I raised my head and the saggy-pants, loose-shirted devil waved. Jaxson was posted outside the door, collecting appreciative stares from the girls walking by.

Sofia hugged him. "Hey, Jaxson. I'm guessing you're here to steal Val away."

"You guessed right."

I slid up and took my best friend's place. Jaxson's spicy-sweet enveloped me as he molded me to his chest.

"I'll catch up with you guys in class," I said.

Logan and Sofia waved goodbye. They were deep in conversation by the time they hit the door.

"So, what brings you here, Van Zandt?"

He kissed my forehead. "I've been too busy at the studio. We haven't spent real time together in a week."

We set off out of the building.

"Is your father working you hard?" I said. "Lately, you don't come home until after I put Adam to bed."

"It's crazy over there. We've signed a bunch of new talent and they all want to have their hands held and be coddled through the process—which is now my job. Dad said I'd be his unpaid grunt until I earn my stripes and he wasn't kidding. I'm fetching lunches, stroking egos, and listening to them record the same track fifty times because the sound isn't *rich* enough."

I bumped his shoulder. "But you love it."

Jaxson cracked a smile. "Shit, yeah, I love it. I'm listening to the best music of this generation, Val, and I'm not exaggerating. We'll be playing these bands while our grandkids run around in the backyard."

My heart fluttered. I loved it when he spoke of our future as an inevitability.

"I'm trying to get you in to listen," he continued. "Dad's tightened up the rules since... you know... sophomore year. Outsiders aren't allowed past the lobby and recording devices don't even make it through the door. But don't worry, I'll get you in." Jaxson draped his arm around me and pressed his lips to my ear. "Maybe we'll even finish what we started the first time."

I poked him in the side. "If you're lucky, and you won't get lucky for a while if you never come home. How long are you going to be doing these hours?"

"It won't be forever. Dad is working on hiring a new intern to back me up when I'm stuck in the recording studio or on the road."

"Good, because I need my Jaxson time."

Our stolen hour at the campus coffee shop was short but sweet. We talked, shared a chocolate macchiato, made out in the back booth, and then Jaxson walked me to Classroom Building Two for my final class of the day.

I paused on the bottom step of the building and drew him in for a kiss. "Here's some incentive for you to come home early tonight," I whispered. "There will be a hot, sudsy bubble bath waiting for you if you do."

"Will you be in this hot, sudsy bubble bath?"

"I will."

He hummed, nodding his head. "And in this bubble bath, will I be doing things to you that aren't allowed in pornos?"

"You better be."

"Then I'll be home at eight o'clock, and you'll be naked and wet at eight oh one."

Jaxson peppered my face with kisses until I giggled.

My feet were encased in lead. That's the effort it took to drag myself away from him and go to class.

General Psychology was held in another big auditorium. The room was packed with freshmen on their first day, all sporting that wide-eyed hopeful look Dior mentioned.

Sofia and Logan beckoned me over to their seats in the third row.

A woman stood behind the podium, giving herself away as Professor Trough. She busied herself sorting through papers and setting up the presentation as the last of the class came in.

"Hello, everyone. My name is Professor Trough and this is"—she pressed a button and her presentation appeared on the screen—"General Psychology. If you're in the wrong class, make your exit now."

I might have chuckled, but two guys actually stood up and shuffled out of the room.

"Today is an easy day," she went on. "I'll tell you a little about myself and my background. Afterward, we'll delve into the course requirements. Any questions?"

No one raised their hand.

"Excellent. Let me take this opportunity to introduce you to my teaching assistant, Mason Brown."

A guy in the front row stood and saluted us. Mason was a rather plain package in his gray sweater, simple jeans, and professional haircut. His most charming asset was his smile. He flashed us one and returned to his seat.

"Okay," said Professor Trough. "Let's get started."

An hour later, Sofia, Logan, and I packed up our things to go.

"Wow," Logan said. "And people say college is hard."

Sofia laughed. "Hopefully tomorrow is like this too."

"Our day isn't over yet," I reminded. "It's our first day as pledges."

"Then I'll see you both on Wednesday," said Logan. "Good luck."

I waited until we were outside and halfway to the Sally house to open my mouth.

"So...?"

Sofia made a face. "So what?"

"So, what did you think of Logan?"

"I think he's nice. Why? What should I think?"

"You should think he's a solid candidate for breaking your dry spell."

She tripped up, coming to a stop. "My dry— Val, I've known that guy for exactly four hours. Moving a little fast, aren't we?"

"How long do you need to know a hookup? I saw him sneaking glances at you through both classes. He thinks you're hot."

She rolled her eyes. "And? It's way too soon to think about hooking up with anyone. I'm not even ready to watch romantic comedies."

I put my hands up. "No pressure. I'm Team Sofia all the way. I just want you to be happy."

The line between her brows smoothed. She looked just like her mom when she wrinkled it like that, but I wasn't dumb enough to point that out.

"I am happy," she replied. "Daddy's doing better. Mom and I are going to dinner tonight. And we're going to crush pledging. How could I not be happy?"

She linked our arms and started pulling me. "Stop worrying about me and let's go. We can't be late on the first day."

We picked up the pace. Cutting through the quad, I spotted Ezra ahead of us, going in the same direction. He was surrounded by four guys.

"Sof, look," I spoke up. "See those boys with Ezra? He told me about them."

"Who are they?"

"All sons of people hoping to get their segment on channel forty-eight. They latched on to him to get close to his mom and they don't even bother to hide it."

"I bet he's used to that." She nudged me. "You better get used to it too. You're an official Evergreenian now. Everyone is looking at their neighbor for what they can get and how it'll improve their status. People have tried to use me to get close to Mom since I was three."

"Are you for real?"

"I wish I was kidding."

"But I won't get caught up in it. It's not like my mother owns two news stations and a restaurant."

"And again, I must remind you who your boyfriends are."

I didn't say anything. Her point landed.

Ezra pulled too far ahead of us to catch up. It was okay. I'd see him later.

We found our way to Greek Row and fell in line with the pack of new pledges going to their frats and sororities. Music poured out of a few houses. Apparently, the first day warranted a party. The lights were on in the Sally house, and through the curtains, people flitted in and out of view, but there was no party.

Sofia and I climbed the porch. My hand closed over the knob just as it swung open.

"Hello, new pledges." Reagan, of all people, beamed at us over the threshold. "Please, shoes off and join us in the living room."

We toed our shoes off and pushed them toward the pile. A low murmur of voices floated out of the next room along with a heavenly smell. We walked into the living room and almost a dozen heads snapped up. Three of them Keily's, Mai's, and Palmer's. One of them Blair's.

"Sit," Reagan said. "We'll be with you in a minute."

Mai, Keily, and Palmer squished up tighter to make room for us. I let Sofia sit and perched myself on the edge of the couch.

The aroma came from the yummy spread on the coffee table. Drinks, chocolate chip cookies, banana bread, and other treats.

"I swear, it's like, just ask me to marry you already," I said under my breath. "This wooing is making a girl blush."

Sofia stifled a laugh. "Do all pledges get treated this well?"

"The movies say no."

She picked up a slice of banana bread and handed it to me.

"So, they gave you a bid."

I froze with my mouth half open. Blair eyed me from across the room, her face unreadable.

"Looks like it," I replied.

She wrinkled her nose. "Then we need to talk."

"Do we?"

"Yes," she snapped. "After the meeting. Meet me outside."

"Are you going to beat me up?"

She pulled a face that—annoyingly—made her look cute. "What the hell are you talking about?"

Sofia and a few other girls clapped their hands over their mouths, hiding their amusement.

At least some people think I'm funny.

"Fine," I said aloud. "We'll talk after the meeting."

"As will we."

The room snapped to attention as Leighton strode into the room. She struck me with a smile.

"Speak to me after this, Valentina."

How am I in trouble on the first day?

"Okay."

Leighton turned her attention on the room. Reagan and two other girls fanned out behind her. They were each holding boxes. With those three at her back, the height difference was stark. She wasn't the shortest person in the room, but she didn't have much on the girl who was.

Despite this, Leighton surveyed us like she was ten feet tall. The breath-stealing smile was gone. In its place were a firm set to her lips and serious eyes.

"Hello, ladies," she began. "You are our lucky dozen and I believe that deserves a round of applause."

Blair clapped enthusiastically and the other girls quickly joined in.

"If you were fortunate enough to have syllabus day," Leighton continued, "you'll be happy to know this will be more of the same. The real work starts on Wednesday."

Leighton snapped her fingers and her entourage sprang into action. They went around passing something out. When Reagan got to me, she placed a booklet on my lap titled "Zeta Rho Sigma."

"For the next ten weeks, you'll endure tests, training, studying, and bonding. The Sallys are the best sorority on campus for the simple reason that we seek, cultivate, and acquire the best. At the end of these eight weeks, the best among you will become our sisters," Leighton said. "I wish I could say it will be all twelve of you, but this year, we are only looking to add six new additions to the Sallys."

Whispers broke out among the girls. I wasn't fazed. A part of what made groups like these so popular was their exclusivity.

"I'm sure your next question is: How do I ensure I'm one of them?" Leighton pointed to my lap. "This is the first step. You're holding our charter, history, values, and rules in your hands. This is what makes the Sallys, the Sallys. Study this book like there'll be an exam, because there will be.

"At any time, in or out of the Sally house, sisters will approach you and test you on the information in the book. If you answer incorrectly, you can trust that will count against you. Any questions?"

Palmer raised her hand. "When will you start testing us?"

"You have a one-day grace period. Wednesday, come prepared."

My eyes bugged. I had to be ready to spout this thing by heart after one day?

"One more thing, we're hosting a joint activity with the Sams the weekend after midterms. It'll be a weekend trip to a ranch an hour away. You have to get yourself there, but we arrange a carpool. It's mandatory, so put it in your schedule now. Any questions about that?"

Palmer's hand flew up again. "What are we going to do there?"

Leighton smiled. "It's just a fun boys-versus-girls game we like to do. There's a course, some challenges, and you'll win prizes at the end."

"Sounds fun."

"You all will love it." She clapped. "That's all I have for now. Spend the rest of the hour snacking and getting to know each other. Valentina."

I jumped.

"Can we speak outside?"

Leighton left the room, expecting me to follow. I did.

We stepped out onto the porch and she turned those unreadable orbs on me.

"Please, sit."

We moved over to the deck chairs. The whole of the street spread out before us. Students darted across the pavement going in and out of other houses. Skateboarders chanced their tricks. Girls walked arm in arm talking about what, I'd never know. A flurry of noise and activity, but the silence on this porch was profound.

What could she possibly have to speak to me about already?

Her first sentence went straight through me. "You're probably wondering why we gave you a bid."

"Actually, I am."

She nodded off to the distance. "I can guarantee it's not the reasons you're thinking. Sally Hollenbeck was an incredible person. She stood up when others would have run or hidden away. I like to think that kind of strength is in all of us, that we just need the right circumstances to draw it out."

Leighton's gaze snapped to me. "You've experienced those circumstances. The news of what went on at Evergreen Academy spread through the country like wildfire. Everyone knows what they did... and what you did. *You* stood up when others would have run. You proved yourself a Sally before you ever learned of this house."

I swallowed, forcing my tight throat to unclench. Leighton was correct. Of all the things I thought she'd say, this did not make the list.

"Thank you," I rasped. "I appreciate that."

She inclined her head. "I won't lie to you. There was some push-back due to you having a son. Not because we fault you for being a young mother. We look for sisters who can make the Sallys their priority. Whereas for you, your son will be your first priority."

"Always."

"I expect nothing less. I, for one, see this as a good thing." She pointed over her shoulder. "Half the pledges in there are dreaming of the parties and the gold star on their resumes. They're not serious, but you are. You've learned responsibility, making sacrifices, and putting another's needs before your own. These traits will get you over the finish line, if that's what you want. Is it?"

"It is," I said clearly. "If you know all about me, then you won't be surprised to hear my life hasn't been normal. I want the simple college life with my friends and a community of people who are on my side."

Leaning in, Leighton put her face so close to mine, I tensed. "We are on your side. Sallys are sisters for life. We'll help you, defend you, and be the ones to back you up while others keep their heads down. That's one thing you'll never have to worry about, Valentina. If you become one of us, the Sallys will never abandon you."

I blinked. Leighton didn't.

She fixed on me with an intensity that stirred mixed feelings. I had endured years of the world being against me and she knew it. Leighton reached inside and pulled out everything I wanted but couldn't put into words. There was only one thing I could say.

"I will become one of you. This is the house—the community—for me."

EZRA

"You are expected to know everything in this book by Wednesday. Will that be a problem?"

The other pledges traded looks, uncertainty flashing on their faces like a neon sign. No such emotion crossed my features. A smile hung on my lips as I bobbed my head along with the president. Valentina once called me a mannequin. It stung at the time, but her ability to see through me was what frustrated and captivated me back then. Like a mannequin, people saw what I chose to display and nothing more.

"You're required to do two brother activities a week," the president continued. "This counts as one. You can knock out another by coming on our run, hitting the gym with us, signing up for a study team, or something else on the weekly lists we send out."

His instructions faded into background noise as I studied him. Nu Alpha Theta's president, Aiden Connelly.

Son of Jolene and Robert Connelly, owners of a small but popular local restaurant. No story surrounding those two. Aiden himself got in on a football scholarship and drove Somerset to victory three times. He became the president of the Sams in his junior year. Also, no story, except as a local feel-good piece.

"That's all for now, gentlemen." My interest in him stopped there, but I could see why others would want to get to know him. His height and muscles said jock. His ability to carry a conversation said charm and intelligence. His light dusting of freckles and the dimple in his cheek said attractive. Aiden Connelly was the hometown hero everyone loved.

"Now eat, chill, and do whatever you want for the rest of the hour," he finished.

Aiden walked out of the room, followed by his brother, leaving the pledges to their own devices.

An elbow in my side drew me out of my musings.

"Can you believe this?" Miles asked under his breath. "No way anyone can memorize this entire thing in a day."

Austin leaned around me. "The guys who believe that won't even try, and they'll be weeded out in a week. The Sams are the hardest frat to get into for a reason. They're only taking half of this group, man. Be in the right half."

"Of course, I will," Miles amended quickly. "I got this. I didn't get any homework today, but I know what I'll be doing tonight."

I made no move as they talked over my lap. The only problem with being a mannequin man was that I couldn't tell the hangers-on to fuck off.

But I can get some air.

"Be right back, guys." I heaved myself up and walked out, moving fast in case one of them got it into their head to follow me.

I darted down the hallway between the stairs and the kitchen. There was nothing back here except for a bathroom, the back door, and the entrance under the stairs that led to the basement.

Ducking under the stairs, I leaned against the basement door and released a breath. Only one day to memorize this shit for the random questions they were going to throw at us was crazy. Plus, they wanted another hour of my time on top of the homework I'd been assigned.

No syllabus day for me. My physics professor gave us two chapters to read and my Cultural and Historical Foundations professor wanted three more on top of that. All of this *and* Mom asked me to escort her to a banquet this weekend—which meant brushing up on the attendees. Plus, somewhere in there I needed to carve out time for Val.

There was too much on my plate. Why did I join this frat?

You know why. You joined for Val.

Sighing, I let my head fall back against the wood. My eyes fluttered shut as the truth of it sank in.

Everything I told Valentina the day I signed up was true. The Sams had a great rep, this would look good on my resume, and the opportunities for useful connections were endless, but the truth was that none of that mattered.

My future was guaranteed, so I didn't need a polished resume. Making connections wasn't a problem when people freely approached me looking to get close to Mom. There was nothing the Sams had that I needed. No, I was here because Valentina was right next door and this was something we could do together.

She and Jaxson had their music. They'd blast it in his room and dance around the carpet. Val loved learning about computers from Maverick. And she and Ryder could stay up until sunrise talking about everything.

Val and I danced, talked, and learned from each other, but we didn't have anything that was just ours.

I groaned. *Maybe we can share my massive insecure streak. What the hell am I doing here? I'm piling all this shit on my plate to spend more time with a girl I live with and see every day. I should call it now before the hazing starts.*

"Ezra?"

My eyes snapped open.

"Where did you go, man?"

I bit back a curse. Why couldn't these guys leave me alone?

The sound of heavy footfalls got louder and closer. I could tell it was the whole pack.

Thinking fast, I yanked open the basement door and slipped inside. I closed it without a creak just as one of them appeared in the sliver of the doorjamb.

Turning around, I surveyed my hiding place. I was atop a landing. A steep wooden staircase led down to a concrete floor. I saw nothing else, though dim light floated up the stairs and reached as far as the fifth step.

Through the wood, I heard my name tossed around the hallway. *If dropping out means shaking those guys loose, then my mind is made up. I'll wait here until they give up.*

"...no choice..."

A voice drifted up the stairs and whispered in my ear. I wasn't alone.

"They had to take Teagan."

"Now?"

"Yes. Now."

I frowned. *Who is that? What are they talking about?*

Inching closer, I bent over the edge of the landing and strained to hear. I recognized one of those voices.

"How do we explain it? What do we tell people?" he hissed.

I didn't know that voice, but I sensed his anxiety like it was my own.

"She was Sawyer's girlfriend. We can't pretend like she didn't exist!"

"Keep your fucking voice down."

The command jolted it loose. That was the president of the Sams.

"You don't need to worry," Aiden continued. "They'll tell us what to say. They always do. Besides, Sawyer will be gone soon enough."

Gone? Who is Sawyer? Who is they? And why does the name Teagan sound familiar?

Silently, I placed my foot on the step, and then the next. I needed to get closer.

A heavy fist pounded on the door.

"Ezra?" Austin shouted. "Are you in there?"

I bit my lip hard, penning in a flood of curses.

"Who the hell is that?" Aiden snapped. "Caleb, go tell the pledges the basement is off-limits this week. We can't let them see that."

Let us see what?

"Yes, Aiden."

Footsteps sounded in the small space, approaching the staircase—and me—fast.

Moving faster than I ever had in my life, I ripped open the door and threw myself over the threshold. Austin jumped back, nearly tumbling into Luca and taking them both out.

I grabbed the handle, pretended to close it, and then flung it open again just as Caleb appeared.

"Whoa," I breathed. "What's down here?"

Caleb waved. "Hey, guys. Sorry, but the basement is off-limits." He came up and closed the door behind him. "The board for keeping track of pledge points is down there and we can't have you see it."

"No problem," I said. "Let's go, guys."

The boys gave me matching confused looks, but thankfully, they didn't say anything. We went back to the living room and they descended on the food, all right with their world.

I accepted the soda Austin shoved on me with an automatic thank you. I might as well buckle in. I wasn't going anywhere.

VALENTINA

"This place is like my second home," Helena said. "College is hard. Being away from your family is hard. Adjusting to hardcore studying, partying, and this adulting thing is hard."

Sofia and I chuckled.

The three of us had claimed a spot on the couch with half the loaf of banana bread. Helena was one of the junior sisters, and she'd been cracking us up for the last hour.

"But it's easier when you have people to do it with you," she finished.

Sofia's arms encircled my neck. "I agree. Ready for hardcore partying, studying, and adulting, Val?"

"I guess I'd better be."

Helena patted my knee. "I've got to go. My friends and I are meeting up in the student union. It was great to talk to you guys."

We waved her goodbye.

Sofia got up and took her spot. "So...?"

I raised my brows. "What?"

"What did Leighton want to talk to you about?"

"Oh, that. She just wanted to assure me I got a bid on my own merit. The Sallys like me for me. Not for my boyfriends or best friend. It was cool of her to pull me aside."

She shook me. "You see? I told you."

"In between your reality checks."

"Yes, but I still said it first."

Someone tapped me on the shoulder.

I twisted around and found Blair standing over me.

"I'm leaving."

I made a face. "Okay?"

Blair's lips twisted with impatience. "We were going to talk, remember?"

"Oh. Right." I got to my feet. "Be right back, Sofia."

"Do you want me to go with you?" she asked.

"No, I'm fine."

Blair was already walking off. I pushed through the girls mingling and sharing snacks to follow her out onto the porch. Blair sat on the deck chair I was in only an hour before.

"Here's the thing," she announced before I took a seat. "I didn't believe you or that Palmer girl and her friends would even get in."

"Yeah. We knew that."

She flashed a look and I made a show of buttoning my lip.

"Like I was saying," she continued, "I didn't think you'd get in when I said all of that stuff. But now that you're here, we should try to be friends."

What? I can't have heard that correctly.

"Excuse me?"

She pointed over her shoulder. "The sisters have to live in that house together and they don't want pledges who can't get along with the other girls. They'll cut us rather than deal with three and a half years of drama. I *will* become a Sally. I'm not letting a silly tiff about nothing get in the way."

Blair stuck out her hand. "If you're willing to forget about it, so am I."

I shook with no hesitation.

"I'm more than willing. I want to be friends with everyone. Drama is the last thing my life needs."

"Good." Blair dropped my hand. "Some of the pledges and I are going to have lunch at the Palm Court once a week. Join us."

"I'll try."

She strode off without another word.

I should go too. It's almost dinnertime and Adam will be missing me.

I went inside, said goodbye to Sofia and the girls, and then got in my car to go home.

Adam rushed into my arms the moment I set foot in the living room. From the trays of food and movie streaming on the big screen, he didn't get a chance to miss me that much.

Maverick rose from his seat and kissed me.

"How did it go today?" I asked.

"My classes or Adam's?"

"Both."

"Adam got a sticker for the picture he drew of his house, and I have three chapters to read and a short essay due Wednesday."

"Got any time to cuddle up with me before you get to work?"

He kissed me softly. "I always have time for you."

Adam, Maverick, and I were just sitting down when I heard the front door open. Ezra appeared moments later in the entrance.

"Ezra," I said. "Come sit. Tell us how it went with the Sams."

"That's exactly what I'm going to do. Val, can you come with me to our bedroom, please?"

My smile dimmed. *What's that look on his face?*

"Okay. I'll be right there."

I kissed Adam and passed him over to Maverick. I met Ezra in the hall, taking him in properly. My always-perfect Ezra was less than today. His hair was windswept and sticking up. A look I found cute on him, but that he'd never let slide in public. The biggest giveaway was his untucked shirt.

"Ezra, what's wrong?"

"In our room," he said simply. He took my hand and led me up.

My anxiety heightened with our ascent. Had something happened to his family? Did something happen to mine? Why wouldn't he talk about it in front of Maverick and Adam?

By the time we reached our bedroom, my skin prickled with a thousand needles. I couldn't take any more bad news. Our lives were supposed to be starting over.

Ezra shut the door and I burst.

"What's going on?" I demanded. "I haven't heard from Ryder or Jaxson. Are they okay? Is it your mom? What is—"

"Whoa," he cried. "Slow down, Val. It's nothing like that. No one is hurt."

I let out an audible sigh of relief.

"Well... that I know of."

Stiffening, I said, "What is that supposed to mean?"

Ezra grabbed my shoulders and steered me to the bed. He sat us both down.

"I overheard something strange in the Sam house today. At first, I brushed it off, but as I kept thinking about it, I got the feeling something was wrong." He squeezed my shoulders. "Do you remember the girl from the Sally booth? Wasn't her name Teagan?"

"Yes," I said slowly. "Why?"

"At least three guys were in the basement, taking about a Teagan. One of them was the president."

Basement? President?

"The president, Aiden—" He tossed his head. "I can't be sure, but it sounded like he said they had to take her. They had to take Teagan."

"Take Teagan?" I repeated. "Who is 'they'? Take her where?"

"I don't know. You tell me, Val. You were in the Sally house. Did you speak to Teagan?"

"No, but... I tried." Fragments of my conversation with the president came back to me. "I wanted to talk to her during rush. Leighton said she didn't know who I was talking about and there was no sister named Teagan."

Ezra's brows snapped together. "Val, that's not true."

"Why? She could have been a volunteer just helping out for the day."

Ezra shook his head, even harder that time. "Val, when she spoke about the Sallys she used the word 'we.' *We* want you. *We'll* be lucky to have you. Why would she have said that if she was just a volunteer?"

"Because she— She could have—" My explanations sputtered to a stop. "That is weird, isn't it?"

"It gets weirder. One of the guys was really nervous about it. He kept saying 'What do we tell people?' and 'We can't pretend she doesn't exist.'"

"Pretend she doesn't exist?"

He nodded, face grave. "Then of all the things to reply, Aiden goes with *they* will tell them what to say."

"They will tell them what to say?"

I was repeating things like a dimwit. I knew I was doing it and that I should stop, but my brain wasn't supplying another response. What was Ezra telling me right now?

"Val, it gets even worse," he said. "The nervous guy brought up her boyfriend and Aiden brushed it off saying *he would be gone too.*"

"He would be gone—" *Stop repeating everything!* "What does that mean?" I cried. "Why would he say something like that?"

He threw out his hands. "That's what I kept asking myself. The conversation was strange any way you look at it. I couldn't think of any reasonable explanation for it, so I asked one of the brothers if they knew a Sawyer and he pointed down the flipping hall."

"Sawyer is in the fraternity?"

He nodded. "I can't be certain it's the same Sawyer they were talking about, but it's not that common a name."

I pressed my fingers into my temples, trying to make sense of what he was telling me.

"Did you talk to him?" I asked. "Sawyer."

Ezra blew out a breath. "I tried. I asked if he had a girlfriend named Teagan and he said he wasn't dating anyone. I asked if he knew any Teagan, and again, no. I finally asked if he was going somewhere—leaving the house or the school. The guy looked at me like I was nuts and walked off."

"Maybe they were talking about a different guy."

"But talking about what?" he pressed. "What did it mean that he would be gone soon? And what the hell happened to Teagan?"

"Okay, just hold on, baby." I cupped his cheek, gently stroking his cheekbone. "We don't know that anything happened. There are a lot of sisters in Zeta Rho Sigma. Leighton could have forgotten her. Let me ask the other girls who were manning the booth that day where she is."

I felt him untense beneath my palm. "You're right. Of course, you're right. This is why I came to you." He pulled my hand away and kissed it. "But you were there today. Did you see her?"

I shook my head. "But she could have been in class, out with friends, on a date, who knows. What those guys said could mean so many things," I continued. "After Evergreen, we're hardwired to think there's a dark meaning behind every twitch and wink. Let's not jump to conclusions."

He laughed mirthlessly. "You have a point. This is Somerset, not Evergreen. There is an explanation and Teagan and the right Sawyer will give it to us."

"That's right." I stood and pulled him up with me. "Now, let's go downstairs, eat, and get started on our homework. I've got an entire charter to memorize by Wednesday."

A ghost of a smile crossed his lips. "They're making you do that too?"

"Yep. It's going to be a long night."

Chapter Four

*V*alentina

It wasn't a long night. It was a long three weeks.

I thought reading the Sally handbook five times in two days was tough. Who was I kidding? That was nothing compared to four classes, daily homework, taking care of Adam, weekly lunches with Blair, four boyfriends, and *bonding* activities.

"Let's go, ladies! Pick it up!"

Sweat dripped down my back and soaked the band of my shorts. I sucked in hard, desperate breaths that burned my lungs.

"How much... farther?" I wheezed.

Sofia stumbled along next to me. Dark, reddish strands stuck to her damp forehead. Her face flushed a deep cherry red that concerned me.

"We're not even c-close," she said. "We have a whole mile left!"

I almost threw myself on the ground right then.

Sofia and I stupidly signed up for morning runs to knock out a half hour of bonding. It seemed like such a perfect idea at the time. We didn't have early morning classes, getting in shape would do us good, and it'd be a great time to chat and get to know everyone.

What fucking fools we were.

No one told us the morning run was a proper, full-out sprint around the campus with the hounds of hell—I mean, Reagan and Patricia—at our backs shouting at us to pick up the pace every time we fell behind. The sisters also forgot to mention we had to run three miles.

Sofia and I wanted to quit a mile into our first run, but Leighton made it clear quitting would not reflect favorably in our points.

"Are you the type of women who back out of your commitments?" she said to us. "Because women like that don't embody what we stand for."

"Just give it time," Sofia called to me. "We'll get used to it."

"Sof, I cannot deal with your positivity right now. I'm literally dying," I shrieked.

Palmer laughed—or I think she laughed. She could have been gasping for air.

"One more mile, Val. Mai," she said. "We can do it."

By some miracle, we did do it. Our group of thirteen crossed the quad and huffed the last few feet to our finish line, the fountain's rim. Sofia and the other five pledges collapsed on the rim, sucking in deep lungfuls of air.

I didn't stop.

I hit the rim, climbed up, and tipped over the edge. Blessedly cool water enveloped me to shouts and exclamations. Three blissful seconds of peace awaited me at the basin of the pool. I enjoyed every bit of it until a strong grip on my arms pulled me up.

Leighton deposited me on the rim. "Stop messing around, Val, and do your cooldown exercises."

"Yes, Madame President," I mumbled.

She winked and moved on to Blair. I rubbed the place where she grabbed me when her back was turned.

"Wow, that girl is strong."

Sofia, the only one who heard, hip-checked me. "You're telling me. I went to the gym with her last week and you should see what she bench-presses. Don't let her size fool you."

Sofia and I did our cooldown under Reagan's watchful gaze. When she was satisfied, we were released.

"I wish Teagan's replacement was as nice as she was."

"Teagan wasn't replaced," Sofia reminded me. "She moved back home because her mom was sick. Something I completely understand. Still, it must have been a relief to Ezra. From the way he described the conversation, it sounded creepy."

"It did. I'm glad there was a reasonable explanation."

After my talk with Ezra, I asked the Sallys who had manned the booth that day what happened to Teagan and they explained that she went home. They even showed me Teagan's Facebook page and the photo of her curled up in a hospital bed with her mom. Leighton not knowing her also had a simple explanation.

Teagan Kainer was actually Elizabeth Teagan Kainer and Leighton never got close enough to the sophomore to remember she went by her middle name. And after three weeks passed and Sawyer was still kicking around the Sam house, Ezra accepted that he overreacted.

"Do you mind if I shower in your dorm?"

"You don't have to ask," she replied.

The two of us went back to her place, cleaned up, and then headed out to class. Our day was far from over.

Fall had Somerset in its grip. The wind shook loose colorful leaves like raindrops. I put out my hand, letting them fall on my palm.

"Sof, can I say something?"

"What's up?"

I chewed my lip, hesitating. *She's your best friend. If you can't talk to her, who can you talk to?*

"Pledging the Sallys is nothing like I expected," I rushed out. "All this running, pop-up questions on the charter, and Blair taking the macarons off my plate and replacing them with cucumber sandwiches."

"Ugh. Did you talk to her about that?"

"Twice. Both times she said we're close now and friends don't let friends cheat."

"Cheat at what?"

"The diet I didn't know I was on."

Sofia clapped her hand over her mouth, but not quick enough.

"Don't laugh at me," I cried. "I can't shake the gremlin loose. She's so determined to become a Sally, she is *making* everyone be her friend by any means necessary. She got my number somehow and she texts me random trivia about her life. Palmer said she showed up at her dorm the other day for a surprise shopping trip."

Sofia was full-blown laughing now.

"It's because you're obviously impervious to her charms, so she's working harder," she said. "This is better than having an enemy, though, right?"

"I haven't decided yet."

Linking our arms, she drew me in and rested her head on my shoulder. "As for the other stuff, this isn't what I expected either. It feels like we have five classes instead of four. I've started running at night to get more practice in and I read the charter every night to make sure it's fresh. It's why I can't wait for the Close Enough party next weekend. We're overdue for some fun."

I laughed. "The Close Enough party. Seriously, who thought of that?"

"No clue, but I'm all for Halloween a month early."

Halloween a month early meant I had to source five costumes, a sitter, and spare time to decorate the Sally house. All the same, I was excited. Next weekend, the Sallys and Sams were throwing a joint party for all who could come. Just from hearing Leighton talk about it, I knew it would be epic.

The Sallys would have real food, dance music, and drinking games. The Sams were buying the candy, playing rap and EDM, and providing a pool. People would flow from house to house as they pleased, decked out in costumes.

Together we walked through the student union for the building right behind, Classroom Building One. As we climbed the steps, I noticed someone waiting for us.

Logan held up his treats. "Hey, Sofia. Hope you're hungry."

"Oooh. What did you get me?"

"Cinnamon twists and an Irish crème latte."

Logan and Sofia had taken up this game over the last few weeks. It started with her buying a dozen donuts and sharing them with us, and ever since, they'd taken turns bringing each other treats.

"And nothing for me," I said as Sofia nibbled on a twist.

Logan laughed. "Do you recall two weeks ago when I gave you a cupcake and the giant you were with threatened to squeeze my head like a pimple?"

"Maverick didn't say a word," I protested.

He leveled two fingers at his face. "It was all in the eyes, Val. He didn't have to say a word. Half of your boyfriends are twice my size, and the other half glare at me like they can take me anyway."

Laughter bubbled out of me. "They are not that bad."

"They are that bad." Logan sidled up to me, made a show of looking around, and dropped his voice. "But I got you a muffin anyway. Tell no one."

This close I breathed in his musky scent. He slipped the little package into my hand like we were doing a drug deal.

I shook my head at him as he walked off with Sofia. He was incredibly goofy, bordering on dorky, but he made Sofia laugh. There was also the fact that he was hot.

Sofia's giggles floated over their heads and filled the hall.

She wasn't ready for a relationship just yet. When she was, I had an inkling a date with Logan wouldn't be far behind.

The three of us grabbed our usual seats up close and personal to Professor Bude. I listened to snippets of Logan and Sofia's conversation as I got out my notes.

"How is your dad doing?"

"He's feeling a lot better," she replied. "Dad and Mom have been taking walks around the property to keep him moving. Mom says it's great spending time just the two of them and talking about something other than work."

"It's awesome you and your mom are getting closer."

She groaned. "Yesterday Mom told me she can't wait until his heart is healthy enough for sex because she has needs. We have reached too close."

The two of them cracked up.

"All right, front row," Bude spoke up. "Settle down or share the joke."

Sofia and Logan fell silent.

"Hmm. For some reason, no one picks the latter option," he said. "I'm starting to think it's because I'm the butt of the joke."

Now we did laugh at him. Bude was a good guy and a great professor. I was grateful three times a week that I chose his class and not the taskmaster that Ezra had to pick to fit into his schedule.

After an hour dissecting story structure and how it applied to classic literature, the three of us packed up our things and left.

We stepped outside to fresh air and beaming sunlight. In unison, we turned our heads up to the sun like worshipping sunflowers.

"Want to go back to my dorm, Val?" asked Sofia. "We have an hour to kill and I'd rather do it on my couch in front of the television."

"Yes to that."

"May I join you guys?" Logan asked.

"Sure." Sofia bumped into him. "As a thank you for the twists, I'll let you in my cookie stash."

I sucked my lips between my teeth and bit down hard. Grinning like a loon would embarrass them both. I'd keep it inside how cute I thought the two of them were.

"Yo, Logan."

We turned as a guy in a leather jacket and ripped jeans jogged up the steps. He looked straight at me and threw me a nod like we were old friends.

"Shawn," Logan said. "What's up? Make it home okay last night?"

Shawn smirked. It looked good on him. So did the worn clothes and beat-up sneakers. Between the piercings, tattoo poking out of his shirt, and the up-to-no-good glint in his eye, he was firmly on the hot side.

"I made it to *a* home last night, but it wasn't mine," he said in a slight accent I couldn't place. He grabbed Logan's hand without waiting for him to put it up and thumped their chests together. "Introduce me to these lovely ladies."

"This is Valentina and Sofia."

"Sofia." He turned the name over in his mouth, seeing how it tasted. "I danced to a song about you last night, Sofia. Sofia." Shawn threw his head back. "So-fi-a-a-a-ah!"

I edged away. Was this guy for real?

Shawn stopped singing and flashed her a grin. "I bet that song was made for you."

"You mean the song by Alvaro Soler where Sofia broke his heart and he's singing about being better off without her?"

That wiped the smile off his face. "Is that what the guy's saying? Damn. Why does he sound so happy about it?"

Logan rolled his eyes. "It might have helped your flirting attempt if you had looked up the English translation to that song."

Shawn's grin came back like it had never left. "I know that for next time." He tipped an imaginary cap to us. "Have a good day, ladies. I've got to get to class. See you, Logan."

"Nice guy," I said after the door closed on him.

"He is," Logan said. "Shawn is in my astronomy study group. He got me a B on the last test. He's a smart guy."

"Shall we go?" Sofia asked.

"Let's do it."

We took the party to Sofia's room. Logan whistled as his eyes swept over the space.

"Um, yeah. This is way nicer than my dorm."

"You should see her bedroom at home," I piped up.

"That would be cool."

Eyes huge, Sofia mouthed something to me behind his back. Probably that she was going to kill me.

I hid a smile as I flipped over on the couch and left them to talk.

EZRA

"Mom?"

I wandered through the hall, calling for the woman who birthed me.

We need an intercom system in this place. Better than me shouting all over the house for her.

I reached her bedroom and peeked inside. The room was immaculate as always. The bed made, the nightstand organized, clothes tucked away in the closet, and her awards lined up on the mantle. The only thing that could be termed as cluttered was her picture wall. Dozens upon dozens of photos covered the wall that shared her television. Photos of her through the years. Photos of me and Brian. Photos of the people she'd met, interviewed, written about, or exposed. The life of Amelia Lennox was on that wall.

"Mom?"

No one answered.

I pulled out my phone and dialed Cora. She could always be relied upon to answer on the first ring. Today was no different.

"Ezra, what's wrong, dear?"

"I can't find Mom and I'm looking at her phone on the nightstand. Have you seen her?"

"She's down here, love. In the breakfast nook."

Ducking inside, I grabbed Mom's phone and then went back the way I came. "You're the best, Cora. If I wasn't taken, I'd run away with you."

She harrumphed. "You'd run into two hundred pounds of my husband if you tried, cheeky boy. Now, come and get your mother. You have to leave soon."

I wound through the halls of my home, collecting memories along the way. The hardwood floor that bore my tiny footprints as I learned to walk. The living room where Mom gave me elocution lessons. The jungle gym out back that Jaxson, Maverick, Ryder, and I climbed on and pushed each other off of.

It's amazing we didn't break our necks.

I ran my fingers along the molding. I used to picture raising my kid in this house and giving them all the same memories. Who knew I'd end up in the home Ryder never invited us to, the four of us together with Valentina? Any version of the future with her in it was vastly better than the ones I'd imagined.

Mom and Cora looked up from their tasks when I walked into the kitchen. Cora waved with her steak knife.

"There you are, sweetie," said Mom. She shut her laptop and pushed it away. "Ready to go? I got the three of us a reservation at Bianchi's."

"My favorite," I replied. "But I still don't understand why was I summoned for lunch."

"Do I need a reason to take my favorite boys out to lunch?"

"You have a reason for everything, Mother."

Laughing, she swatted my arm. "Don't be fresh. I'm not nearly so calculating."

I wisely didn't reply to that and handed her the phone.

"Thank you, Ezra. Can you go and find your brother too? We have to leave soon so you'll make it back in time for class."

"On it."

I jogged out of the kitchen and veered left, away from Mom's and my former quarters and toward the guest room. With Cora having her own little house in the back, Brian pretty much had this part of the house to himself.

Brian's door was closed but not locked. I inched it open, peering through the crack. The shower running told me where he was.

"Brian." I went up and pounded on the door. "Hurry up, man. We'll miss our reservations."

"We... need reservations," he called through the wood. "Burger King..."

The shower did its best to drown him out but I got the gist. We didn't need reservations. Burger King would do just fine.

"Wake up from that dream. You know Mom hasn't eaten a fry in nineteen years," I shouted back. "And she still blames me and the pregnancy cravings for breaking her diet."

I couldn't tell if he said something, but I definitely heard him laugh.

A raucous noise startled me. Brian's cell belted some horrible ringtone, most likely that death metal crap he was into. Not for the first time I wondered how two brothers could be so different.

"—answer it," Brian said.

I vaulted over his unmade bed and snagged the phone off the dresser.

"Hello?"

"It's about time," the person hissed. "I've been calling you for weeks."

I frowned. "Who is this?"

"Don't fucking give me that, Brian!"

The guy's snarl raised my hackles. What the hell was he so mad about?

"You said you were leaving to sort some things out and then you'd be back in a week," he bit out. "We're supposed to fly this stuff out in two days."

"Fly what stuff out? Who the fuck is this?"

"Bri—wait. Who the fuck are you?"

The bathroom door banged open. "Ezra, what are you doing?!"

I didn't have a chance to reply before the phone was ripped out of my hand. The snarly guy's shouts were cut off with a click.

"What is wrong with you?" Brian snapped. Water dripped along the harsh twist of his mouth.

"What are you talking about? You told me to answer it."

His eyes flashed. "I said *don't* answer it, Ezra. You and Mom think you have a right to know everyone's fucking business."

Anger licked at my calm. "Relax," I said through gritted teeth. "It was an honest mistake. It won't happen again."

"It better not."

The mask cracked. "You're being a real asshole! Want to explain why you're flipping out over a damn phone call?"

"No," he replied, voice hard. "Just stay out of my stuff."

"Gladly."

I stormed out of the room and blew past Mom on the staircase.

"Ezra? What's wrong?"

"I'm not going anywhere with him," I shouted loud enough for Brian to hear.

"But, Ez— What could have happened in the last ten minutes?" she cried.

I left, got in the car, and drove to campus. I ignored the texts for me to come back and grabbed lunch at school.

I had one class this afternoon and then I was expected at the Sam house to help plan the party. Valentina was so excited about it that she had roped Maverick, Ryder, and Jaxson into going. Jaxson loved a good party, but Maverick was an introvert. Ryder hated everyone except for the people who lived in his house, and parties for me meant being *on* all night.

No drinking, no drugs, and getting out if things got too wild. One day my brand would rival the Media Maven's and when that happened, people could use the Hubble telescope to look for dirt on me and they'd find nothing.

Two hours later, I walked out of my Intro to Journalism class and crossed campus to Greek Row. Along the way, I hooked up with some other pledges.

"Why do we have to help?" Chuck griped. "I bet what they really want us to do is clean up the vomit and used condoms after."

I cringed. "You're probably right."

"We'll wear gloves and suck it up," said his friend, Nolan. "Anything to become a brother. I was talking to my professor about the student interns he lets work cases with him. He heavily hinted that becoming a Sam guarantees my spot. What about you, Ezra?"

"What about me?"

"We're all trying to become a Sam for something. What's your reason?"

"They say they're the best. That's reason enough for me."

"Nice. Well said."

We made it to the Sam house together, but split up in the front hall. Austin spotted me from the living room and came over.

"I texted you," he said by way of hello.

"I turned my phone off for class." *And to avoid Mom.*

"We have to go next door. We're meeting in the Sally house."

Nolan and Chuck reappeared like they'd just gotten the message too. The four of us backed out and walked across the lawn. The noise hit me before the smell. Fresh cookies awaited in the living room along with twenty pledges. I moved inside and there she was.

Valentina covered her mouth to hide her food as she laughed. It did nothing to mask her beautiful, dancing green eyes. Sofia tapped her shoulder and pointed me out. Val stood and came to where she belonged—in my arms.

I kissed her, highly aware of the watching eyes. They forced me to end it much earlier than I wanted to.

"Mmm. And you say you don't taste like chocolate." My voice was barely above a whisper.

Red stained her cheeks. "You weren't talking about my lips and you know it." Val leaned back, squinting at me. "What's wrong? You're upset."

It was a statement, not a question.

How does she do that? There isn't a trace of my fight with Brian on my face. I made sure of that. But she sees through me anyway.

"You know you make me question everything when you do that?"

She cracked a smile. "The only thing you should question is why you're surprised. The woman you love is supposed to know you inside and out." She held my chin between two fingers. "You avoid eye contact with me. That's how I know there's something you don't want me to see in those dark eyes."

I blinked. *Do I really do that?*

"We'll talk about it later," I said.

"Hey, Val." A voice sounded behind us. "Can you help us in the kitchen, please?"

"Be right there." She pecked me on the lips. "Later."

The minute she was gone I noticed Austin staring. He sidled up to me.

"Are you two together?" he asked.

"Yes."

"How long have you been with her?"

"A few years," I replied. *What's with the questions?*

"Are you exclusive?"

My eyes narrowed to slits. "Why?"

Austin backed up. "It's not me you have to worry about."

He took hold of my arm and pulled me to the side. "I recognize her," he said under his breath. "I saw her last week kissing some guy outside the student union. I'm sorry, man, but you should know she's cheating on you."

I pointedly extracted his hand. "What did this guy look like?"

"Massive Black dude."

"The massive Black dude is named Maverick," I corrected, "and he's Valentina's boyfriend too."

He gaped at me, jaw slack. For the first time, something other than irritation broke through.

"I appreciate you trying to be a friend and looking out for me," I said. "But you don't need to worry about me and Valentina. We're solid."

"Right," he muttered. "Sorry."

"Gentlemen, we're in here." I looked up and saw Aiden gesturing at us. "Take a seat."

There weren't many to choose from. Austin squeezed in between two girls, looking pretty pleased about life. I picked a spot on the wall and propped it up.

"So, about the party," Keily began. "I was thinking we could make fingers and fake eyeballs and—"

Aiden waved that away. "Forget about the party. Pledges are on cleanup duty. We have the rest handled."

"What? But, Leighton."

The tiny woman who led the Sallys nodded. "What he said. We're not here to talk about the party."

I straightened. "Then why are we here?"

"There is a more important task for you to complete," said Aiden. "You didn't get details beforehand because we didn't want you trying to prepare."

Leighton picked up the thread. "Every pledge class, Sallys and Sams, has to take the test. Fifty questions ranging across all and any topics. You will have two hours to finish and it starts in"—she glanced at her watch—"three minutes and forty seconds."

This calm announcement didn't elicit the same response.

"Three minutes?" someone bleated.

"We don't get to study?"

"How hard is it? What if we don't pass?" asked Nolan.

Aiden cut him a sideways look. "It's well-known that we take the best, the strongest, and the smartest. If you don't pass this test, you'd better hope the other pledges don't either. The point loss will put you seriously behind."

I sensed Valentina before she took my hand. The sweet strawberry shampoo she favored prevented her from sneaking up on me.

"What's going on?" she asked.

"It's bullshit," I said softly. "They're surprising us with some test that will make or break us."

"Test? Test on what?"

"Any and everything."

"Shit."

"My sentiments exactly."

"Take it into the dining room, guys," Leighton announced. "Sallys and Sams. It's all set up."

Seeing no other choice, we followed the depressed group into the next room. Twenty-four test booklets and twenty-four pencils lay neatly on the table.

Valentina sat and pulled out the chairs next to her. I took one side and Sofia sat on her other. Leighton looked at her blasted watch again.

"No talking. No cheating. No breaks," she said. "Your time starts… now."

I flipped over my book and opened to the first page.

Question One: Does free will exist, or is every action predetermined?

What the hell? The first question and they hit us with a philosophical one that's impossible to answer?

I spared one minute pondering and then wrote something about life being steered by too many random events for order to apply—like my mother forgetting her water bottle at a tourist site, ducking into the nearest restaurant, and meeting the man who would become my father.

I moved on to the next question. A random math theorem I'd never seen before.

Ten questions in and it became clear. This test was created to torture us.

In those two hours, I squeezed every drop of gray matter onto the page, summoning all the knowledge and critical thinking I had acquired over the years.

It wasn't enough.

"Time."

Leighton called it with twelve questions still to go. I pushed the test away in disgust.

"We'll let you know your results after the Close Enough party."

No one said anything. A collection of sallow, glowering pledges trudged out of the house.

"The hell," Valentina said. "Can you believe those questions? 'What is the core message of King Lear?' 'What does each individual owe their fellow man?' They were completely random. We couldn't have studied for that test even if they had warned us."

She lifted my arm, draped it around her shoulder, and tucked herself in. "I used to think I was reasonably intelligent. Staring dumbfounded at ninety-eight percent of those questions cured me of that idea."

"Don't believe that," I said.

We crossed the lawn, putting as much distance as possible between us and the Greek houses. I was more than ready to go home.

"Those were graduate-level questions," I continued. "Stuff that all of us gen-ed-taking freshmen wouldn't know. They made it crazy hard on purpose to weed us out. Only half are becoming Sallys and Sams."

Val sighed. "I bet I know what half I'm in after today."

Chapter Five

*V*alentina

"Hands up, legs apart, Val," Leighton barked.

"Buy me dinner first," I huffed—not low enough.

Sofia snorted a laugh. How she had breath enough to do that I didn't know.

A week had passed since that mind-melting test and life had gone on as usual in the Sally house—with one exception.

Sofia and I had rolled in ready for our three-mile run when Leighton announced we were shaking things up this morning. I basked in four seconds of euphoria till Leighton finished her statement with "backyard workout." That was how I ended up stretching, running, and jumping jacking all over the yard. At least I had a nice view.

Swarming around us, sisters worked to set up for Close Enough. Even in the beginning stages, it was obvious this would be a great party.

Cobwebs hung from skull string lights and spooky paper lanterns hovered above our heads. The Sallys were in charge of the real food for those who didn't want to gorge on candy all night. The sisters took that task and slam-dunked it like they did every other.

The foldout table would soon be loaded down with veggies and green slime dip, mummy jalapeño poppers, cheese puff eyeballs, chocolate cake dripping with blood, pumpkin deviled eggs, and poisoned candy apples.

I offered to help bring these creations to life so I could rack up more bonding points. Anything to get me out of all of this exercising.

Leighton paced before the line of jumping girls, surveying us like a drillmaster.

"Good form, Blair."

"You've been training, Sofia. Your hard work shows."

Leighton stopped in front of me. "That's enough, Val."

"What?" I stumbled out of my jumping jack. "Am I doing that badly?"

She chuckled. "No. You're done for today. Go home, change, and then come back to help with the food. And well done for offering to do more than clean up. It's that kind of initiative that impresses me."

"I can help make the food too." Blair shot in between us. "I'm happy to help."

She let loose the tide.

"I can too, Leighton."

"Me too, Leighton."

"I love to cook."

Leighton held up a hand. "Two volunteers are more than enough. Val and Blair, get ready and be back here by five."

I waved bye to Sofia and escaped through the fence.

My boys weren't home, except for one. The shower was calling my name, but when I arrived, I turned left instead of right at the top of the stairs, heading to Adam's room.

I heard him before I saw him. Laughter spilled through the open door—high and excitable for Adam, soft and tinkling for Caroline. I peered around the frame.

Caroline sat cross-legged on the carpet, arranging Adam's toys in a neat little row. At her back, looking wholly out of place in the colorful toy land, was her ever-present bodyguard. And there was my son, at the foot of his bed, rifling in his backpack.

He pulled out his prize. "Look, Cara. I made this for you."

A smile tugged at my lips. Caroline was a bit of a mouthful for him, so he called her by the cat's name. That Cara also meant love warmed Caroline's heart so much she couldn't stand to correct him.

"This is beautiful," she breathed. "I'm going to hang this on my wall, so I can see it every morning."

"Knock, knock," I called.

"Mommy!"

Adam took a running leap at me. I caught him and spun, laughing as I peppered his face with kisses.

"How was school, baby?"

His mouth turned down in a pout I rarely saw on my son's face. "Bad."

"Bad? Why was it bad?"

"Derek won't stop eating my snacks."

I gasped. "He's eating my baby's snacks? Well, don't you worry, Adam. Mommy will take care of it."

Adam's smile returned fast—everything was perfect in his world again.

Cuddling him to my chest, I buried my nose in his soft curls. This was everything I ever wanted. For Adam's life to be filled with so much love, security, and happiness that his biggest worry would be a few stolen graham crackers.

He was conceived in blood and pain, but while I live, he'll never know either.

"I told Ryder about our cookie thief," Caroline spoke up. "He's going to speak to Adam's teacher on Monday."

"He doesn't have to do that." I set Adam on the carpet and let him run back to Caroline. "He's got a test on Monday. I can handle it."

Caroline shook her head. "Don't you have a test as well? Let Ryder take care of it. I have a feeling he'll enjoy reaming them out."

I chuckled. "I have that feeling too."

Adam pushed his toy car around the carpet, making little *vroom vrooms* as he played. I sat behind him and pulled him onto my lap.

"How is the sorority, Val?" Caroline asked. "Did I ever tell you one of my best friends was a Sally? I had a ball hanging out with her and the other sisters."

"Really? I had no idea." I winked. "Any tips to help me get in?"

"You don't need help. If this generation is anything like mine, they'll realize they're lucky to have you."

"Thank you."

Adam mimed an explosion and added the sound effects to match.

"Are you sure you're up to watching him tonight?" I asked. "It's just a party. If you're tired, I'll stay in."

She waved that away. "I'm fine. Adam and I are going to take it easy tonight. We'll have our dinner in the theater, watch our favorite movie, and then we'll be in bed by nine. If we need anything, we'll call you."

I knew they would be fine. This was hardly her first time babysitting. I just wouldn't be doing my job if I didn't worry.

Caroline transferred Adam to her lap. "Get out of here and enjoy your party. Be a college student."

"Okay." I got to my feet and slowly backed out of the room. "But call if you need me."

"I will."

"He's on this bubble bath kick, but don't let him stay in there for hours."

"Of course not."

I was almost to the door. "He has to eat all of his vegetables. Adam, eat your vegetables."

He wrinkled his nose. "No, I don't like them."

"Listen to Grandma Cara," I said sternly. "Do everything she says."

Adam waved both hands at me. "Bye, Mommy."

I huffed. "And look sadder to see me go."

Caroline laughed. "Go on, you silly. We can't miss you until you do."

Reluctantly, I closed the door on the cute scene.

Our living arrangements left me with my pick of bathrooms to shower in. I went with Ezra's since I stashed our costumes in there the day before.

I left a trail of clothes on the way to the shower. Hot, billowing steam escaped its confines, seeking me. I stepped into the spray and moaned unashamedly. The water beat on kinks I didn't know I had. I danced under the showerhead, soaping my body and indulging a rare moment to myself.

Voices reached me through the open door.

"—put them in here."

That was Ezra. There were only three possible people he could be talking to.

I shut off the water and stuck my hand past the shower curtain for my towel. I dried myself off and then wrapped my towel around my head. I padded out of the bathroom not wearing a stitch.

Ezra and all three possible people looked up as I came in. They stood around the bed; my costume picks laid out before them.

"What the hell is this?" Ryder started.

"Don't you like it?" I picked one costume off the pile and held it up to him. "A vampire for my dark, brooding love."

"What's with this brooding shit? I don't brood." Ryder plucked it from my fingers. He glared at the dark suit and bloodred cape. "Are you going to throw glitter on me next?"

"And which one is supposed to be mine?" asked Jaxson.

Beaming, I handed him his costume. "You're the teddy bear."

Jaxson's face did not mirror mine as he gazed at the furry body-suit. "Because...?"

"Because you're my sweet, cuddly, goofy Jaxson."

"That makes me the mob boss," Ezra spoke up. "Any particular reason why?"

I shrugged. "I like how you look in a suit. Plus, you'll have your hair slicked back, shiny shoes, a devilish hat, *and* suspenders. You're going to look hot."

"He gets hot and I get oversized children's toy?" Jaxson asked.

Maverick reached for the last one. "So, this means I'm Aladdin?" He locked eyes with me. "Is it because I'm brown?"

"Maverick!"

I swung at him. He skipped out of reach of my swat, laughing away.

"Full disclosure," I said. "It's because I look for any excuse to get you shirtless."

The boys shared a look. A silent communication passed between them in a language not even I could translate. The next thing I knew, my choices were changing hands.

"Guys," I cried.

"Sorry, baby." Jaxson didn't sound sorry at all. "The mob boss is all me."

Ezra held up his new outfit. "I was thinking of going as a vampire anyway."

"I'll dig up last year's costume," Ryder threw in.

I folded my arms, inadvertently pushing up my breasts. Four pairs of eyes immediately flicked off my face.

"Who is going to be the teddy bear? It won't fit Maverick."

"You're going to be the teddy bear." Ryder thrust the suit at me. "Yours shows too much ass anyway."

"It does not," I protested. "I'm Tinker Bell. I brought light, love, and magic into your lives." I smiled at my bulky love. "Will you be Aladdin? Please?"

Grinning, Maverick shook his head. "No chance, Val. I only get shirtless for you." He hooked my crossed arms and pulled me in. "I'll wear my football uniform," he whispered. "You like me in that too."

Maverick tilted my head back and brushed his nose against mine. I shivered as he stroked the small of my back.

"Wear the Aladdin costume for me after the party."

A growl rumbled the back of his throat. "I'll wear it for you right now." He didn't look away from me. "Guys, get out."

"What do you mean, 'get out'? This is my room," Ezra reminded.

"All of you, get out," I said, amused. "I have to get dressed. I'm expected at the Sally house to help with the food."

It took wheedling and the promise of an obscene amount of sexual favors, but I got them out of the room and changed into my Tinker Bell costume.

Ezra was waiting for me when I came out.

"I'll take you," he offered. "I'll find something to do at the Sam house. They must need help."

"Perfect." I linked my arm through his. "I've been meaning to ask you about Brian. Have you guys patched things up?"

"No. The asshole still hasn't apologized."

"You should talk to him. He could leave any day now. You don't want him to go before you make up."

"It wouldn't be the first time he took off while we were pissed at each other. We're brothers. We figure it out eventually."

I let it drop. I was sure Ezra was right. They would figure things out in their own time.

We hopped in his car and drove to Greek Row. Turning onto our street, we were met with a surprising—and somehow typical—sight.

"Wow," I said. "Is it me or does that look like Halloween decorations?"

"It's not just you."

We expected to see two houses decked out in Halloween gear. What we found were six houses covered in cobwebs, jack-o'-lanterns on the porches and skeletons hanging from the trees. The houses that were bare had coeds in costumes outside changing that fact.

"It seems all of Greek Row is having a Close Enough party," I said.

"Then the street is going to be packed. I'll tell the guys to come in one car."

Ezra pulled up behind a black van and killed the engine. He sent me on while he called the guys.

Despite the other Greeks' attempt to copy us, the Sams and Sallys proved the original was always better. In the few hours I'd been gone, witches' hats had appeared in the trees. On both lawns, a huge bubbling cauldron billowed greenish smoke. A makeshift cemetery sprouted between our houses, complete with skeletons clawing their way out of their ground.

It was perfect and it wasn't finished yet. I waved to the girls putting out the decorations. They were all dressed as witches.

"Reagan, did I miss something?"

She smirked. "Sorry, pledge. Only the sisters were in on this one. But your Tinker Bell costume is super cute."

I thanked her and went inside. My nose led me to the kitchen, where the cooking was underway. Speakers bumped in the corner, enticing the girls to wiggle around the kitchen while they chopped the vegetables, mixed the cake, and deviled the eggs.

"Val," Patricia greeted. She was the perfect mix of adorable and sexy in her black, floor-length witch outfit. "Right on time. You can help Blair with the jalapeño poppers."

She pointed to Blair's mummy-making station in the breakfast nook. She was seated, gloves on, and ingredients in front of her. I glanced at my watch.

A half an hour earlier than Leighton told us to be here. This girl is committed.

"Nice costume," I said as I sat down.

"Thanks. What a coincidence I decided to be a witch too."

I had a feeling there was nothing coincidental about it, but either way, she killed it. She teased her hair into a wild mane and topped it with a cute, purple hat. It matched her tight spiderweb dress and the purple, interlocking-bone-hands belt.

"These are pretty easy to make," Blair said. She pushed a bowl of jalapeños over to me. "You cut them in half, load them with filling, wrap them in these crescent roll strips, and then we'll bake them for ten minutes."

"I can manage that."

I pulled on my gloves and got to work.

"Patricia?" I asked.

"What's up?"

"What was it like when you pledged? Did you have to run, jump, and take that test too?"

She snorted. "Oh, yeah. You guys aren't doing anything we didn't have to do. If it makes you feel any better, the test is as bad as it gets. I cried after I took it. I was convinced I failed and lost my chance to be a sister."

"But you passed, proving you're a genius."

Patricia finished chopping the vegetables and arranged them on the plate. "Actually, I did fail."

"What? But then..."

"How did I get in?" she finished. She lifted her head and shot me a smile. "I didn't fail as spectacularly as the other girls in my pledge class. A twenty-five to their twenties, fifteens, and zeros.

"All of it was worth it, though," she continued. "The Sallys are my family. They have my back and I have theirs—through everything."

The other four sisters nodded their heads as one.

I dropped my gaze to my soon-to-be mummies. "You don't see that kind of loyalty often."

"I don't know about that," Patricia replied. "You and Sofia have that kind of loyalty. When you become one of us, you'll have fifty Sofias."

I stilled. *When? Did she say when? Does she know something or was it a mistake?*

"Pat," hissed one of the sisters.

She knows something.

I felt Blair's eyes on me. It was the only reason I schooled my face and showed no outward reaction.

I was in.

EZRA

"Damn. You guys know how to throw a party."

Sawyer gripped my shoulder. "How many times does it have to be said? We're the best! Woot woot!"

"Woot woot!" half the party cheered.

The house was bumping, and I meant that literally. The music rattled the walls and shook the Solo cups piled in front of the speakers. Regardless of the competition, the Sam and Sally houses were packed. Most of the dancing was going on in the Sally house, but the getting shit-faced was happening here.

Sawyer took a break from manning the kegs and ended up on the arm of the couch. The five of us took it up. Ryder, Maverick, and Jaxson sat next to me while Val stretched out on our laps. I ran my fingers through her hair, content to be right where I was.

"Shit," Sawyer crowed. "What's going on in there?"

He was referring to the beer pong room, where two girls were dancing on the table. They'd gone up as a fairy and a nurse. Now they were just naked.

"This is next level even for us," said Sawyer. He clapped me on the back. "I've got to get back. Have fun, pledge."

I tossed him a two-finger salute. He was actually a decent guy. Constantly questioning him after what I heard in the basement had resulted in us getting to know each other pretty well.

Valentina poked Ryder in the stomach. He made good on his promise and showed up to the party as a pirate.

"Let's go back to the Sally house," she said. "Everyone is dancing there. I want you to dance with me. All of you."

"It's nice to want things," Ryder replied.

He got another jab for that remark.

"Jaxson, you'll dance with me, won't you?"

"Always, baby."

Valentina smiled up at me. "Ezra?"

"You know Jaxson is the only one who can keep up with you."

Ryder pointed at the beer pong room. "Seems like they can. Why don't you dance with them?"

"You think I won't?"

The smile wiped clean off his face. Hers melted away too, as her smirk widened.

"Looks like fun and you love it when I dance naked for you."

"Val..." Amazingly, his growl could be heard clearly over the music.

Valentina tipped off our laps. She got to her feet and, back to us, reached for her zipper and began pulling it down.

"Val!"

The four of us shot off the couch so fast we collided with each other. Ryder picked up a giggling Valentina and threw her over his shoulder.

"If I didn't know any better, I'd say you were drunk," Ryder said.

"I'm in a good mood," she replied. "And I want to dance with my men." She smacked his ass. "To the Sally house."

"You realize I'm paying you back for that tonight."

"Promise?"

Val started whacking his cheeks like a drum. Amusement bubbled out of me. Discovering the Sallys wanted her had Val bursting with happiness, and her happiness was everything. It was more than everything.

"I'll dance with you, Val." I helped her off Ryder. "Let's go."

I threaded our fingers together as I led her to the other house. Outside, the entire street was thrumming. Music spilled out of every house and people flitted in and out of them, looking like real trick-or-treaters—but in this case, their buckets held alcohol and the trick would be the massive hangover the next morning.

Val pulled me into the living room. Everyone was grinding on each other, but that wasn't my thing—not in public. Instead, she wrapped my arms around her waist and hers around my shoulders.

The deejay played a fast song, but we ignored it and everyone else.

Eyes fluttering shut, she pressed her forehead against mine.

"You weren't really going to dance naked on the table, were you?"

She laughed. "It's good I still have you guessing."

We kissed—chaste, but unhurried.

"Ezra."

I forced myself to pull away. Sawyer stood in the front hallway, waving me over.

"I'll be right back."

Ryder took my place the moment I stepped away.

"What is it, Sawyer?"

He jerked a thumb over his shoulder. "The Sallys need another keg. Aiden said to grab one from the van. Help me carry it in?"

"Sure."

He broke out into a grin. "Thanks, man. I would have asked another pledge to do it, but I saw you first."

Shaking my head, I veered around him and went outside. I scanned the street.

"Which van is it?" I asked. I counted three mixed in with the convertibles and secondhand junkers.

"I don't know," he replied. "Aiden said it would be unlocked." He pointed to the black van parked in front of my car. "I'll check that one. Give me a sec."

Sawyer jogged over to the van. I saw him try the driver's side door. It didn't budge.

"Try the brown van," I called.

He held up a finger. Sawyer continued around back and opened it. His body was blocked by the doors, but I could see his shuffling feet.

"Got 'em," he shouted. His feet vanished. "They're in the back."

I stepped off the path, going to help him.

The back doors suddenly slammed shut. A figure appeared in the driver's seat where none had been before.

"Sawyer?"

The engine kicked to life.

"Sawyer?"

I started shouting when they pulled away from the curb.

I broke into a run as they accelerated, heedless of the college students staggering through the street.

My ridiculous cape fought the wind, pulling against my throat in a near-strangling grip. I ran and ran, but the distance between me and the black van lengthened.

They veered onto the main road, cutting off a green sedan. In a squeal of tires, the driver jerked the car and came barreling straight at me.

I dove out of the way and crashed onto the pavement. Pain exploded in my shoulder. Dazed, I struggled to get up.

"Sawyer! Sawyer!"

The van was gone.

"YES, THANK YOU. THANK you so much. We appreciate you getting back to us. You as well. Goodbye."

Mom ended the call and turned to me. "That was the dean."

"I know it was the dean," I replied, a bit impatiently. "What did he say? Did the police find him?"

"Ezra." Val rubbed my chest slow and soothing. "It's going to be okay."

The three of us were in Mom's living room. She made me stay here after picking me up from the police station two nights ago.

Two nights.

Two nights ago, Sawyer was taken before my eyes. Two nights ago, the police swarmed Greek Row, shutting down the party and questioning everyone. Two nights ago, I was told to hang tight and let them investigate. Two nights.

Mom sat on my other side and took my hand. "They did find him, sweetie. The dean just got off with the police. Sawyer's older sister got into a terrible accident and his parents rushed down to pick him up. He's with his family now."

I gaped at her. "Are you fucking kidding me?"

Mom frowned. "Careful who you're speaking to."

"You can't be serious." I jumped to my feet. "I'm supposed to believe his *parents* pulled him into an unmarked van and tore off with him? No phone call? No heads-up? No time to pack? They just pulled him off the street."

"Ezra, the dean spoke to the police himself."

I threw up my hands. "Then— then— he's lying! He's in on it too!"

"In on it?" Mom shot Val a look as if asking for help. "In on what?"

"Sawyer didn't go outside by chance. Aiden told him to get another keg out of the van. The same Aiden who said he would be gone soon. I explained all of this to the police. Did they even speak to him?"

"I'm sure they did, honey, but they put aside any notion of kidnapping when his parents confirmed he was fine."

"Mom." Hard eyes met hers. "This is not a coincidence. Something is going on and Sawyer is in trouble. You taught me that reality is never what people say and the story isn't what we expect. We keep digging until we find the truth."

The silence stretched between us. Mom held my gaze for so long Val started fidgeting.

"Okay, Ezra," she said. "You're right. The dean gave me the name and number of the officer tracking down Sawyer. We'll call him, so you can confirm it for yourself." She held out her phone. "We don't stop digging until we find the truth."

I released a breath. "Thanks, Mom."

"I'm going to check on Adam," Val said. "Come find me if you need me."

"Alright," I replied automatically. I was focused on Mom and her tapping fingers.

She handed over the phone.

I pressed it to my ear just as he answered. "Hello. This is Officer Noone. How can I help you?"

The name triggered familiarity. I recognized him as the man who interviewed me two nights ago.

"It's Ezra Lennox. I'm calling about Sawyer Burn."

"Oh, yes. Mr. Lennox. Has your dean spoken to you? He assured me he'd pass on the news."

"He did…" I gave Mom my back. "But it doesn't make sense, does it? Aiden sent him to that van and they grabbed him off the street and took off with him. His parents wouldn't do that even if it was an emergency."

"Apparently, his parents did do that," he replied. "I spoke to them myself. They asked me to pass along their apologies for scaring you. They recognize that it didn't look good to an outsider."

"Didn't look good?" I pulled the phone away and stared at it. *Is this fucker serious?*

"Yes, Mr. Lennox," came through the speaker. "A heads-up to you and his frat brothers would have been nice, but their daughter was in the hospital and they weren't thinking straight."

I shook my head. "This isn't right. Aiden—"

"Thank you for bringing up Mr. Connelly. Before Mr. and Mrs. Burn phoned us, we spoke to Aiden at length about the conversation you overheard in the basement. When Aiden said he would be gone soon, he meant from Nu Alpha Theta. Sawyer was struggling to keep up with his workload and the fraternity, so he was thinking of leaving. That's what Mr. Connelly meant."

"You can't be buying this," I burst out.

"Ezra." The warning in Mom's tone was loud and clear.

"I am buying it, Mr. Lennox," he said, a touch of frost lacing his words. "Because Sawyer confirmed it himself."

I froze. "Sawyer?"

"Yes. I spoke to him and he backed up everything his parents and Aiden Connelly said. Now, I appreciate your concern, but I have no more time to waste on a young man safely with his family. If that's all, I'll be going."

I didn't reply. After a beat, the dial tone sounded in my ear.

"Well?" Mom prompted.

"He... spoke to Sawyer," I said softly. "Everything is fine. He's with his family."

"What a relief." Mom hugged me from behind. "Do you feel better, sweetie?"

I nodded.

"Good." She kissed the back of my head. "I'm glad you pushed until you were satisfied. It's what makes you a good reporter and me a proud mama."

"Thanks, Mom."

"Are you and Valentina staying for dinner?"

"Can't."

Mom turned me to face her. "Is this because you and your brother are still fighting?"

"No." I stepped out of her hold. "Val is making dinner tonight. She's giving the chef a night off as a thank you."

"Okay. Tomorrow night."

Mom didn't phrase it as a question.

"I'll try." I kissed her cheek. "Bye, Mom."

"Goodbye, sweetie."

I dropped my smile the minute I left the room. Val and Adam were in the dining room. Adam scribbled on a piece of paper. His little tongue stuck out as he concentrated on his masterpiece.

"Everything okay?" Val asked. "Did you talk to the officer?"

"Val, do you trust me?"

Lines marred her smooth brow. "Do I trust you? Of course I do. Why?"

I motioned at the door. Val picked up Adam and followed me out. I felt her eyes boring into my neck, but I didn't speak until we slammed the car doors shut.

"Sawyer is not with his family. He was fudging snatched and, at the very least, Aiden and the guys in the basement had something to do with it." My grip tightened on the wheel until my knuckles sang for blood. "Something is going on with the Sams and I'm going to find out what." I looked her in the eyes. "Will you help me?"

VALENTINA

"That's it, baby. Just relax."

"Val, this is serious."

I pushed him down, letting the sudsy water envelop him.

The bubble bath was perfect. The water danced on the line of too hot. A sweet berry-scented cloud mingled with the steam.

"I know it's serious," I replied. "But we couldn't talk about it in front of Adam. Now we can."

Sitting on the rim of the tub, I draped my legs around Ezra's shoulders and tilted his head back. He gazed up at me, those dark eyes more tempting with the storm that raged within them.

I placed a light kiss on his nose. "I hope our children have your eyes."

"Babe, focus. They took him. They snatched a person off the street and they're getting away with it. Sawyer was— Sawyer *is* a good guy and we have to help him."

"So, let's think this through." I pressed my palms against his chest and moved down, up, and down again—relishing the bumps and dips of his body beneath me. "The president of a fraternity had one of his brothers kidnapped. Why?"

His eyes flashed. "I thought you believed me."

"I do believe you, baby."

I dipped lower. My nipples brushed his cheek and rippling electricity shot through me.

Focus, Val. With how pissed he looks, this bath won't end the way you want.

"But we need to understand what's going on here," I continued. "Why Sawyer of all people? Was he wealthy? The son of someone important? Did Aiden have a grudge against him?"

"No, I— No."

A bit of Ezra's rigidity leaked away under my hands and questioning.

"His family isn't rich," Ezra went on. "I mean, I don't think they are. I don't know much about him, but rich people tend to wear it, and Sawyer wears clothes from Walmart. If they were looking for ransom money, there were plenty of other Sams who were better targets—me included."

"See," I said. "We're getting somewhere. We know this can't be about money, so what about revenge?"

He shook his head. "If Sawyer pissed off Aiden or the other brothers, they did a great job keeping it secret. It seemed like everyone loved the guy." He sat up straighter. "Now that I think about it, Aiden loved him most. Sawyer showed us all up in the brother bonding activities. He lifted heavier, ran faster, and beat our times. Aiden was always saying we needed to push as hard as him."

"Okay," I said slowly, mind churning. "If Aiden held him up as a shining example, why would he have masked men snatch him off the street?"

Ezra slumped back. "I don't know, Val. None of this makes sense. The police say they spoke to him and his parents, but Sawyer didn't rush out there because he got a call from his mom. Aiden sent him to that van."

My hands drifted lower, seeking his length almost of their own accord. A soft sigh escaped him and I—

"Were his parents in on it?" He tossed his head. "No, that's ridiculous."

I pulled back at the last second. Ezra's mind was on one thing right now.

"They wouldn't have to kidnap their own kid. And they definitely wouldn't be a part of some black van, midnight escape."

"But his parents told the police they took him," I said. "Why would they do that?"

An awful thought occurred to me. My wandering hands stilled. "Do you think they're being threatened? They have to go along to get him back."

"Maybe that's exactly it," Ezra said, face grave. "Aiden spoke of a 'they' down in the basement. One thing we know is Aiden and the brothers didn't leave the party. Someone else drove off with him. *They* drove off with him."

I resumed my massage. "Do you have any idea who they could be? Have you seen Aiden talking to someone suspicious or overheard anything else?"

Ezra shook his head and his thick, raven locks tickled my clit. I bit my lip as I shifted away.

This is serious. Sawyer's life may be on the line. We can't—

"Did you like that?"

"What?" I glanced at Ezra and lit upon his upside-down smirk.

"You're so bad, Val." His reprimand rumbled out his throat, low and deep. "A man may be in trouble and you're trying to get off."

Heat rivaling the warmth of the bath flooded my cheeks. "I'm not—"

Arching his back, Ezra pressed his head between my legs. "And that's why we're meant for each other. It's all I can do to string two sentences together when you're touching me like that." A hand grabbed my wrist and tugged me down. "Finish what you started."

I pulled free. Ezra's growl lasted only as long as it took me to stand, twist around, and dip into the water. A smile spread across my lips as I straddled him.

"We are meant for each other," I said. "I know you, Ezra, and your instincts about people are never wrong. Something happened to Sawyer and we're going to find out what."

I closed around his length. He hissed, eyes darkening.

"Which we'll talk about after," I said.

I stroked him, loving the feel of him hardening to my touch.

"On your knees," he ordered.

I rose up, intending to turn around. Ezra took hold of my waist and pulled me closer. He held my gaze as his tongue flicked out and teased my nipple.

"Who told you to stop?"

My hand picked up the pace.

I bragged often and unashamedly about my sex life to Sofia, and why shouldn't I? Four guys and four different personalities in and out of bed. Ezra was my dark prince. All the things I'd done that were considered taboo; I did with him first.

My first time in a car behind a restaurant. Ezra.

My first time in a bathroom stall while attending a celebrity fundraiser. Ezra.

My first time bent over the living room couch while everyone slept peacefully upstairs. Ezra.

My first, second, and fourth sex toy was a gift from Ezra.

He wanted it when he wanted, how he wanted it, and he wasn't afraid to take it.

How he wanted it now was harder, tighter, and faster. I knew my man.

His grunts got louder. They poured out of his mouth and vibrated my sensitive nipple.

Heat pooled in my lower belly. I loved the power he had over me.

I cupped my breast with my free hand and forced his attention on the other one. Ezra obliged without hesitation, swirling his tongue around the rippling flesh before taking me in his mouth.

"Ezra," I rasped. "Ezra, please."

He knew what I was asking for. I felt his smile against me.

"Go back where you were."

I scrambled over him. The pressure in my lower belly made me clumsy, but Ezra helped me prop on the rim. I spread my legs for him. Water dripped down my body, mixing with my weeping pussy.

Ezra raked the length of me—wet, stretched out, and legs wide. He licked his lips like he couldn't wait to feast.

"What do you think?" Ezra pressed a kiss just above my knee. "Should I tease you?"

"No," I rushed out. "Please, no."

"But I like teasing you." A kiss. Then another. Then another. Each one getting closer to where I wanted him to be. "Drawing out every kiss, lick, and thrust. You cum when *I* say."

Ezra sank his teeth into my soft skin. Just a playful nip, but the effect it had on me was no game.

I trembled. The last of my self-control dangled off a cliff by its nails.

"I share your body, your time, and your love," he whispered. "But these orgasms are all mine. Mine to tease from you. They're mine to lick from you. And they're mine to pound from that tight, wet pussy."

My chest heaved with rapid pants. He hadn't done anything to me yet, and I was aching for him.

"Ezra," I near pleaded. "Do it."

Ezra kissed the tiny space between my thigh and lower lips. "I will... but not yet."

My self-control snapped. I flicked my little neglected nub and Ezra's hiss sounded as loud as mine.

"Don't you dare."

Unheeding of the warning, I dipped inside. I savored my rebellion for all of two seconds.

Ezra moved fast. Water sloshed over the rim, soaking our clothes as he grabbed my waist and spun me around. He bent me over the edge, ass in the air.

My feet couldn't find purchase. Ezra gripped my legs, holding me securely.

A moan ripped from my throat as he swiped his tongue through my lips. Pissing him off had the best consequences.

He tasted and teased me, darting in and out of me, and then moving down to seduce my clit. My cries encouraged him.

"Ezra, yes. Just like that." My nails scraped against the tile. "It's yours, baby. Take it."

"Not like this," he rasped. "Up."

Ezra pulled me back into the tub. He settled me on his lap, re-claiming our earlier position.

"Like this."

My heart thrummed with anticipation. Ezra rarely let me ride him. He liked to be in control and I liked when he pushed my head into the pillow and pounded me from behind.

I offered my thank you. Our lips connected in a feverish kiss that pulsed heat through my veins. Being with him was everything and more.

Ezra moved in the midst of our kiss and positioned himself at my entrance. I sank down, taking all of him inside me.

I started moving—slow at first as we found a rhythm. Ezra came up as I came down, syncing perfectly.

"Faster," he ordered.

I bounced on the balls of my feet, giving him exactly what he asked for. Our sweet, strawberry bath sloshed out of the tub and added a noisy chorus to my feverish moans. His tongue brought it so close and now my orgasm was cresting fast.

"Fuck, Val," he forced out. "Is there a more perfect sight than you bouncing on my cock?"

I laughed, albeit breathlessly. "Yes. You."

Droplets ran down Ezra's flushed cheeks. His inky-black hair shone with iridescent, soapy streaks. His hungry, ravaging eyes and soft pink lips begging to feast on me, consume me, tear me apart, soothe me, cherish me, and put me back together again.

Ezra was light and dark. Savage and gentle. The side the world got to see and the part of him that was all mine.

"Cum for me, Val. Give me one more."

I couldn't have denied him even if I wanted to. Ezra was slamming into that spot relentlessly and my belly clenched tighter and tighter, riding the building pressure. I was no better—bouncing out of control on top of him.

Ezra released me and sank beneath the surface. I hit that spot again and sunbursts exploded in my vision.

I threw my head back, my mouth open in a silent scream. Wave after wave of muscle-wracking pleasure contorted my body until my cries were anything but silent.

I slumped against the tub. Soft hisses escaped me as the last of my orgasm seeped out of me like the heat from our bath.

Ezra rose out of the water. "We can put that on our list of firsts. Underwater orgasm."

I laughed. "That was only a first for you. Jaxson and I took care of that a while ago."

"Shit. I just can't keep up with you, Valentina Moon." Ezra snaked an arm around me and drew me to his chest.

I snuggled in, perfectly content in our tepid bath. "Now that we got the sexy portion of the evening out of the way," I said, "we should figure out what we're going to do about Sawyer. How are we going to find him, Ezra?"

Worry flushed out my ardor. If Ezra was right, and I believed he was, an innocent guy was snatched off the street and the police weren't trying to find him or go after the ones responsible.

"We don't have anything to go on," I continued. "Aiden's been lying his ass off, and since the cops are buying it, he's got no reason to tell the truth."

"Going at him again wouldn't be smart," he agreed. "I gave myself away. He knows I overheard him in the basement and that I'm suspicious of him. I have to let him and everyone else think that I believe the official story."

Ezra ran his finger down my spine. "Val, what if it's not only the Sams? Aiden talked about Teagan in the basement. They spun a nice story about why she left, but nothing holds up after what happened to Sawyer."

I went rigid. "You think the Sallys did something to Teagan? But I saw the photo of her with her mom."

"And Officer Noone *spoke* to Sawyer. But he never met the guy. He could have been talking to anyone. And you met Teagan one and a half times. The story they gave you could be just as fake. We both need to do some digging. Quietly."

"Ezra... have you thought about what this means?" Tendrils of fear worked their way through me. "They made two people disappear and we don't know why or what's being done to them. I thought we left all of this behind in Evergreen."

"I did too, baby." He held me tighter. "I did too."

Chapter Six

"Val, that can't be true." Her hold on my legs constricted. "Why in the world would they do that?"

My muscles strained. Every ounce of energy I had poured into lifting me off the floor.

Who in the hell invented sit-ups?

Inch by inch, I drew closer to Sofia's stricken face. "Fifty."

I collapsed onto the floor. That morning, I walked into the Sally house just as Leighton, Sofia, Paisley, Blair, Keily, and Mai were walking out. I immediately swung around and offered to join them at the gym. The day before, I called Sofia about our suspicions about the Sallys. She was busy with her father, so she swore we would talk about it as soon as we saw each other.

"Val, what you're suggesting is insane," she hissed. "Sororities and frats don't just disappear people. Why would they?"

I scanned our surroundings just to be safe. Somerset's gym boasted new, state-of-the-art equipment and a closed-off room for women only. Sofia and I slipped inside and took up a corner to do our workout. The other girls didn't follow us, and from what I could see, no one in the women's room was paying us any mind.

"The why is what we can't figure," I said. "I don't know anything about Teagan, and from what Ezra could tell, everyone liked Sawyer. We don't understand why they would have them kidnapped."

Sofia was still hanging on to my knees. She leaned over me, clutching tighter. "Val, even bigger than the why is the how. You can't just snatch a person out of their life and keep going like everything is normal. They have family, friends, classmates, and professors who would notice. I can't even imagine what it would take to fool all of those people."

I nodded along. "Of course, you're right. I've been thinking about that and if their families believe they have to keep silent to get them back, they'd spin a tale to the police. Wouldn't you?"

"Well, yeah, but— But why?" she cried.

I braved one more sit-up and put my arms around her. She trembled in my hold.

"I wish I knew, Sofia," I said softly. I nuzzled her cheek, trying to send waves of calm into my best friend. "We can go around and around this trying to understand why, but I can barely fathom that this is happening. All I know is that I trust Ezra. He overheard that strange conversation with Aiden and then Sawyer is sent on a beer run that he never comes back from. Something is wrong and I'm going to help him find out what."

"Okay, okay. I just—" She paused and took a breath. "If you're right, we can't stand by and do nothing. Just promise me we won't act without proof."

"We?"

She swatted my hip.

"Ow," I whined.

"Of course we. I'm on your side always, but the Sallys have been nothing but nice to us. Paisley stayed up until two in the morning last week to quiz me for my chem test. Before we accuse them of being some kind of high-heeled mob, let's see if we can't prove Teagan and Sawyer aren't where they say they are."

"Absolutely," I agreed. "For all we know, the Sallys are as clueless to whatever is going on in the Sam house. They could be swallowing Aiden's lies like everyone else. Too much has happened for us not to be suspicious of Aiden Connelly, but we are giving everyone else the benefit of the doubt."

"Okay, good. What do we do now?"

"Ezra is digging up more on Teagan and Sawyer. He's going to track down their parents and speak to them himself. He wants me—"

Sofia swatted me again.

"Us," I corrected. "He wants us to lie low and see what else we can find out. Everyone was at the party, so someone else took Sawyer. We have to figure out who 'they' could be."

She nodded. "I'll talk to the girls and see if they know anything. I'll be discrete of course." Sofia jiggled my legs. "I don't want us to be so jaded from high school that we think everyone has an ulterior motive. That said, I have yours and Ezra's back no matter what."

I dropped a kiss on her forehead. "I love you. Do you want to be a part of my harem?"

Laughing, she shoved me back. "Shut up. Besides, I don't share. That's why I'm your only best friend and I'll fight any bitch that tries to take the title."

We fell to the floor, cracking up.

"Sofia. Val."

I flopped onto my stomach and spotted Leighton in the doorway.

"Why are you in here?" she asked. "All the rowing machines are free. Come join us."

I raised my hand. "Question. Are you trying to kill me?"

Leighton's soft, throaty laugh rang out in the tiny space. "We are trying to make you the best you can be, Valentina Moon. That's what sisters do." She motioned for us to come. "Afterward, we'll get tacos. My treat."

"I'll do anything for tacos."

She chuckled again as she ducked out.

"She's so nice," Sofia said. "It's hard to believe she'd have anything to do with this."

"I hope none of the Sallys are involved." I got to my feet and helped her up. "I can admit it, Sof. I want to be a Sally. I want the parties, taco dates, staying up late studying, and being a normal college student. Normal," I repeated. "For once, can that not be too much to ask."

She slipped her hand into mine. "The sooner we find out what happened the other night. The sooner we can get back to normal."

EZRA

"Bye, Ezra. Bye, Rick." Adam waved, his face beaming as his preschool teacher led him to class. "I miss you!"

The two of us waved from the Evergreen Preschool sidewalk. Matching expressions on our faces. Val was worried about putting the responsibility of fatherhood on our shoulders. She didn't have to be. Everyone who meets this kid falls in love with him.

"Bye, Adam," I said. "Have fun in school."

"He looks just like Val when he smiles," Maverick said.

"He looks just like Val period. She gave birth to her clone."

He chuckled. "All right. We've unloaded the kid. Finish what you were saying. Why do we have to go to MMBC?"

"*We* don't," I corrected. "I have to go, but I can drop you on campus."

Maverick leveled me with a steely look. With his bulk, it was even more intimidating.

"Want to stop fucking around and tell me how I can help?" he asked. "You're my brother and Val's my girlfriend. I'm going with you."

"I have a brother," I replied, fighting a smile. "Your ass looks nothing like him."

Maverick chuckled. "You have four brothers and it's hilarious seeing people's faces when you say I'm one of them."

"Let's get a few heads scratching at the station."

The two of us piled into the car and peeled out of the parking lot. Maverick picked up the conversation as soon as we were on the road.

"Do you think the whole frat is a part of whatever is going on, or just Aiden and the other guys that were in the basement?"

"You were at the party," I replied. "When I came in shouting about Sawyer being taken, the brothers were freaking out. I can't believe that all of them are that good at acting. This must be confined to Aiden and the guys he knows he can trust. Caleb was down there and another guy that sounded nervous about the whole thing. So, two guys for sure."

"Well, those two and... Sawyer."

"What?" I shifted away from the window to catch his look. "What are you talking about?"

"I've been thinking about what you heard that day. The nervous guy was freaking out because he didn't believe they could pull off pretending Teagan didn't exist. How could they if she was Sawyer's girlfriend?

"But if Teagan is the Sally that *dropped out to be with her mother*," Maverick said, taking his hands off the wheel to throw in air quotes. "Then Sawyer did go along with it. He told you he didn't even know her."

My mouth fell open but nothing came out. *Holy hell. He's right. Sawyer swore up and down he never dated a Teagan. He must have known. They took his girlfriend and he did nothing. Why?*

"I can't explain that," I finally said. "But I can tell you he didn't know he was going the same way as her. Otherwise, Aiden wouldn't have needed to lure him to the van. Sawyer could have just packed a bag and driven off into the sunset. Trust me, he didn't know he was going anywhere that night."

"They take his girlfriend, he keeps quiet, and then they take him? And you have no idea who 'they' is?"

I shook my head. "Val grilled me too. I don't have to tell you how big that campus is, Rick. Aiden and I don't have classes together. We don't see each other at all outside of the Sam house. And when I'm there, he doesn't go shooting his mouth off or meet masked men on the lawn. I wouldn't know anything at all if I didn't end up on the wrong staircase at the right time. I don't know much about this guy or what he's into. That's why we're going to MMBC. I'm changing that."

Maverick stopped before a red light. Taking his eyes off the road, the look he gave me belied his seriousness. "If this is what we fear it is, you need to get out of that frat, Ezra. You and Valentina. You don't want to go up against a guy who can make people disappear."

What could I say in reply? Maverick was right. A good reporter didn't strike until they had all the facts. The more I collected about Aiden, the clearer it became that a strike would not end well.

We didn't talk for the rest of the drive. Maverick rode up to the security guard who took one look at us and opened the gate. My friends and I were regular fixtures around MMBC's news station.

MMBC. Media Maven Broadcasting Company.

I said us Lennoxes weren't modest.

"Pull into Mom's parking spot," I said. "She's at the restaurant to-day vetting a new chef. Brian, the lucky bastard, gets to eat every-thing off his menu."

Maverick turned into the spot directly in front of the station and killed the engine. "Why didn't Mama Melia share the love? I'm very good at vetting five-star chefs."

"Are you kidding?" We climbed out of the car and made for the fifteen-story building. "She's loving all this quality time with Brian. This is what it's like not to be the favorite."

He laughed. "Cheer up, mama's boy. Brian never stays that long. You'll have her all to yourself in no time."

I snorted. "I don't know about that. It's been weeks and he's showing no signs of leaving."

"Doesn't he have a wife and kids to get back to?"

"That's what I'm saying."

The two of us stepped into the lobby and locked eyes with Mom.

It was hard not to. The portrait she hung over the reception desk seemed to track everyone who stepped into the lobby.

"Glenis?"

An elderly woman with powdery cheeks and cat-eye glasses peeked over the reception desk. "Ezra, Maverick, how are you boys?"

"We're good. We have to run upstairs for a minute." I winked at her. "Don't get any more gorgeous until I come back?"

"Silly boy," she cried, cheeks pinking. She scanned us through in a flurry of giggles and hand flapping.

Maverick laughed at me under his breath. "Does Val need to be worried? When are you and Glenis making it official?"

"Mom's third lesson: people open up to a charming smile."

I pushed the button for the elevator. It dinged open on command.

"One of these days," he said, "you have to tell me all of these lessons."

"I'm afraid they're a Lennox family secret."

He clapped my back and propelled me into the elevator. I straightened with a wince. Maverick had yet to get his head around his strength.

"What are we doing here?" he asked. "What in this building is going to tell us about Aiden Connelly and Sawyer Burn?"

"Not what. Who." I pressed the number for the very top floor. "Ever heard of an assignment desk editor?"

"Should I have?"

"They are the ones who track developing stories and send out reporters to cover them. Mom's has been with her since the beginning and his—"

The elevator opened and a rush of noise flooded in and drowned me out. The floor was a flurry of activity. People charged around the cubicles, talking to coworkers, at coworkers, and over coworkers. It was amazing. In this tiny section of the world, nothing else mattered but the news.

I motioned toward the back. "This way."

Maverick and I weaved through the glorious chaos, collecting nods, hellos, and handshakes as we went. Everyone knew who I was and I knew them.

The cubicle nearest the office at the back contained a small desk loaded down with papers, and a tall, buttoned-up guy working to sort through them.

"Hey, Mike," I said. "I can't wait to see pictures of the honeymoon."

The assistant rose from his desk—and kept rising and rising and rising. Mike rivaled Maverick for height, but the similarities ended there. He was thin, gangly, and by far his best feature was his smile. A smile he couldn't get rid of since he married his girlfriend of three years.

"Are you sure?" asked Mike. "I've got about three hundred."

"Oh." I pointed over my shoulder. "Then Maverick can check them out."

He laughed. "You know you can go in. Nolan is inside."

I didn't even glance at the editor's door. "Actually, it's you I need to speak to. Got a minute?"

His brow inched up his forehead. "I do. What's up?"

"Maverick, this is Michelangelo Barker," I introduced. "He is the unseen puppet master of this place. The Lucius Malfoy to Mom's Voldemort."

"Do you realize you just compared your mother to a genocidal maniac?" Maverick shot back.

I ignored him. "So here it is, Mike. There is something strange going on in my fraternity, Nu Alpha Theta. Otherwise known as the Somerset Sams."

Mike immediately reached for a notepad. "What do you need me to find out?"

"I know a little about the president, Aiden Connelly, but I need to know everything. He's involved in a kidnapping."

Mike's pen stilled. "Kidnapping? Someone was kidnapped? Ezra, you need to call the police."

"I did," I replied. I pointed at the notepad for him to write this down. "Sawyer Burn was taken off the street Friday night. People claiming to be his parents told the cops they were responsible, but I was there. Mommy and Daddy were not in that van."

"The hell? What's going on?"

"That's what I need to know. Track them down. I want to talk to them myself. And while you're at it, look into Elizabeth Teagan Kainer."

He scribbled faster than I spoke. "Kainer, Connelly, and Burn. Got it. I'll do a deep background, tap into a few sources, and have something for you soon."

"You're the best, Mike."

He waved me off, his mind already on the task as his fingers flashed across the keyboard.

"I thought we were seeing a news editor," Maverick said.

We headed back to the elevator.

"Nope. A news editor's assistant. He tracks all the little details and that's exactly what I need right now. I can't interrogate the brothers or Caleb without it getting back to Aiden. I want him kept in the dark while I gather information. No one is better at that than Mike."

Someone caught my eye.

"Cyrus, you look like death warmed over," I said. "Go home."

Cyrus Giles, Mom's newest, and therefore hungriest reporter, let out a laugh choked by phlegm. "I'm fine," he said. "Besides, I'm meeting with a source from Senator Worth's office today. I don't have time to be sick."

I ground to a halt. "Senator Worth? What's the angle?"

Cyrus gestured for me to come closer. Maverick and I ducked into his cubicle.

"The senator's been pushing this new foreign aid bill hard," he whispered. "But my source hinted there may be more in it for him."

Austin's dad. What is the senator up to?

"Keep Ms. Lennox apprised of the situation," I said. "She's bringing him on for a segment to speak about that very bill."

He bobbed his head. Cyrus's red-rimmed eyes shone with eagerness. "I'm on it."

Maverick waited until we were in the elevator to speak. "If anyone is Amelia's Lucius Malfoy, it's you."

VALENTINA

"Are you sure we should go?" I asked. "If there was ever a perfect time and place to make people disappear, dragging them hours away to a ranch in the middle of nowhere fits the bill."

Sofia shoved her makeup kit in the duffle. "Benefit of the doubt, remember?"

She had been reminding me of that a lot. A week had passed since the Close Enough party and it brought midterms with it. Lately, the Sally house was a museum of textbooks, highlighters, coffee mugs, and exhausted coeds. Everyone was too focused on their tests to worry about anything else, so my clumsy attempts at questioning were shushed.

Ezra stretched out on the couch and rested his head on my lap. "We can't refuse to go," he said. "But Mike will have something for us soon. Any day now."

The three of us were in Sofia's dorm. She was packing. I was getting in last-minute study time before our English Lit test, and Ezra was sneaking me kisses when her back was turned.

"Leighton said it will be fun," Sofia continued. "Obstacle courses, music, hanging out, and showing the boys up. Perfect way to celebrate getting through midterms."

"Sorry to disappoint, Sof," Ezra spoke up, "but if anyone is getting shown up, it's the Sallys. One of the brothers gave it away that the big prize is a spring break cruise for the winning house. The losing house has to fundraise to pay for it."

Sofia's compact slipped through her fingers. "That's the prize? Oh my gosh, that's epic," she gushed. "You shouldn't have told me, Lennox. Now I'm ten thousand times more motivated."

I shook my head. "Have you guys forgotten you can buy your own trip *and* a fleet of cruise ships to go with it?"

"That's not the point," they said at the same time.

I rolled my eyes.

A teasing grin came to Sofia's lips. "But Ezra forgot he loses even if he wins. There's no way you want to be trapped on a boat with your frat brothers while Valentina waves you off from the dock."

"Damn. You're right. Especially if Aiden is there." He smiled up at me. "How about you and I go on our own cruise?"

My fingers tangled in his hair, delighting in the silky smoothness. "Like you have to ask."

"The whole point is brother or sister bonding," Sofia said. "If they're 'cleared from suspicion' by then, you'll want to come with the Sallys, Val."

"Or you could come with us," I replied, quickly warming to the idea. "Forget the competition. Let's plan our own cruise and spend spring break together."

"You want me on your floating sex vacation?" She planted her hands on her hips. "We both know you and Ezra won't leave the suite."

"She's got a point," Ezra said.

I flicked his forehead. "Then bring a date along and hole up with him," I said to her. "By March, you'll be in a much better place about the breakup. You'll be ready to date. Maybe even ready to date—"

"Don't say it."

"—Logan."

Sofia pinched the bridge of her nose. "You said it."

"Who's Logan?"

"He's this guy in our class," I told Ezra. "He's super nice and fond of giving Sofia treats."

"Is he the guy Maverick told me about? The one handing out cupcakes?"

I laughed. "You boys really tell each other everything."

"Can you boys tell each other *and* Val that I'm not interested in Logan." Sofia crossed the room and plopped on Ezra's lap. "He's cute and sweet, but he's not for me."

"Since when is cute and sweet not for you?" I reached out and pushed her hair behind her ear. "You deserve sweet and cute."

She gave me a lopsided smile. "I know I do. It's just that Logan is... too nice. It's not fair to compare every guy to Zane, but he was sexy and worldly. He was the kind of guy that held open my door and handcuffed me to his bed."

Ezra shifted. "Maybe I should let you guys talk alone."

I clapped my hand over his mouth. "When did you decide Logan was friend-only material?"

She shrugged. "I guess a few days ago I realized if there was going to be a spark, I would have felt it by now."

Soft kisses tickled my palm, spreading goose bumps up my body. *The kind of guy that handcuffs and holds open doors. A guy like Ezra.*

"I understand. The right guy is worth waiting for." I nudged her arm. "But don't say no to the floating sex vacation just yet. You might meet someone you like by then."

She nudged me back. "You might give in to a spring break celebration with your sorority sisters by then. We'll see who wins out."

I heaved a sigh. "No one is winning anything if we don't get through midterms. Pass me my psych book, please. Ezra can quiz me in between kisses."

"Yes, please," he agreed beneath my hand.

Sofia went back to packing and I resumed studying. The torment was nearly over. I had two exams that day and one the next day, Friday. Afterward, Sofia and I would hop in a car with Mai, Keily, and Palmer and drive up to the ranch.

That night, I went from room to room packing. Not having my own bedroom worked fine for the guys. In my case, it meant my things were scattered all over the house.

I followed the melody pouring down the hall to Ryder's bedroom. I poked my head inside.

"Don't mind me," I said. "I'm just here for my pajamas."

The tune stopped anyway. Ryder closed the piano. "Val, we need to talk."

"Do we? About what?"

He jerked his head at the couch.

Ryder gave his old room to Adam, but his new one was no less magnificent. Our bed sat on a raised platform accessed by carpeted steps. Next to it was the book nook. This was Adam's favorite spot for the love of curling up with Ryder in the armchair while he read him to sleep.

Beneath the bay windows, his piano had the spot of honor where it caught the morning light. Some days I'd wake up to his playing and my sleep-fogged mind would mistake the man bathed in sunlight as an angel.

Ryder didn't have a lot of pictures or posters around the room, with the exception of the photo of me that he put on the piano. It was a close-up shot of my face partially buried in a pillow. My hair fell over my eyes, but my smile couldn't be hidden.

He loved that photo for what the camera didn't show. The fact that I was naked and he was inside of me when he took it.

"What's wrong?" I asked. We climbed on the couch and Ryder opened his arms for me to get comfortable.

"You know what's wrong. All of this stuff with you, Ezra, and the Sams. Why are you still pledging?"

Sighing, I rested my head on his chest. "Because we don't know what's going on yet. The Sallys and the other Sams could be just as clueless to what Aiden did as the rest of us. Sof and I like the sorority. We want to get in."

"What you wanted was a normal college experience," he said. "Kidnappings and secret basement meetings are far from normal."

"I will have a normal college experience after we find out what happened to Sawyer. He may be in real trouble and no one is looking for him."

"And you have to be the one to do something about it?"

"No, the police will do something about it. We just have to find proof."

"Nothing I say will convince you to drop this, will it?"

I scooted up and kissed his chin. "Ezra asked me for help, so... no. Nothing will stop me."

He held my gaze for a silent stretch. In his eyes, I saw the battle rage. His need to protect me and his faith in his brother.

"Then tell me how I can help," he said.

"I will." I curled my hand around his neck and closed the distance between us.

We shared a kiss that lit the flames of my desire. Packing went straight out of my head.

"You busy?" I whispered.

I felt his grin against my lips. "For what we're about to do? Never."

"THIS IS GOING TO BE so much fun." Keily danced across the lawn and shook her ass at a group of Sams. "Get ready to pay for me to lounge in my bikini sipping mai tais on the way to the Bahamas."

The boys whooped.

"I consider that a good cause," one of them shouted.

"Forgive her," said Mai. She stepped over the threshold, carrying the cooler like it was nothing. "She's never been on a cruise. Suddenly, she's loving Leighton for making us train the last several weeks."

Mai, myself, and the other pledges were on the porch organizing our backpacks, food, drinks, pillows, and everything else we needed for the weekend.

"Is that why we've been working out? For this weekend?" I asked. "What are we going to be doing?"

"Pat said there's an obstacle course," Palmer spoke up. "That's the big challenge. If the most girls make it through first, we win."

"That actually sounds fun."

"All right, ladies." Our illustrious leader came out of the house flanked by three sisters. Once again, they coordinated their outfits and left the pledges out. Pink and black striped shirts flashed the words "Sallys Dominate" to everyone.

"The sisters already know, so this information is for the pledges," said Leighton. "There are two bunkhouses and the main house. The bunkhouses have bathrooms and showers, but the kitchen is in the main house. You can go in and get food whenever you're hungry and you'll have to because no one is cooking for you. Our day starts early at six a.m., so don't make the mistake of partying all night. Any questions?"

We shook our heads.

"Great. Let's get these cars packed up and head out." She pointed at Mai. "You and Reagan have vans, so we're putting the coolers and packs in your cars."

"All of this? But I'm taking Val, Sofia, Palmer—"

Leighton held up a hand, cutting her off. "Whoever doesn't fit in your car will ride with me. I've got four empty seats."

"Ooh." Blair leaped over the cooler and grabbed my arm. "Val and I will ride with you."

"So will I," Sofia threw in.

Keily skipped up the path. "Me too, Leighton."

"That's settled."

I shot big eyes over Blair's head. Sofia nodded imperceptibly. I knew we were having the same thought.

The pledges heeded their orders and packed up the vans. Twenty minutes later, I was sliding into the passenger seat of Leighton's blue convertible.

"This is a nice car," I said. "My boyfriends wanted to get me one just like it."

"Did you turn them down?" she asked.

"They have cars, plus my mother-in-law's car, plus the two cars sitting in the garage that Ryder abandoned when he traded up. I'm not hurting for a ride. They like to spoil me, but I have to draw the line somewhere."

"Do you?" Leighton flicked my earring. "But only at cars."

Her teasing pulled a laugh out of me. "Cars and lots of other things too, but not diamonds. Never diamonds."

Sofia stuck her head between us. "Val's decked out in a different flavor of bling every day. You should have seen her at Evergreen. The only person on the planet to make a yellow uniform look good."

"Second person on the planet," I corrected. "Sofia looks amazing in everything."

"You two are disgustingly cute," Keily said. "I've known Mai and Palmer since kindergarten and I don't like them that much."

We busted up as Leighton pulled out of the parking space—all except for Blair.

"Did you just say mother-in-law?" Blair asked. "You're married to one of them?"

"No. I just call Caroline my mother-in-law because I love her. She's done so much for me and my son."

Keily was next to push her face between us. "Is it rude to ask how it works for you guys? I've been dying to know."

I shrugged. "I never had a boyfriend before them, but I'm sure it's like being in any other relationship. We fight and argue like everyone else. We do little things to show we care. We plan our future and look out for each other. Most people do that with one person. I just do it with four."

"Well said," Leighton replied.

I smiled at her. As far as sorority presidents go, Leighton had been a great one. I appreciated the little things she did for sisters and pledges alike. As well as her understanding when I had to put Adam before pledge activities. At the top of her list of good qualities, she did not express an ounce of judgement over my relationships. To be fair, none of the other girls said anything out loud, but I was well-trained in the awkward silence. Leighton never gave off those vibes.

I really hope you're not a part of whatever happened to Teagan and Sawyer. Because it turns out I like you.

Keily hummed. "Can I admit something?"

"You will anyway," Blair said under her breath.

"I'm talking to two guys right now and I'm thinking I'll give Val's brand of dating a try. They're both cute and they say they're cool with it. Why not?"

I laughed. "I've inspired a revolution."

"What about you, Sofia?"

"Ooh. We've gotten to the portion of the drive where we talk about boys," Sofia said. "Sorry to disappoint but there is nada happening in my bedroom lately. Besides, breaking up with one guy wrecked me. I couldn't imagine three or four guys dumping me."

Keily hissed. "You have a point."

"I couldn't do it either," Blair added. In my rearview, I saw she addressed the window. "Even if I wanted to, my boyfriend wouldn't go for it."

"I didn't know you had a boyfriend," I said.

"He's home in New York."

"The distance must be hard for you."

"Yes."

"Tell us about him."

"He's handsome, smart, and I miss him every day. What else is there to say?"

Her reflection in my mirror said as much as her clipped response. She did not want to talk about him.

I let it drop. Sofia and I knew enough about her already. This car ride was a chance to peel away Leighton's layers.

"And you, Leighton?" Sofia asked. "Are you seeing anyone?"

She sighed. "I don't have time between classes, clubs, and being president. It's alright though. I'm not big on relationships."

"You're not? But you're always saying the relationships we make with the Sallys are everything."

"Romantic relationships," she corrected. "The picket fence, kids, and husband aren't in the cards for me. It's not the future I want, so I don't get serious. My hookups are fleeting but the bonds I make with the Sallys are forever." She smiled into the rearview mirror. "You girls will see. There's nothing like having fifty sisters who'll do anything for you."

"Does that mean we're in the final six?" Keily tried.

"Now that would be telling."

"Are you guys hungry?" Sofia asked. "I packed some sandwiches in my bag."

"Yes."

"Sure."

"I'm starved."

"Fair warning," she continued. "It's an apple, turkey, and brussels sprouts sandwich. I had no choice. I made them at home and Dad can sniff out the unhealthy stuff like a bloodhound."

"Pass."

"No, thanks."

"I'm not that hungry."

Sofia swatted my arm. "Eat my sandwich, Val. It tastes better than you think."

"Sofia, I love and would do anything for you, but I will *not* eat that sandwich."

Leighton swatted me too. "You guys are too mean. I'm sure it tastes delicious, Sof. I'll have one when we get to the ranch."

"Thank you." I heard the crinkle of food being unwrapped. "We have an hour to kill," Sofia said. "Want to play a game?"

"How about 'would you rather'?" Keily offered. "I love that game. I stump everyone."

That worked as well as any other game. Sofia and I needed to keep Leighton talking. We didn't expect her to reveal any deep, dark secrets, but at least we could get to know her better.

"You first, Keily," I said.

"Okay. Would you rather win ten thousand dollars or let your best friend win one hundred thousand dollars?"

"Best friend," I said.

"Best friend," Sofia agreed.

"I would rather win," said Blair.

"Best friend," Leighton said.

"Best friend for me too," Keily threw in. "All of them would share it with me, so win-win."

I admit none of those answers surprised me. *Someone ask something really difficult.*

"My turn," said Sofia. "Would you rather marry someone you love or marry someone who loves you? Just to be clear, in both cases it's not reciprocated."

"Oh, that's a tough one," Keily said. "It's soul-destroying being with someone who doesn't feel the same, but then, who would want to spend their life with a person they don't love?"

"Marry someone I love," I said. "I'd win them over in the end."

Leighton chuckled. "I like that, Val. Take what you want and make it happen. But I've got to say, someone who loves me. I could rely on their faithfulness and loyalty, and that's what matters most in a relationship."

"That's a good point," said Keily. "I pick someone who loves me too."

"Someone I love," Blair said.

"Someone I love," Sofia agreed. "Blair, it's your turn."

"Alright." My perfect view of her granted me the chance to see her slight smile. She'd recovered from her earlier mood. "Would you rather have freedom or safety?"

"Damn," Leighton said with a laugh. "You ladies don't mess around. I'm going with freedom."

We all said the same.

Blair tapped my shoulder. "What's yours, Valentina?"

"Would you rather know *when* you'll die or *how* you'll die?"

A chorus of hisses went up.

"Yikes," said Sofia. "Definitely not when."

"But what if I find out I'm hit by a car," Keily said. "I'd be a twitchy, paranoid mess whenever I went outside for the rest of my life."

"Unless you peacefully die in your sleep," said Blair. "I wouldn't mind knowing if that was my fate. I pick how."

Sofia and Leighton said how. Keily chose when.

"I'm going with when," I said. "I want to know how much time I have left with the people I love, so I make every day count."

"Wow, Val," said Sofia. "Why do I feel like you're winning a game that can't be won?"

I laughed. "Leighton's turn."

"I'm under pressure to come up with a good one after yours. Let's see." Leighton actually stuck out her tongue as she thought. "Would you rather save the lives of five people you love or a thousand people you don't know?"

Silence blanketed the car.

"If there was an award for stumping us," I muttered, "you win."

"You don't have to answer." Leighton was relaxed as she weaved through traffic. "It's a hard one."

"No, I'll answer," said Sofia. "It's awful but... I'd save five people I love."

"Me too," said Keily and Blair.

I sighed. "I would too. Wow. This question is similar to a few from the test you gave us. It was just as hard to answer then."

"The test is brutal," Leighton stated. "But we don't give it out to be cruel. Questions like that tell us how you think and what kind of person you are. Even the tricky math questions. Are you someone who takes what they know and applies it as best they can? Or do you give up and skip the question entirely?"

I found myself nodding. In a way, it made sense.

"And you?" I asked. "How did you do on the test?"

"Eighty-five percent."

Keily whistled. "That's why we call you Madame President."

Leighton cracked up. "Don't be too impressed with me. I'm a philosophy major. Questions like 'What do we owe our fellow man?' are ones I love to wrestle with."

"What do we owe our fellow man?" Sofia put in.

"Blair asked if we would choose freedom or safety, but I say people are owed both. We should be able to live the lives we want and do so free of violence and abuse. A woman should be able to walk through an alley at night and make it home safely. A child should live in a home where they are safe, fed, and cared for. Sadly, we cannot expect these things, but people deserve them."

My gaze drifted to the window. *She is right... but this is not that world.*

"It's getting kind of heavy," Keily spoke up. "Let's play something else. 'Guess the song' is easy. Whoever shouts out the name and artist first is the winner."

"What do we win?" Blair asked.

"How about we *don't* have to eat Sofia's sandwiches and the loser does?"

"Hey!"

Just like that, the pall washed under our giggling. The hour-long drive passed quickly with music, games, and more questions ranging from silly to scandalous. Leighton played and joked with us. She belted along to the radio and didn't hesitate to answer Kiely's "How many people have you slept with?"

When we pulled up to the white-bricked, two-story, ranch-style home, I hopped out and ran to Ezra.

He was standing among a group of brothers next to their van. He saw me coming and opened his arms to catch me.

"Miss me?" he asked, grinning.

"Always." I hopped up and wrapped my legs around his waist. "Take me somewhere private, please."

"Private?" he whispered. "We haven't scoped out the best places to have sex yet."

I nipped his nose. "That's not what I meant, silly. And we're not having sex here."

"We'll see about that."

Ezra did as commanded and carried me away. Wide, open fields stretched out around us. There wasn't much to see, but charming touches here and there made the property quaint. An old-fashioned water trough was the centerpiece of a small flower garden. A huge oak was the only thing blocking the view. It withstood the breeze while the tire swing hanging from it swayed with the wind. Ezra placed me on it.

"Leighton is not involved," I announced. "Whatever shady shit Aiden is into, she had nothing to do with it."

"How can you be sure?"

"You're not around her, Ezra. She's nice, funny, and tough. More than that, she's not about to let anyone mess with the Sallys. She believes in loyalty even stronger than I do. One conversation about what we owe each other as people and I know she wouldn't be a part of hurting Sawyer or Teagan."

"Okay. I trust your instincts." He peered over his shoulder. "But there could be other Sallys who know more than they're saying. I'm working on getting closer to the brothers, but I have to be careful. I can't push too hard."

"Why?"

Ezra's eyes locked on to mine. "Because Aiden knows I don't trust him."

EZRA

Val's friend shook her ass at us. "Get ready to pay for me to lounge in my bikini sipping mai tais on the way to the Bahamas."

Colton wolf-whistled. "I consider that a good cause."

I kept my mouth shut and my eyes averted like a good boyfriend. I wasn't stupid enough to do something that would stop Val shaking her ass at me.

"Ezra."

The voice stopped me cold.

"Get in here."

Slowly, I looked toward the house where Aiden stood on the porch, eyes fixed on me.

"Now," he finished.

I hesitated. *What does he want? He hasn't spoken a word to me since the Close Enough party. He's been smiling and strutting around the house like nothing happened.*

He can't do anything to me, another voice reminded. *Not in broad daylight.*

The fact that I needed that reassurance chilled me. Who the hell was this freckled-face nobody? How did the person I dismissed as irrelevant from day one become the center of this mystery?

"Are you waiting for something, Lennox?"

Snapping out of it, I picked up my feet and climbed the path. Aiden disappeared into the house, expecting me to follow.

I stepped in the doorway in time to see the hem of his shirt go into the living room. I slowed down and cautiously rounded the corner.

"Put these in my truck." At his feet were two red coolers. "In the back seat. Don't let it block my view."

"Sure, Aiden."

I bent and grabbed the handles.

"We don't have a problem, do we, Lennox?"

I froze. Aiden's voice was soft—almost casual.

"What do you mean?"

Aiden moved out of the corner of my eye. I sensed his presence behind me, then the doors clicked shut.

"I got an interesting call today," he continued. "Someone—he wouldn't give his name—rang up the Silverton chief of police and asked questions about me. My connection to Sawyer and Elizabeth. And if anyone around me has ever... disappeared."

Michelangelo.

I slowly straightened as he reclaimed his spot before me.

"I guess he couldn't have known my dad and the chief are old poker buddies. Robert called me right after he hung up."

Aiden's smile didn't reach his eyes, but it reached me. Unease skittered up my spine as we gazed at each other. His hands were in his pockets—his stance loose. But the atmosphere was charged like a man facing a rearing serpent.

"Was it you?"

"No," I replied. My expression gave nothing away and, thanks to Valentina, my eyes looked nowhere but at him.

"Really?" He cocked his head. "And you're not having anyone else look into me either?"

I shrugged. "Not me."

"That's good," he went on. "Because you and I settled this whole thing with Sawyer. You believed that I did something to him, but then you heard the whole story and accepted you were wrong."

He was telling me, not asking me.

"Absolutely," I said lightly. "You know if you ask me, maybe the police sat down and had another think. Sawyer went out to that van because of you, and you were the one predicting he'd make a sudden exit. One of them must have decided to do a little digging to be sure."

"They didn't," Aiden said without skipping a beat. "The police know he's with his family. They've moved on."

"You can't be sure of that."

"I can."

"Well, someone clearly has more questions," I shot back. "Like what exactly were you talking about in the basement."

He quirked a brow. "Is that a question?"

I kicked the cooler out of my way and shortened the distance between us. "Yes."

Aiden's smirk was level with my eyes. "Refresh my memory? What did I say exactly?"

"You know what you said. You're asking to see how much I overheard and just how deep a hole you need to climb out of." I returned his smirk with one of my own. "Very good, but I can't be beaten in a verbal joust, Connelly. If you've got an explanation for what you said in the basement, let's hear it."

An expression flashed across his face—too quickly for me to read.

"I have the same one for you that I had for Noone. Sawyer couldn't handle the pressure and he planned on dropping out. Teagan went home to be with her mother. That's it. Let it go." Aiden's eyes flicked down. "And put that cooler in my truck, pledge."

He sidestepped me.

"I hope whoever is checking up on you believes that story," I said.

The soft click of the door was his reply.

As requested, I packed up the cooler and then climbed into Austin's back seat. Music, laughter, and conversation buzzed in my ear as background noise. My mind couldn't connect to it.

He knows. I see in his eyes that he knows I'm digging into him. The only question is... what is he going to do about it?

"WHAT WILL HE DO, EZRA?"

I drew the blanket tighter around us.

The front of the ranch wasn't much to look at. The same could not be said for the back. It had everything. The bunkhouses held enough beds to sleep all of us, on top of couches, a microwave, a rug, and across the walkway, shower facilities. In addition, we had a picnic table, aboveground pool, and the fire pit that Val and I were cuddled in front of.

It was just us. Everyone else trudged to the bunkhouses to get some sleep in anticipation of the real reason we were here—the impressive obstacle course that took up the rest of the property. There were two bunkhouses. Officially, one for boys and one for girls, but no one was enforcing it and I'd like to see them try to stop me from sleeping with Valentina.

I buried my nose in her neck. "He's not going to do anything."

"You can't know that." She twisted in my arms and I saw the worry etched in her face. "If I didn't know it before, his chat with you sealed it. He did something to them. What if he tries to do it to you?"

"He can't." I pulled her in, pressing our foreheads together. "I've gone to the cops about him. I've told my mom about him. I've even got someone looking into his past. If I go missing now, he's the first one they'd drag into an interrogation cell."

She grabbed me and gave me a scorching kiss. So hot heat ignited beneath my skin.

"You better believe I'd burn that house down with him in it if anything happened to you," she said, voice hoarse. "But I won't pretend I'm not freaked. If it wasn't Sawyer who told the cops he was fine, who was it? If they spoke to his actual parents, why are they lying? There's too much we don't know and it puts us at a disadvantage in every way."

"Mike is working on it. There is nothing this guy can't find out. If he can't get to the information, he'll have a source who can. Once he tells me what we're dealing with, we'll have information to take to the police."

She made a low, frustrated noise. "I can't talk about this anymore. It's making my head spin. Say something to make me smile, please."

"All right. How about this? We've never made love in front of a fire."

"That's not true." A smile tugged at the corner of her mouth, achieving my goal. "We took that vacation over the summer. The hotel we stayed in had a beautiful fireplace and I distinctly remember you and me rolling around on the rug."

I glanced over her shoulder. "I'm talking about a real fire. A crackling, smoldering pit and you and me rutting next to it like cavemen. Getting dirty and hot and—"

I cut myself off. My cock twitched, responding to my on-the-spot fantasy.

"No." Val's lips skated across my cheek and found the shell of my ear. "Keep going."

The sound of my zipper drawing down could hardly be heard over the crackling flames.

"It's always a hard choice," I said huskily. "Whether to put you on your knees or lay you on your back."

Val was gentle as she freed me from my confines.

"Staring up at me. Your legs clinging to my waist. Your cheeks flushed. Those lips..." I caressed the object of my attention, parting her mouth slightly. "Those lips pink and swollen having just been wrapped around my cock." I hissed as she swirled her finger around the tip. "Valentina Moon, you on your back is the most beautiful thing I've ever seen."

"Ezra," she breathed.

My tongue flicked out, tasting my name on her lips.

"But you on your knees is so delicious it should be a crime," I went on. "That pert little ass in the air. The sweat from our bodies trickling down your spine as I ram into you over and over and over." My voice cracked as Val picked up the pace. Fire rollicked in her emerald eyes—bewitching me, burning me, promising all I needed was right before me. Suddenly, I had to have her right there on that lounge chair.

"Off," I ordered.

Val didn't ask what I meant. We shuffled beneath the blanket, highly aware of the people sleeping not twenty feet away from us. Soon, her shorts and panties were pooled at my feet.

"I won't be on my knees or my back," she whispered, a trace of teasing in her tone. "I hope that doesn't disappoint you."

"We haven't even gotten to how much I love you bouncing on my cock. I could write a damn book."

She giggled. "I don't know how you do it, Ezra Lennox. All these things I thought I'd never do and then a few words from you and my clothes are off. Somehow I always give you what you want." She pressed a kiss to my cheek, then my lips. My body coiled with anticipation as she pressed me to her entrance. "We can cross rutting in front of a fire off the list."

"Val?"

We stilled.

"Val, there you are. Leighton says you have to come inside. We wake up in five hours." Keily walked right up to us. "What are you guys...?"

Keily glanced at my feet. "Oh."

"It's not what you think," Val blurted.

She chuckled. "Yes, it is. I'm sorry, I'm an idiot. You two keep doing what you're doing and I'll tell Leighton you're sleeping in the boys' bunk." Keily winked at me. "Just don't get too loud."

Her friend skipped off like it was no big deal. Val buried her face in her hands.

"Holy hell," she groaned.

"The blanket covered us. She didn't see anything."

"That's not the point. We just got caught having sex."

"We got caught *before* having sex." I smacked her backside. "Now we're going to have sex."

"I think the mood is lost, don't you?"

"No," I protested.

Val clambered off me anyway. "I'm sorry, love. We can go camping—just me and you. I'll let you do anything you want to me in front of the fire."

I held out my hands, willing her into them. "What do I have to do to make you get back on my lap?"

Gripping the chair handles, she leaned over and gave me a soft peck. "Rewind time and seduce me faster."

I was less than pleased trudging after her to the bunkhouses. Val veered off to the boys' bunk while I went into the bathroom and masturbated.

She was waiting for me in the bottom bed. I curled up next to her, relaxed by her warmth despite desiring her with every molecule of my being.

Eventually I drifted asleep to her soft breaths on the back of my neck.

VALENTINA

"Get up!"

I bolted upright, nearly smacking my head on the top bunk.

"Everyone up," Aiden repeated. "Ladies, back to the Sallys. From this point on, we're rivals. Boys, get dressed, eat, and meet up behind the bunks."

Palmer, Mai, and I dragged ourselves out of our shared beds and wandered over to the Sallys' bunk. In there, Leighton was shouting the same thing at the bleary-eyed girls.

I saved her the trouble and started getting ready. I was the first one in the main house cooking my breakfast.

Sofia came in and hugged me from behind. "How much do you love me?"

"Enough to make you an egg sandwich."

"You're the best."

Sofia sat at the farmhouse table and plopped her head down.

I cooked me, her, and Ezra a quick breakfast while the other girls streamed in. He deserved it after having his sex fantasy dashed last night.

"Eat quickly," said Leighton. "We're doing warm-ups on the front lawn and then we'll get started."

I finished plating our food and moved over so the other girls could get in. Sofia raised her head to tear into her sandwich.

"How exactly are we doing this?" I asked Leighton. "I took a look at the course. Do we really have to complete that whole thing?"

"If we want to win, yes."

"So, if the most girls finish first, we get the cruise," Blair said. "Sounds easy enough."

Leighton swung her leg over the bench and joined us. Sofia handed her one of her sandwiches which she accepted with a thank you.

"You'll go two at a time," Leighton said. "One guy, one girl. If a Sally gets through the course first, it's one point for us. Doesn't matter how many times you fall on your ass. You just need to finish. It'll take a while to get through all of us, but afterward, the real fun starts. We've got music, a cooler full of beers, and marshmallows for s'mores. Do me proud and then we'll celebrate."

"Are you doing the course too?"

"Everyone is. The Sallys are in this together."

We finished our breakfast with renewed vigor. The Sams tromped in as we headed out and I snuck Ezra a kiss for good luck.

"The first kiss in the many it will take to make it up to me."

I grinned. "Does breakfast bring me closer?"

"It's a start."

"Come on, Val." Blair grabbed my hand and pulled me the rest of the way.

The Sallys gathered next to the water trough. By now, I knew the routine. We stretched and then launched into our jumping jacks, getting our hearts pumping.

The sun rose on the course, lighting up the morning dew blanketing the field like frost. Some of the boys and girls shuffled tiredly about. The same could not be said for the brothers and sisters. They formed neat lines in front of Aiden and Leighton—backs straight and hands clasped behind them.

Aiden handed Leighton a clipboard. As he leaned in, he held his board in front of his mouth and whispered something to her.

"Listen up," she said, drawing back. "By now you know how it works. Finish the course first and you win a point for your house. The pairs have already been assigned, so don't ask to go against your friend. We don't need anyone getting hurt out here, so be quick *and* smart. No pushing, shoving, or touching your opponent in any way. If we see that shit, you're disqualified. Understood?"

"Yes, Leighton," we chorused.

She swept out her hand to encompass our playground for the day. "You'll start by climbing the low wall and then it's on your hands and knees through the tunnel. After the tunnel, you climb the ladder, leap across the stepping stones, swing over the ditch on the rope, go through the ducking lane, walk across the balancing bridge, and finally it's an all-out sprint to the finish line. Any questions?"

There were none, so she kept going. "We'll do the pledges first, then the brothers and sisters, and finally Aiden and I will go. First up, Mai and Xavier."

I sought Ezra through the sea of boys. We came together and held hands.

Mai and Xavier took their places at the starting line. The boys and girls separated and formed on opposite sides of the low wall. Ezra and I stayed together.

"How much do we care about winning?" I asked.

"Enough to want to see Richards go down!" he shouted at my best friend's back.

She spun around, middle fingers up. "You wish, Lennox! You'll be eating my mud!"

"I did not know this girl was so competitive," I mumbled.

"You missed the prep school years," he said with a laugh. "Sofia is fierce and she's going to be sobbing in the mud when the Sams win!"

"Say it to my face!"

My eyes crossed lamenting how I ended up with such dorks. "Should I leave you two to your trash talk?"

"Nah. Leighton's burning a hole through our heads, so I better shut up."

Ezra wasn't lying. Leighton's flashing eyes closed my mouth too. When she was satisfied we'd be quiet, she walked up to the finish line. "You two know the rules. We will be watching. Play fair. Push through. Fight hard. Ready?"

"Ready," they said together.

Aiden blew his whistle and they were off.

As though we were tethered to them, the Sallys and Sams trailed the first runners of the day, skimming along the course.

It wasn't a pretty sight. Neither one of them knew what they were doing. Mai slowed down on the first obstacle. It took her three tries to swing her leg over the wall and jump down to the other side. Xavier was already through the tunnel. Mai dropped to the floor and shimmied through, quickening her pace.

Xavier raced to the stepping stone. Six raised platforms that he had to jump across to get to the ditch. He leaped, overshot it, and smacked the dirt.

"Xavier? Xavier, are you okay?" one of the guys shouted.

Leighton and Aiden didn't move. Their eyes were glued to their clipboard and whatever they were writing.

"I'm fine," he shouted back. "I can do it."

Mai sailed over his head.

Xavier looped around and raced across the stepping stones again. He made it through but the fall severely set him back. There were two ropes to swing across the ditch and two ducking lanes, but only one balancing bridge.

Mai climbed over the wall, then ducked beneath the beam, and then climbed over another. She had the hang of it after the third vault, and ducking beneath the low beams did not slow her down. She was first to reach the balancing beam—just a hair before Xavier—but since he couldn't touch her in any way, he lurched back.

Slowly and carefully, she climbed the beam and inched across. The beam was the width of my hand and about five feet off the ground. The fall wouldn't kill her, nor would it be pleasant. She took her time and Xavier huffing impatiently at her back didn't faze her.

She touched down on the ground and ran. Xavier scrambled off the beam and sprinted after her, but quick little Mai was too fast for him. She started whooping a foot from the finish line.

"Mai wins!" Leighton shouted. "First point to the Sallys!"

Keily and Palmer rushed their friend. They scooped her into the air, chanting like she won the Olympics.

"Next up, Colton and Mary."

The pledge obstacle course race progressed from there. Boy versus girl facing off for a prize most of us would not partake in. Somewhere along the way, people forgot about that and were having actual fun. The groups cheered from the sidelines, making up chants and ribbing the other side.

They were into the competition, but they weren't taking it nearly as seriously as Aiden and Leighton seemed to.

The presidents followed each pair through the course, jotting things on their clipboard as they did. After each race, they huddled together to consult before calling the next pair.

"What are they doing?" I asked. "It doesn't look like they're using a simple point system."

Sofia and Ezra lounged next to me on the grass. Both had finished their obstacle race and come out the winners. They basked in a much-deserved break, drinking water and nibbling on watermelon I brought out from the main house.

"We're still pledges," Sofia said. "We're probably racking up points for the Sallys and for ourselves."

"If that's the case, I pray they take more than winning and losing into account, because I predict a faceplant in my future."

Ezra bumped me with his damp forehead. "You're going to do great, Val. You'll win... but it won't be enough to save your team."

"We're only behind by four points," Sofia shot back. "Don't pack your Speedo just yet."

"Next!" Aiden bellowed. "Valentina and Austin."

"Win this for us, Val," Sofia said.

I saluted. "Yes, ma'am."

Austin and I met at the start line and shook hands. I didn't know much about the senator's son except for Ezra's unfiltered thoughts about him. He told Ezra I might be cheating on him and I wasn't sure if that made him a good friend or nosy as hell.

I looked him up and down.

One thing I do know is the guy is built. He won't go down easily.
"Ready?"

"Ready," we shouted.

The whistle blew. I took off.

Vaulting over the low wall was easy. I made it over first and dropped on my hands and knees for the tunnel. The small, echoey chamber amplified the Sallys' cheers—Sofia's loudest of all. I stuck my head through the other side and met Austin's gaze. He had closed the distance fast.

In front of us was a ladder made up of large, evenly spaced logs going up on a slight incline, and then down at the same angle. It looked simple, but I'd seen three separate pledges slip and bust their ass. Properly planting your feet was more important than speed on this one.

I gripped the log with that thought in mind.

Hand, foot, hand, foot, hand, foot. I crawled up the ladder.

Austin bounded up, jumping from log to log—

—and mis-stepped.

His foot went through the gap and he landed hard, smacking his head with an audible crack that made me gasp.

I stopped. "Austin, are you okay?"

He blinked dazedly at me, body tangled up in the logs. "Wha...?"

I crawled back down.

"Val, what are you going?!" Blair shrieked. "Keep going!"

Ignoring her, I grabbed his arm and helped him out. "You hit your head pretty hard. Can you keep going?"

He nodded. "I'm okay. Thank you."

"It's a ladder," I said. "Climb it like one."

Carefully, he adopted my position. I didn't move until he had it—much to my team's chagrin. They screamed louder than ever for me to keep going. Only Leighton stood silent, writing—what I would never know—on her clipboard.

I reached the top and quickly scrambled down. Recovering fast, Austin was right on my heels. We hit that rope at the same time. Sofia was in my ear as I swung over the mud and raced to the ducking lane.

"You got this, Val! Go, go, go!"

Over, under, over, under, I passed through the lane.

This is actually kind of fun.

Our final obstacle loomed. The balancing bridge.

Austin and I jumped over the last wall to the beam. This was make or break. If I wasn't the first one across, the chances of me winning were slim. Austin huffed next to me, pumping his arms. We were neck and neck... and then Austin pulled ahead.

That's it. I lost.

We reached the balancing beam and out of nowhere, Austin slowed down.

Surprise rattled me but I didn't have time to think as I set foot on the beam. Arms out on either side, I made my way to the other end and jumped down.

"Yes, Val!" Ezra shouted, uncaring of his teammate. "You got this!"

I heard the thump from Austin behind me. Putting on a burst of speed, I raced over the finish line to raucous cheering.

Sofia and Ezra ran at me. I looped back and ran to Austin instead.

Austin was doubled over, sucking in deep lungfuls. Sweat clung to his forehead and the reddish bruise that was beginning to show. Otherwise, he looked fine.

"Why did you do that?" I asked. "You let me win."

Austin peered at me through the curtain of his hair. "You would have anyway. My stupid self slipped on the ladder and you came back for me. The win went to the right person."

"But—"

He shook my hand. "Good match, Val. Thanks again."

Austin loped off just as my friends got their hands on me.

EZRA

I rescued Val from the crowd of girls and planted a kiss on her that earned catcalls.

"You were amazing."

She beamed. "Thank you, but..." Val glanced behind her. "I know he didn't make a great first impression, but Austin's a decent guy. You should give him another chance."

"Should I?"

My phone buzzed in my pocket.

"Yes, you should." She nuzzled my cheek. "Listen to your girl-friend."

I hummed. "I'll do whatever my girlfriend wants if she'll find a spot with me and make up for last night."

"Well," she drew out. "I could do with a shower... and some com-pany."

"Let's go."

We hurried across the field. There were more people needing to go through the course which made this the perfect time to steal away.

Val went into the bunkhouse to get our stuff. I hung back to check my phone.

Mike: Call me as soon as you can.

Visions of sudsy showers and bending Val over in the spray van-ished.

"Val, go in without me," I called. "I'll be there in a minute."

I wandered off to the fire pit, dialing Mike on the way. He an-swered after one ring.

"Mike, what did you find?"

"It's good you got back to me right away." He didn't seem put out by the lack of hello. "Ezra, what exactly is going on here?"

"That's what you're supposed to find out. Did you contact Sawyer's parents? And what did you find out about Aiden?" I looked across the field where the Sams and Sallys battled it out. "The guy is fucking shady. My chat with him yesterday proved it."

"Chat?" His tone sharpened. "What did he say to you?"

"Not much of anything. But the way he stood there, grinning like he knew I couldn't touch him."

"You can't."

"Excuse me?"

"You can't touch him, Ezra. You shouldn't be involved in this at all. Does your mother know you're looking into this?"

His scolding blew me back. "My mom? Yes, of course. I told her about Aiden and Sawyer."

"Really?" Mike didn't sound like he believed me. "She knows that you, nineteen years old and a freshman journalism major, are digging into this story?"

I seized on one word. "So, there is a story. Tell me what you found out, Mike. It's not like you haven't before."

"Sliding you some background info on a woman your mother wants to impress at a banquet is a lot different than this. Let it go."

"What's the story, Mike?" I asked through clenched teeth. "This is serious. Sawyer could be in trouble."

"He's not," Mike replied without hesitation. "He's fine and so is Elizabeth Kainer. There is no story. Hit me up the next time you need research on a socialite. Bye."

"Mike—"

He hung up.

Chapter Seven

E*zra*

Jaxson turned on our street.

"He's not calling or texting you back?" he asked.

"No," I replied. "And if he thinks I'm not seeing that as suspicious, he's a fudging idiot."

A sharp thump to the back of my seat drew my attention. Adam was deep in his tale, relaying everything Val missed over the weekend. He couldn't have heard what I said, but it didn't stop her from giving me the evil eye.

"Sorry," I said. "But I know he found something, and it must be bad if he's acting like this."

"It must be," Jaxson agreed. "Mike might be trying to protect you. Maybe you should do what he says and leave it alone."

I couldn't believe what I was hearing.

"You can't be serious," I said. "Two people are missing."

"It's messed up, but I don't see what else you can do. Aiden's on to you and it's looking like this is getting dangerous." Jaxson glanced up at the mirror. "You agree with me, don't you, baby?"

"Let's talk about this when we're alone," she said simply.

"Whatever you say. Want me to drop you both home?"

"Drop them home?" I repeated. "Why? Where are you going?"

"We," he corrected. "Your mom asked me to bring you by the house."

I checked my phone. "She didn't call me."

He shrugged.

"Yes," Val said. "Drop us home. It's almost time for our nap."

"I don't want a nap," Adam cried immediately.

"Then Mommy will take a nap. You can cuddle with me and keep me company."

"Okay."

I stifled a laugh at Adam's instant agreement. He fell for that every time. Once she got him in bed, he'd be out in ten minutes flat.

Jaxson drove home and got out to kiss Valentina and Adam bye. I climbed out of the car too.

"I'll drive myself," I told him. "Chill out with Val."

"Normally I'd jump on that," he said, "but Amelia asked me to come too."

"Why?"

"Again, I don't know."

I gave in and slid inside. I didn't mind that much.

Jaxson's car was even more impressive than mine—and that was saying something.

His dad hooked him up with a bright red Ferrari whose doors opened like bat wings. The horsepower on this thing was insane. Zero to sixty in three seconds flat and an engine that purred all the way. Jaxson fitted it with tricked-out speakers and unbeknownst to the love of our lives, he and I liked to race on the back roads with the music blasting.

I once said no one would ever find dirt on me even if they whipped out the Hubble telescope. That wasn't technically true. There was some dirt, and if anyone looked, they'd see Jaxson right next to me creating it.

"Let's give this girl a workout after we visit Mom," I said.

"Read my mind." Jaxson groped for the glove compartment. "I've got the perfect soundtrack. Worship me now or later, but I'll take my praise."

He flung a disc on my lap. My eyes bugged.

"Cosplay Meltdown," I said. "Is this—"

"Songs from their soon-to-be-released album," he finished. "On second thought, I'll have my praise now."

I gaped at him. "Your dad will go fucking mental if he finds out you have this."

"Nah, we're cool. Gael slipped me this after the session and asked me to give it a listen. Dad is still shushing and calling me junior. He doesn't trust me yet, but Gael thinks I have good instincts."

I shook my head. "I'm the one who is going to graduate from a great university and be the biggest name in news, but *you* will still have a better life than me. How is that fair?"

He laughed. "We'll both be with Valentina, so I say our lives will be just fine."

Jaxson turned onto the winding path leading to the Media Maven's manor.

We went inside and found her in the living room with Brian. My brother sat in the armchair, messing around with his phone, while Mom watched her segment on TV.

"I believe I was summoned."

"Ezra, sweetie." Mom turned off the television and rose to give me a hug. "How was your bonding activity?"

"Less bonding and more boot camp. It was fun though. The Sams won the spring break cruise."

"How exciting." She put her arm around me and led me to the couch. "It'll be good for you to have some fun guy time."

"I'm not going," I admitted. "I'd rather take Valentina on a cruise."

She clapped. "Why don't we all go? Make it a family trip."

"Uhh... Like I said, I'd rather take my girlfriend on a romantic cruise."

Mom knocked my forehead. "Cheeky. You used to love spending time with me."

"I still do," I said with a laugh. "So, what's up? Why did you need me and Jaxson to come over?"

"I needed you to come over, but since Jaxson was picking you up from campus, I figured now was my chance to pass along his father's birthday present." She waved him on. "It's in the kitchen, Jaxxie. Cora made him a yummy coconut cake too."

"Sweet. Thanks, Mama Melia."

I shook my head. Maverick and Jaxson insisted on calling her Mama Melia. It didn't help that my mom loved it.

"Is everything okay?" I asked after he left.

"I was going to ask you the same." Mom's charming smile melted away. "Sweetie, explain to me why I got a call from Michelangelo telling me you asked him to look into this Sawyer Burn situation."

Stiffening, I glanced at Brian. His eyes were on his phone, but his fingers were still.

"I had to." I looked at her full on. "Someone had to."

"The police have spoken to you, Mr. Burn's parents, *and* Mr. Burn himself. He was not kidnapped, Ezra, and sending my employees on wild goose chases—"

"Wild goose chases? Mom, I was there. Sawyer was kidnapped. How can you not believe me?"

She folded her arms. "How can I not believe a college student with no money, connections, gang ties, or criminal record had a man kidnapped and then persuaded his parents to perpetuate a lie? I am a reporter, Ezra. *We* are reporters. And what is the first rule?"

"Mom—"

"Tell me the rule."

I gritted my teeth, refusing to answer.

Mom waited.

The air was charged and would ignite under the slightest charge. Brian trained on us, though he wisely did not speak.

Her stare did not waver.

I bit back a curse. I couldn't win a battle of wills with her when I was five and didn't want to eat my spinach, I couldn't win now.

"We report the story as it is," I ground out. "Not as we want it to be."

She inclined her head. "Precisely. Multiple sources have confirmed Sawyer is fine, but you refuse to believe it. You've made up your mind that this Aiden character is a villain because you're clinging to part of a whispered conversation and an offhand order to grab a keg."

I jumped to my feet. "I'm clinging to a hunch. There is something off about him, Mom. I know it as surely as if Aiden confessed. Sawyer was taken that night and Aiden was behind it!"

Mom's face was hard and unwavering. "The facts do not support your hunch."

"Yes, they do," I snapped. "Fucking hell! I was standing ten feet away when it happened!"

"Watch your language, young man."

Frustrated fury zinged through me. I suddenly felt hot and uncomfortable in my skin, like thousands of fire ants marched beneath my flesh. "Why don't you believe me? You know me, Mom. I was there. Those were not his parents and it can't be a coincidence that Aiden spoke about him leaving and then he's just gone."

She put out her hands. "Okay, Aiden had him kidnapped. Why?"

"I don't know."

"How did he fool the police with a call from his parents and Sawyer himself?"

A growl ripped from my throat. "I don't know. Obviously, he's working with someone. They took him and they faked out the cops."

"Again, I must ask why." She stood and faced me down. "If you do not have a why, you do not have a story."

"I'm trying to get a why but Mike freaked on me and— Hold up." I walked away. "Why did Mike lose his shit? He called me up going on about what I got him into, then he brought up my age and experience when that never mattered to him before."

My eyes narrowed. "He found something, didn't he? Something he or *you* are trying to protect me from." An awful thought flashed through my mind. "Or maybe they got to him too."

She threw up her hands. "Ezra, listen to yourself! I will not fit you with a tinfoil hat, sweetie. It would clash horribly with your eyes."

Heat flooded my cheeks. "I'm not a conspiracy theorist."

"They got to him too?" she repeated. "That sounds remarkably like what a conspiracy theorist would rant."

"Aiden is behind this. I won't stop until I prove it."

Mom bore down on me. "I'm telling you to stop."

"No."

"For fu— Ezra, I am your mother. You will do as I say."

I held her glittering, angry gaze unflinchingly. "I said no."

Holding my stance, I braced myself for a fight.

Mother straightened to her full height, turned her back on me, and walked out.

A silence so heavy it crushed me, filled the room.

"Well."

I jumped.

"That could have gone better."

"Don't start, Brian," I growled. "I'm not in the mood."

"You would be if you let this go. You don't have any proof."

"I have what I saw and heard."

"And the police have a statement from the guy you're trying so hard to *rescue*. Mom is right. You're twisting everything to fit what you saw and heard because you don't want to accept you have it wrong."

His words were a cheese grater on my nerves. "Why are you even here?" I snapped. "Don't you have a wife and kids somewhere? It's been over a month. Go. Home."

"Don't be like that," Brian said, softening his tone. "You're my little brother. I'm trying to look out for you."

"You're about nineteen years too late."

He flinched. "Okay. Fair enough. But if you don't hear anything else we say, hear this: If Aiden Connelly is what you think he is, he's very dangerous. The way you're coming at him—painting yourself as the obsessed nutcase and him as the innocent being harassed—is not smart."

"I—"

"—speak to him. Maybe he'll listen to you." Mom stormed into the living room and shoved her phone at me. "It's your father."

"Ezra? Hello, Ezra?" My father's heavily accented voice poured from the speaker. "Are you there?"

I put the phone to my ear. "I'm here."

"What is all of this fuss?" Hakim was groggy like he'd just woken up. He most likely did. It was four a.m. in his part of the world. "Why aren't you listening to your mother?"

"You don't understand, Dad. I'm pledging this fraternity and..." I filled him in on the whole story, beginning with the conversation in the basement and ending by replaying Aiden's and my chat over the cooler.

"Why would his parents say he was fine if it was not true?"

"I don't know," I burst out. "People keep asking me the questions like I'm the one who kidnapped him."

"From what I am hearing, there is no proof of kidnapping."

"I was there. I saw them take him."

"You can't be certain of what you saw," he argued. "Did he scream, call for help, or try to run away?"

"He— I— No, but the street was so loud. I couldn't hear him call for help."

"If he did."

"He did. He must have. Something happened to him that night and I'm going to prove it."

"Nothing happened, Ezra."

My already frayed nerves unraveled. "What would you know, Hakim? You're seven thousand miles away."

"Do not call me Hakim. I am your father."

"You're not my father. You're a stranger on the other side of the phone who is calling me a liar."

"Ezra!" Mom cried.

I flung the phone away. Rage licked at my heels and spurred me out of the room, the house, and off the property.

My phone went off. I took it out, dropped it on the street, and didn't look back.

VALENTINA

"You're going to have to talk to them at some point," I said softly.

"At some point, but not today."

Ezra lifted me and placed me on the bed. I let him rest his head on my lap.

Anger radiated off of him that his two-mile walk hadn't cooled. He came back and roused me out of bed with Adam.

"I'm sorry your family ganged up on you." I gently massaged his temples, willing his muscles to relax.

"You believe me, don't you?"

"You know I do."

He caught my hand and pressed a kiss to my palm. "Brian was right about one thing," he whispered. "I have to play this smart. That chief of police tipping off Aiden was a setback. He won't let his guard down around me knowing I still suspect him."

"What do we do now?"

"I... don't know. Mike won't help me. Mom won't help me. And I have no clue where to start?"

My mind cast about for an idea. "Michelangelo. What was he doing that we can't do ourselves? Maverick is a hacker. We can track down his..."

I trailed off as he shook his head.

"I went to Michelangelo because I didn't think I was at the point I needed a hacker. I know all the players. I just wanted Mike to track down Sawyer's parents, Aiden's family, and Teagan to talk to them. Human interaction like reporters do. Instead, Mike's acting strange and he ratted me out to Mom. I think he found something and it scared him. I don't want Maverick to find the same thing."

I dropped a kiss on his temple. "Maverick is smart, my love, and that's what you said we need to be. If there's something to find, he'll find it without attracting attention *or* turning on you. That's what we need."

"You're right, but—"

"No buts. Just relax, cool off, and then we'll talk to Maverick."

"Okay." At last, he let go. "That's what we'll do."

CONVINCING EZRA TO sit back and wait for Maverick to find something turned out to be the easy part. The hard part fell on Maverick. The weeks marched toward finals and every day Maverick had to tell us he found nothing.

"Nothing?" Sofia said. "How can there be nothing?"

Our textbooks sat abandoned on her coffee table in favor of steaming tea mugs and fancy cookies she pilfered from her parents' house.

"Maverick found a number and address for Sawyer's parents," I said. "We called the number and it rang... and rang... and rang. The number is old and so is the address."

"And Aiden?"

"Oh, him. We found plenty on Aiden Connelly," I said with a trace of bitterness. "He's the football star, high school valedictorian, and the best guy you could ever meet. At least that's what is kicking around social media and in his old school records. We were hoping for a buried high school therapist report on Aiden being a latent sociopath, but no such luck."

"Are you serious?"

"Yep. He doesn't have a record. He grew up in the nice part of town, and in high school he only got detention once for being tardy. He's clean."

Sofia poked me with her pink toes. "Except, he's not."

"Except that."

"What about Teagan? Your text said Maverick found something on her."

"Teagan is where it gets interesting." I lowered my voice even though we were alone in the room. "The official story is that she dropped out to be with her mom, right?"

"Yes," she said slowly.

I shook my head. "The mother of Elizabeth Teagan Kainer passed away over a year ago. Maverick found her obituary."

"What?" she hissed. She hurriedly put her tea on the table. "Is he sure?"

"They ran the news in the town's paper. It's legit. On top of that, Teagan did not have any other family. We don't know who to ask about where she is."

"Her mom is gone," she said again. I wasn't sure if she heard the rest. "But the Sallys told us..."

I looked away. "I know. Either Teagan lied to them or they lied to us. We have no way of knowing which."

"Pledging is almost over, Val. They're going to choose the six girls to become sisters this week. If they pick us, what do we do? All of this stuff is freaking me out and I wanted normal."

"You want to be a sister, Sof. I admit it, I do too. You asked me to wait for proof and I still don't have it. If they don't pick us, it won't matter." I put my hand over hers. "If they do, we'll go with our gut."

She flopped on the couch like a puppet whose strings were cut. "I hate this. I want that on record."

"It's on there."

"Good. Pass me my tea, please."

I handed her the mug. "I love that we're munching on tea and cookies when we're about to meet Blair and the girls for brunch."

She laughed. It was a welcome sound. "We had to get rid of the evidence quickly. Mom can sniff out when I steal her cookies."

We finished eating our contraband and headed out. Our brunch place was close to campus. Blair picked it out and we had to give her points for the cute, old-timey teahouse theme and delicious food. I showed up every week just for their muffins.

"Hello, girls." Yvette scurried out from behind the register. "Your table is all set up. I've got your muffins under the warmer, Val, and a pot of oolong tea brewing for you, Sofia."

Yvette was a short, round woman who gave the best hugs and wore a different colored wig every week. We quickly became her favorite regulars. Twelve girls eating almost everything on the menu and tipping heavily. Her face lit up whenever we came through the door.

Blair, Mai, Keily, and Palmer were seated and nibbling on their rolls.

"The other girls are running late," said Mai. "They got held up at the stand."

"The stand," Sofia said. "I'm still bitter about us losing the obstacle course race. We were so close."

"Lost by three points," I said. "One thing's for sure, we can hold our own with the Sams."

"But now we have to stand outside in the middle of November selling hot cocoa and brownies," Blair added. "I can't wait until pledging is over. It's not fair we have to do all the grunt shifts."

"Speaking of which, Patricia has me down for eight to ten tonight," said Sofia. "Want to keep me company, Val?"

"I'll come after I put Adam to bed."

"How bad is it working at night?" Keily asked. "You must be freezing."

"It's not so bad," Sofia replied. "I bundle up nice and tight. Plus, at that time I get a lot of couples. They're sweet strolling around arm in arm and snuggling up in the cold. I make a decent amount from them."

"We've raised almost nine hundred dollars so far," Mai threw in. "At this rate, we'll hit our goal by the end of January."

My phone chimed. I dug it out of my purse.

Reagan: You forgot your English notebook at the house.

Me: I've been looking all over for that! And in a house like mine it takes days.

Reagan: LOL. It's safe and sound. Pick it up tonight.

Me: Thanks.

"Does the couple-ogling mean you're ready to date?" Keily waggled her eyebrows at Sofia. "Or at least take a few guys out for a ride."

Sofia hid her smile behind her napkin. "Okay, so... there may be a guy."

I bolted upright. "What? Who? What guy? Where?"

She leveled me a pointed look. "This is why I didn't tell you. He's just this guy that I've seen around. We've talked like three times and

I don't even have his number. It's nothing to get excited about," she added quickly, seeing the beaming smile stretch across my face.

"What's his name?"

"Hudson."

"Where did you meet him?"

Bright spots of pink colored her cheeks. "At the stand. He's come by for hot cocoa a few times and we got to talking."

"A hookup or boyfriend material?" Keily asked.

Sofia's blush deepened. "Definitely boyfriend material."

"I have to meet him," I announced.

"You know you will. By introduction or stalking."

She knows me well.

"Does this mean Logan is officially in the friend zone?" asked Palmer.

She lost her smile. "He kind of always was. He's dropped hints a few times about taking me out to dinner or watching a movie in his room just the two of us, but I've said no. I'm sure he's not expecting anything."

I squeezed her hand under the table. "Don't worry about him. Logan can date anyone he wants, but he can't find a friend like Sofia Richards anywhere else. He should consider himself lucky."

Sofia leaned on my shoulder, silently passing on her thoughts in our own language.

"More about Hudson," Keily said. "What's he look like?"

"Tall, but not too tall. I hate straining my neck to kiss a guy." Sofia's eyes glazed over. "He fills out a shirt, but he's not too beefy and I swear his eyes sparkle when he grins.

"He's also got arrogance dripping from his pores. We got into a whole argument about the upper class hoarding resources and forming monuments to excess like the town of Evergreen."

"Did you tell him you were from Evergreen?"

"Yep, and he said that was obvious. It was written on my Prada sneakers and did I really think six-hundred-dollar *trainers* counted as dressing down? Oh and he's British," she cried. "So, he's extra cocky with that stupid accent."

Mai and Keily shared a look.

"Are you sure you like this guy?" Mai asked.

"Handcuffs and chivalry," I said under my breath.

Sofia whacked me under the table.

Brunch continued in the same vein. We talked relationships, school, classes, and the one thing that brought us all together, the Sallys. Soon, the other six girls arrived and joined in. Color me less than impressed when Blair proposed these meetups for her own gain, but weeks back, my attitude changed. Dare I say it, I considered them my friends—Blair too.

And I want them to be my sisters. I don't know what happened to Teagan or Sawyer and I desperately hope the Sallys don't either.

EZRA

"Dude, you haven't seen your mom yet, have you?"

Adam and I looked up from our work.

Adam's homework was to match up the number of stars to the right digit. Mine was a ten-page essay on ethics in journalism.

Ryder came into the kitchen and pulled out a seat. "She's calling me now. She wants to know how you're doing and if you're eating enough."

"No," I said. "I haven't called her."

"Have you talked to your dad?"

"Nope."

I had a new phone and a new number. My mom got her hands on it within a week. It didn't stop me from hitting ignore.

He shook his phone at me. "He's also calling me. Nice guy. We had a chat about his trip to Greece."

"Great. Is that all?"

Amusement colored his features. "Are you going to be mad forever?"

"Not forever," I said lightly. "Just until they admit they were wrong."

"Parents don't do that."

"Then I'll be mad forever."

He snorted a laugh. "How about until tonight? Your mom wants you to come over. She's having Cora make your favorite."

"Can't."

"Because?"

"I'm going to the Sam house tonight. Aiden's giving us a pop quiz to see if we've got that charter memorized."

"That should take an hour. Maybe two." Ryder stood and collected Adam. The little boy settled in his arms easily. "Deal with it, Ezra. Your mom cares about the truth more than anything. Make her see it."

I jerked a chin at Adam. "You don't have to take the kid. We were hanging out."

"Mom requests his presence." Ryder backed toward the door. "Think about what I said, man."

I sat unmoving for a long time, staring at the chair he vacated.

My favorite song by Cosplay Meltdown pierced the silence. I knew before I looked that it was Hakim.

I turned off the ringer and returned to my paper.

VALENTINA

"Do you think Hudson will come tonight?"

I arranged the brownies and chocolate chip cookies near the front. The chocolate would reel them in and then cupcakes and steaming hot drinks would finish the job.

Our bake sale stand was simple and cutely decorated. One of the handier sisters knocked together a proper wooden booth with an overhead sign and a solid square bottom that didn't let the wind pass through to our legs.

We scooted our chairs all the way in and wrapped comfortably in our blankets. The temperature wasn't unbearable. A solid sixty degrees blanketed our sleepy university. It was the wind whipping our hair and seeking us through our layers that was the problem.

"I never know," she said. "It depends on his shifts, but if he comes, we'll see him."

"His shifts?"

"He works for the school as a night janitor and maintenance man. He started a few weeks ago and doesn't go to school here. He's twenty and is finishing up his degree at the community college." She twisted around. "That's his shed."

I followed her line of sight to the small wooden shed behind us. "And now it all makes sense."

"What makes sense?"

"Why you're happy with the night shift *and* why you've set up in this spot when we usually put the booth closer to the quad."

She laughed under her breath. "I could deny it, but there would be no point. If he comes, he always drops by and we talk. I've been looking forward to those talks."

I rested my head on her shoulder. "Still, it can't be fun for you sitting around for two hours not knowing if he'll show. This time doesn't work for any of the other girls, but if you want me to keep you company—"

"Val, you're doing the morning shift after Adam goes to school. That's the only time that works for you. Being there for him is more important than slinging hot chocolate with me. Besides, I don't mind the quiet. It's well lit. I can read, listen to music, do homework, and when he's here, talk to Hudson."

I gazed around the cozy little pocket of campus. There were plenty of lamps casting a soft orange glow. We were positioned next to one of the walkways that led directly to Greek Row. Not as close to the quad, but I could see it in the distance.

We spent the hour and a half talking and selling treats to passing couples and stragglers heading back to Greek Row. Hudson didn't make an appearance but I was content to meet him when Sofia was ready. She was feeling her way with the opinionated, handy Brit. I didn't want to make it complicated.

"I have to pack up all this stuff and take it back," she said. "I usually text one of the sisters to come and help. Do you mind?"

"Course not. I need to drop by the house anyway."

It took only two trips. Sofia and I walked in with the food and then Reagan and Pat got up and followed us out to get the booth.

"How did it go tonight?" Reagan asked as we placed the stand on the back porch. "We're sorry to stick you with the late shift. You've been such a good sport, Sofia."

"I'm happy to do it," she said. "Honestly."

"You also clear about fifty to eighty bucks a night," Pat added. "We're going to hit our goal in no time."

"Now that we're talking about cruises," Sofia said. "Just because we lost doesn't mean we can't go on our own trip. What if we fundraise enough for two spring break cruises?"

"Hmm. I like the way this girl thinks," said Reagan.

The four of us entered the toasty house. Sofia shrugged out of her jacket and hung it on the coat rack.

"Are you staying, Sof?" I asked. "I'm just grabbing my notebook, but I can walk you back to the dorm."

"Stay, Sofia," Patricia spoke up. "We'll walk you back."

"Okay, thanks."

Reagan pointed down the hall. "Your notebook is in the living room. On the coffee table."

"Great." I moved around them. The doors were shut, but the light peeked through the curtains. I stepped inside and lit upon Blair, Mai, Keily, and Palmer.

"Hey, guys. What's up?"

Keily blew out a breath. "I'm shitting it over the test. I've read that charter backwards and forwards, but I bet it all goes out of my head."

"Test? What test?" Blair and I asked.

"The pop quiz we're taking on the charter tonight," Palmer explained. "Isn't that why you're here?"

I looked at the coffee table and noted the distinct lack of a notebook. "I guess so."

Blair shot up. "No one told me about a test. Pat was lending me her notes for my psych test tomorrow."

A smooth voice sounded behind me. "You will get the notes and I've got your notebook right here, Val." A cool hand gripped mine and placed something in it. "Sorry I had to steal this out of your backpack. We couldn't tell all of you there was a test or you might have spread it to the other pledges."

"Why shouldn't they know?" I asked.

Patricia, Reagan, Devon, Sloane, Callie, and Leighton walked to the front of the room.

"Because they're not pledges anymore," Leighton said. "Congratulations, ladies. You're our final six."

EZRA

I parked my car a few houses down in front of Beta Kappa Delta. A guy in a dreadlocks hat lay passed out in a chair on the lawn.

Why didn't I pledge this house? He's not worried about anyone snatching his ass.

"Ezra?"

Austin stuck his head out of the car and waved. His ride looked a lot like Jaxson's although I'm sure it didn't run him one point four million dollars.

And if it did, the senator certainly has something to answer for.

Austin fell in step with me. We walked the short distance to the house in silence.

Valentina insisted I should give him a chance. Somehow, I wasn't seeing the good guy under the asshat that namedropped his dad all over me to get close to Mom.

I bit back a sigh. What the hell. If Val wanted me to give him a chance, I would. But just one.

I reached the front door first and held it open.

"Ready for the test?" I asked.

Austin scrunched up his face as he crossed the threshold. "Test? What test?"

"Aren't you here for the test?"

He shook his head. "I forgot my comparative government textbook the other day. Do we have a test?"

"Gentlemen." Leo emerged from the dining room. "They're waiting for you in the basement."

"For a test?" Austin bleated. "Why didn't anyone tell me there was a test? What's it on?"

The brother just pointed down the hallway.

Groaning, Austin stomped off without a fight. I didn't follow.

"Since when can we go in the basement?" I asked Leo. "I thought it was off-limits to pledges."

A look crossed his face that I couldn't read. "It is. Hurry up."

My feet stayed rooted to the spot and soon his expression morphed into one I did know—annoyance.

"Is there a problem, Ezra?"

Something is going on.

Aiden isn't going to pull anything, another voice said. *He's playing the innocent game and Austin is down there too as a witness. I'm sure it's fine.*

"No," I said. "There's no problem."

Head up and body relaxed, I followed in Austin's path.

I'd thought about going into the basement again every time I set foot in their house. Once or twice, I'd tried the handle just to see if I'd get lucky. It was always locked. Whether it was because of pledge points or something more sinister, Aiden did not let anyone down there.

Until now.

I closed my hand over the knob and turned. The door gave way under my touch, beckoning me through.

I stepped into darkness. A flickering glow crept up the stairs, but wasn't strong enough to make it all the way. Neither were the murmur of voices.

Climbing off the last step, I took in the scene.

The basement itself wasn't much to look at. The worn couches, television, and pool table were what I expected. The eight men in hooded blue robes fanned out before a kneeling Austin, Colton, Lincoln, Luca, and Miles were not.

"Ezra Lennox." One of the robed men gestured to me. "Kneel."

I surged back. "The fuck I will. What the hell is this?"

Austin shot big eyes at me, shaking his head.

"There is nothing to fear." Aiden's voice slithered out of the middle robe. "Join us... brother."

"Brother?"

He can't mean...

Austin nodded. It was us. We were the chosen six.

"Kneel."

I knelt.

From my place, I peered into the hoods. Easton stood on Aiden's right. He nodded imperceptibly as our eyes met. My presence here pleased him.

It confused me.

Why would Aiden choose me after what went down? I've kept quiet and maintained my mask while I waited for Maverick to dig things up, but the two of us are far from friends. This doesn't make any sense.

"Ten weeks," Aiden began. "For ten weeks we tested your strength, stamina, intelligence, and bonds of brotherhood. And in those ten weeks, you six have proven yourselves to be high above the rest."

Shared smirks passed down the line of kneeling boys—all except for me. I fixed on Aiden's shadowed face.

"Membership in Nu Alpha Theta is not given, it is earned." Aiden passed his hand over us. "You, gentlemen, have earned your place here. You have earned the right to take the final test."

I stiffened. *Final test?*

"Easton, they're ready."

Easton's hand disappeared into his robe and emerged holding six envelopes.

"Open it when I say," Aiden ordered.

Easton placed the sealed blue missive on my palm. My name was written in neatly printed letters on the top.

"We've tested you for many qualities," Aiden continued, "but tonight we test you on the most important quality of all: trust.

"If you do not trust your brothers and know deep down that they trust you, then Nu Alpha Theta cannot thrive. We are only as strong as the bonds we share."

It was difficult to see his eyes through the hood and candlelight. All the same, I could have sworn Aiden was looking at me.

"Brother Ian, please begin."

The brother at the end of the row stepped forward and dropped his hood. He cleared his throat and said, "I've been sleeping with my stepmother since I was eighteen. My father believes the baby she had last year is his son. He's mine."

My jaw dropped. *What the fuck did he just say?*

"Thank you, Brother Ian," Aiden said calmly. "Brother Matthew, if you will."

My eyes widened as Ian stepped back and Matthew took his place. "My parents were bankrupt and on the brink of losing their house. I burned down our family grocery store for the insurance money. They still don't know it was me."

Austin whipped around, gaping at me like I could explain what was going on here.

One by one, the brothers stepped forward and revealed awful, dark, deep secrets.

"I was in a hit-and-run."

"I was in a gang. We knocked over every mom-and-pop store on my street."

"I paid someone to take the SATs for me," said Easton.

Aiden stepped forward.

I held my breath. *Is this it? Will he admit what he did?*

"Thank you, brothers," he said. "We honor the trust you've given here tonight."

Disappointment burned in me. Of course not. That would be too easy.

"The test is simple," he said to us. "To become a brother, all you have to do is return this trust with your own. In the envelopes... are your secrets."

"What?" Luca blurted. "What are you talking about?"

"Nothing is truly hidden," he replied. "I found the secret you keep buried and I put it in those envelopes. If you stand up and share it with us, you're in."

I flung the envelope away like it burned.

A secret I keep buried? What could he know? He couldn't know!

Sickening emotions flooded me to a parade of horrifying possibilities.

My off-track racing with Jaxson. My love of risky sex with Val.

Or a secret on the level of the horrible ones we heard. The woman who molested me all those years ago... and where her body is.

My stomach heaved at the thought. *Aiden can't know about that. He couldn't know anything about me. I'm too careful.*

The little blue envelope leered at me from the carpet, the information within taunting.

"No one knows what is in those envelopes except for me." Aiden's words slid into my ear. "Not the brothers. Not anyone. If you refuse to share it, I'll let you walk out of here right now and no one else will ever know what that note said."

He swept out his hands as if to embrace us. "But if you stand up and return the trust that was given to you, you can count yourself a brother, and a Sam, for life.

"Colton."

Colton looked at us for help. None of us could give it.

With hands that shook, he opened the envelope and took out a single cream card. His face went white as a sheet.

"N-no," he rasped. "I can't—"

"Then leave." Aiden's tone was unforgiving.

"This isn't the whole story! She—"

"Read it or go, Trent. Those are your options."

Colton squeezed his eyes shut. I thought he might cry.

"I... was—" He stopped. Yes, he was definitely crying. "I was accused of r-rape."

Luca shot away from him. The shock on his face mirrored my own.

"I was never charged because my accuser disappeared. But it's not what you think!" he burst out. "I didn't do anything! She was my ex. She lied to get back at me for dumping her."

Aiden acted like he didn't hear him. "Luca Esposito."

Luca straightened. "I don't have any secrets," he croaked. "None like that."

Aiden waited.

Slowly, Luca opened the note. His jaw slackened as he read. "How did you...?"

"Read it or leave, Romano."

"But I haven't told anyone," he cried.

"I won't repeat myself."

Luca flushed red under the candlelight. Every muscle of his being strained to keep his secret in.

"I'm gay!" he shouted under the white flag of surrender.

"Miles Beck," Aiden continued.

Miles opened his without protest. Aiden would not grant mercy, so why plead?

"I stalk my neighbor," he said tonelessly. "She doesn't know about the hundreds of photos I've taken of her."

"Lincoln Iona."

Lincoln read his so softly we barely heard, but it was still loud enough.

"My father cheats his clients. We bought our third beach house with the pension he stole from an elderly couple."

"Austin Worth."

Austin looked at me.

Why does he keep looking at me?! I can't save him! I can't stop this!

My nails dug sharply into my palm as he tore open his envelope. A sudden urge to snatch and tear it up overcame me. This was wrong and their supposed "show of trust" didn't change it.

"Austin, don't—"

"My father, Senator Worth, funnels foreign aid money into his own businesses overseas? That's not true!" Austin reared up. He threw the card in Aiden's face. "You have no proof!"

The president didn't flinch. "I have proof, Austin, but I doubt you want to see it. Sit."

Austin stumbled back onto the couch like the command was a physical blow.

Then Aiden turned to me. "Ezra Lennox." He reached up and finally dropped his hood. Aiden bore into me with an intensity that put my hairs on end. "Read it."

He doesn't have anything on me. I know he doesn't.

The envelope whispered to me, daring me to test that theory. Or maybe that was Aiden.

"Read it, Ezra."

My body moved of its own volition—bending, reaching, closing around the final secret.

I opened it.

My brother's gambling problem landed him in deep with a dangerous cartel. If they find him, they'll kill him.

The words blurred. A loud, high buzzing sounded in my ear, drowning out Lincoln's cries.

It's a lie.

The paper crumpled in my fist.

It has to be a lie.

"Read it, Ezra." Insistence made Austin's voice louder. "Go on. Tell us!"

I didn't get the choice to refuse.

"Don't you trust your brothers?"

The swirling emotions. The stomach-wrenching pain. The sheer horror of this cruel act. I took it all... and locked it away.

Getting to my feet, I gazed calmly into Aiden's eyes—the mannequin man once again.

"No," I said evenly. "I don't."

His brow twitched. "What? Do you think it's a lie? It's all true, Ezra. I have proof."

"I'm sure you think you do."

In front of everyone, I folded the note and put it in my pocket.

"It's been a fun semester, gentlemen," I said to the room. "But on further thought, I don't believe this fraternity is for me. Good luck to you." I glanced at the men kneeling on the floor. "You'll need it."

I turned my back on them.

"I didn't say you could leave, Lennox," Aiden snapped.

Giving no sign I heard him, I marched up the stairs. Heavy footfalls followed me.

"Ezra!"

I threw open the door. I made it as far as the front hall before he seized me.

"You're not even going to ask how I found out?"

I spun around and roughly knocked him off. Aiden recovered fast. He grabbed my collar and shoved me against the living room door. I gasped as his forearm pressed down on my neck.

"You were smart not to read your secret. I was never going to let you become a brother," he hissed. "Did you think you were the only one who has hacker friends?"

My eyes flared for more than lack of air.

A grin spread across his face. "Yeah. I know you haven't stopped digging into my life, Lennox. Lucky for me I can play that game too. Finding Luca's porn stash and Miles's creepshots took a minute. You weren't so easy." He punctuated his sentence by pressing harder.

"A little rich boy like you can afford the best of Maverick Tech. I couldn't get into your computer, but your big brother isn't nearly so protected." Aiden tsked. "He's really been incredibly stupid. It's amazing he's made it this—"

My hand flashed. I viciously jabbed my thumb in his soft, vulnerable eye.

"Argh!"

Aiden released me instantly. His arms flew up to clutch his face and I grabbed hold of one and twisted. Changing our positions, I shoved Aiden face-first into the door and yanked his arm behind his back.

"You fucking move and I'll break it," I said into his ear. "Now who's the stupid one? You didn't think the little rich boy would pay someone to teach him to fight?"

Of all the responses I expected from Aiden, laughter was not one of them.

He shook in my hold, wracked with guffaws.

"Well played," he said. His breath fogged the glass. "I did not expect this. My fault for losing my temper."

I lifted his arm higher, feeling the socket strain. His laughter cut off with a pained grunt.

"Don't make the same mistake, Ezra," he forced out. "I'll keep your brother's secret. All you have to do is stay the fuck out of my fraternity and my life. It's a fair trade."

"I don't buy your bullshit. My brother doesn't smoke, drink, or even cross lanes without fucking signaling! You expect me to believe he gambles *and* owes money to a cartel?"

"We all have our vices." His red eyeball rolled in its socket, seeking me out of the corner of his eyes. "It's all there on his phone and laptop. The promises he'll find a way to pay them back. The panicked emails to sweet Amina. Just say the name Sons of Slaughter and smell him shit his pants. That's all the proof you need."

His words lodged in my mind, pulverizing my certainty. Sons of Slaughter? Could this be true? Did Brian do this?

I shook myself. *No. He's my brother.*

"You're lying." I bore down harder. "I know my brother."

"Test me, Ezra, and *everyone* will know him," he snarled. "The cartel doesn't know where he is, but I can change that in a second. Your brother will spend the rest of his life in your gated ivory tower because the second he steps out, they'll put a bullet in his head."

"You're lying!" The scream tore from my throat.

"Go on. Test my bluff. We'll see who is lying."

My breaths eked out in hard, rough pants. The hands holding him trembled.

I read people too well to not pick up on the smug, self-assured confidence lacing his tone. He believed he was telling the truth.

"Why are you doing this?!" I reeled back and smashed him into the door again, again, and again. A side of me no one had ever seen, splintered and formed in a darkened classroom as a helpless child begged her to stop, broke free of its cage.

I slammed his head onto the door again. Blood spurted from his ruined nose, staining the glass.

"All this because I dug up your valedictorian speech and a photo of you at the town's parade?" I shrieked. "And now I know without a fucking doubt that there's more. There's so much more," I forced out. "You did do something to Sawyer."

Aiden laughed. A broken nose didn't slow this psycho down. "Don't worry about Sawyer. He's in, what they call, a better place."

Shock made me loosen my hold. "You killed him?"

He took his chance. Aiden spun and threw me off. I bounced off the opposite wall, punching the air from my lungs. Through a watery lens, I saw him dust off his robes. He wiped his blood on the sleeve.

"Whatever happened to Sawyer," he said evenly, "you won't find out because you're done. You're not investigating him, Teagan, or me anymore. Say it."

My lips peeled back in a snarl. I should have snapped his arm when I had the chance.

"Say it," he demanded, "and the Sons of Slaughter won't visit Evergreen. No one will find out about your brother and we'll all go back to our lives like none of this happened."

"I'll stop," I croaked. "I'll forget I heard your names."

He smiled—and the blood staining his face tainted it horribly. "See? That wasn't so hard." Dropping his head back, Aiden took a deep breath and let it out slow. "You know, I love this part of pledging," he said conversationally.

The change in tone threw me. My eyes narrowed as I balled my fists.

"All you pledges are on your best behavior for ten weeks. Then a few sentences in an envelope reduces you to the crumbled pieces of your masks." His eyes flicked over my head. "I wonder how your girlfriend is handling it."

"Valentina?"

Is he saying they are...? Right now?

I raced out of the house; Aiden forgotten.

"Valentina!"

VALENTINA

"We are sisters in more than blood, friendship, or name," Leighton said. "What binds us is even stronger—loyalty and trust."

Blair, Palmer, Keily, Mai, Sofia, and I knelt on the living room carpet. Twenty minutes ago, it was a cozy space of movie nights and study sessions. The candles, drawn curtains, and the long, dancing shadows of the women standing before us turned this space into something else entirely.

A shiver went up my spine. Bound in loyalty and trust? What did that mean?

"Reagan." Leighton bowed to her. "If you would begin."

"Thank you, sister."

Reagan moved in front of us. "My stepfather and his brother raped me repeatedly from nine years old until a social worker took me away at twelve."

Gasps filled the room.

"Reagan, oh my gosh." I jumped to my feet and she gently pushed me down.

"It's alright, Valentina. I'm okay."

She walked back to the mantle. Confusion niggled me as Patricia took her place.

"I used to shoplift," Pat said. "Little things at first. But I graduated to pickpocketing when I realized I could get away with it."

"What's going on?" Sofia asked. "Why are you saying these things?"

"Do not interrupt," Leighton said. "It will make sense soon."

I slowly sat back on my heels. Underneath the table, I reached for my best friend's hand.

One after the other, the sisters revealed their deepest secrets. Not a thing made sense... till Reagan revealed the envelopes.

"I want to make it clear you do not have to reveal these secrets. If they mean more to you than your place here, you may walk out the door and no one will stop you," said Leighton. "Only I know what is written, so I will know if you lie. Reveal your secret and become a Sally, or leave Zeta Rho Sigma and never come back. The choice is yours."

Leighton looked at me and I went rigid. Just as quickly she moved on to the end of the row. "Mai Nguyen."

Mai hesitated to take her envelope.

"I suggest," Leighton said smoothly, "that none of you beg, snivel, or plead. I won't be impressed and it will not change your options. Your sisters named their secrets with their heads held high. Do the same."

Mai's hand shook so badly she dropped the envelope on the first try. She picked it up again and ripped it open. "I slept..."

Mai truly tried to hold her head up as tears dripped down her face.

"I slept with my TA for a better grade on my midterm."

"Mai?" Keily breathed. "You wouldn't—"

She touched her shoulder. Mai roughly shoved away.

"Keily Baas."

Keily was clearly torn between wanting to comfort her friend and running away.

"I have two boyfriends and I... use both for their money," she read. "I'm d-desperate to fit in with my new rich friends." Shame burned her face. Rocking back, Keily drew her knees to her chest and dropped her head on them. She looked like a small child shutting the world out.

"Palmer Holbrooke."

Palmer rested one hand on Keily's head as she read hers. "My father has..." She stopped. Her eyes grew huge as she scanned the paper over and over. "This isn't true."

"What did I say about sniveling?" Leighton's hard, unforgiving tone was foreign to me.

"This is a lie," Palmer cried. "You can't just make stuff up!"

"We both know it's not a lie, Palmer," she replied. "I got the truth from you. You have two options. Choose."

"What does it say?" Mai croaked.

"It doesn't matter because it's not true. My father doesn't have a second family." She leveled a shaky finger at Leighton. "Have you been spying on me? That's illegal! I could—"

Leighton waved her away like she was an annoying gnat. "Blair Davenport."

"I have no problem reading this," Blair said over Palmer's noise. "I've done nothing to be ashamed of. Neither has my family."

She unfolded the envelope and tugged out the small cream card. She cleared her throat. "My b-boyfriend."

I caught the trip and the slight widening of her eyes. She recovered and kept going.

"My boyfriend is my best friend's father. He's married and... we've been sleeping together... since I was... sixteen."

I cringed with every word she labored to get out.

"I make videos... of... myself ma-ma-masturbating."

Tears filled her eyes. It was obvious to me Blair did not consider for a second that Leighton would unearth this secret.

"And send them to him," she finished.

With deliberate movements, Blair put the note back in, stuffed it in her pocket, and knelt on the carpet. She held her chin up even as wetness dripped down her face and soaked her collar.

"Sofia Richards."

I found my voice.

"That's enough," I cried. "This is wrong. Sofia, you don't have to do this."

She squeezed my fingers. "It's okay, Val. You know everything about me. I don't have dark secrets. Nothing in this envelope can hurt me."

She opened it before I could stop her.

"My mother sold my intellectual property to competitors for a cut of the profits. All in a bid to one day amass enough to buy them all out."

Sofia stuffed the card back and tossed it on the table.

I studied her. She seemed fine.

"Valentina Moon."

Reagan placed the envelope in my hand.

I should walk out now. I can't make a grand speech about not having secrets. My secrets have secrets. They have repercussions that can destroy lives and bring my world crashing to its knees.

And you're too well protected for Leighton to have found out, a voice whispered. *She could never know the worst of it.*

I peeled back the flap, hanging on to my conviction.

It shattered as my eyes landed on the four typed bold words.

How...

I stopped. Stopped breathing. Stopped moving. Stopped thinking.

"Valentina." Leighton's voice reached me from far away. "Is there a problem?"

Raising my head, our gaze connected in a spark that charged the atmosphere. I read the challenge in her eyes as plainly as the betrayal that shone in mine.

I pressed the card to my chest and spoke without breaking our connection. "I was raped when I was fourteen. My rapist gave me an STD."

Keily gasped. "Oh my gosh. Adam—"

"Don't," I snapped. "Just don't."

She fell silent.

Leighton inclined her head. "Thank you, ladies. I know how hard it must have been. It was difficult for me and the sisters who came before you. Believe us when we say, we appreciate the bravery you showed and the trust you put in us. After tonight, we will never speak of this again." She held out her hands. "Rise, pledges, and become sisters."

The girls rose on legs that trembled and fell into the arms of the sisters.

"The worst is over," Pat announced. "We've got cupcakes, brownies, and wine in the kitchen. Let's celebrate."

Reagan walked up to me, arms out. I sidestepped her and strode out the door.

"Where are you going, Val?"

I paused on the welcome mat. "I'm leaving," I said blankly. "I'm out, aren't I?"

"Did I say you were?" Leighton turned me around. "It's true you broke the rules and didn't say what was on your card but"—she winked—"I won't tell if you don't."

I blinked. "Why would you give me a pass?"

She leaned in so close her forehead brushed my nose.

"Because I want you, Valentina," she whispered. "I wanted you from day one."

"Wha—"

Bang! Bang! Bang!

I stumbled into Leighton jumping away from the door. My heart galloped out of control.

"Valentina! Valentina, get out of there!"

"Ezra?"

The doorknob rattled furiously. "Valentina!"

"Get that," Leighton said, sounding almost bored. "You can miss the celebration, but I expect to see you tomorrow to talk about your new responsibilities as a Sally."

She walked off, leaving me stunned.

Who the hell is this girl? I don't know her at all.

I unlocked the door and Ezra shoved inside. My love's perfect veneer had been broken anew.

His hair was a mess. His eyes huge and bulging.

"We have to get out of here. Their initiation—"

"It's too late," I said. I gently cupped his cheek. "It's done, baby."

"No."

Ezra took hold of me and pulled me outside. Out on the concrete steps of the neat shiny homes, he gathered me in his arms. We hugged tightly, our faces buried in each other's necks, and drawing the only comfort that could sustain us.

"What did yours say?" I whispered.

"It said… that I was molested."

"Oh, Ezra." Tears leaked from my eyes. "I'm so sorry."

"It's okay." His voice was low and raspy. "It's not like no one knows. What about you?"

My nails dug into his shoulder. "I don't know how but… it said I am a murderer."

Chapter Eight

E*zra* "They hacked us, Val. They got everything they needed from our phones, computers, all of it." I punched the dash. "Shit!"

Val put her hand on my thigh. "Ezra, why don't you pull over? You shouldn't drive like this."

"I can't. I have to keep moving. I want to be as far as possible from that place." I veered through the lanes, pushing my speed to the breaking point.

"Aiden told you they couldn't crack Maverick Tech," she reminded. "So how did Leighton know to put that in my card?"

I shook my head. "I doubt Leighton cracked what Aiden couldn't. There's one way she could have gotten it and it's from the person sitting in a jail cell cursing you for ruining their life."

"Oh my gosh, you're right." Val let out an audible sigh of relief. "That's the only explanation."

"I'm done with the frat, Val. I didn't read my card. Aiden kicked me out." The half lie ached like needles in my throat.

I have to tell Val the truth, but I can't until I talk to Brian. There's a chance Aiden is wrong. I need my brother to tell me he's still the man I know.

"He's disgusting for manipulating you," she said. "If and when you tell people about your assault is your choice. Holding it over your head to become a brother was a line he shouldn't have crossed. It's a line Leighton shouldn't have crossed either. She made them reveal terribly personal information."

"Is Sofia okay?"

"I'm not sure. I'm going to call her as soon as we get home."

"I'm going to drop you home." My white-knuckle grip on the wheel tightened. "I need to go to my mom's."

"All right. But then come back and let me make you feel better."

This is Val. She knows me. She knows when I need her.

The suffocating pain began to ease.

"I love you," I said.

"I love you too."

I took Val home and waited for her to go inside.

My head was a tangled mess driving to my mother's house. What do I say to Brian? What if it's true? You don't get a name like Sons of Slaughter for trafficking in fluffy kittens. How much danger is my brother in? And my sister-in-law and nieces?

Aiden's threats were too specific to be false. And Brian was still here. Weeks and weeks when his longest stay since he was eighteen was two.

I burst through the front doors.

"Are you alright, Master Ezra?" asked our butler.

"Where is Brian? I need to speak to him now."

"Let me get your mother," Evan replied. "She wanted to know the minute you arrived."

I put him out of my mind as he scurried off.

"Brian?" I called. "Brian!"

"Ezra?"

I skidded to a stop just short of the living room. Mom stepped into my path. She beamed at the sight of me.

"Sweetie, you came."

"Mom, I can't right now. I have to find Bri—"

She grabbed me in a strangling hug. "I'm so sorry, sweetie. Our fight got out of control and I was not at my best. I should have heard you out."

Her apology burrowed beneath my single-minded focus. "I appreciate it, Mom. Thank you." I tried to pull away. "Can we talk about this later?"

"Yes, we'll talk later." She cupped my cheek, smiling at me like my eyes held Christmas morning. "I have a surprise for you."

"I can get it later too," I said. "I need to talk to Brian."

"Brian is in the dining room, love. He's waiting for us to start dinner."

"Okay." I made to go.

"No." Mom snagged my sleeve. "Come with me."

Frustration pounded my patience. "Mom, give me a minute. Brian and I—"

"Hakim, he's here." She pulled me into the living room. "Ezra is here."

My feet planted to the spot. A man with a neatly trimmed salt-and-pepper beard and sparkling obsidian eyes rose from the armchair.

"Meet your son," Mom said.

"My son," he repeated. "My Ezra."

I willed moisture into my throat. "Who... are you?" I asked dumbly.

Mom laughed. "You know who he is, sweetie. Go ahead." She gave me a tiny shove right into his arms.

Hakim enfolded me to his chest—whole and real and warm.

"My eldest son," he whispered, voice choked. "So long I've waited for this day."

My nose buried in his blazer, inhaling a scent of ginger, lemongrass, and fresh clean soap.

My father's scent, my dull mind supplied.

His beard tickled my forehead.

Hakim's beard on my forehead. His arms around me. Him here... in front of me. Not a voice in my ear or a face on a screen.

"I'm sorry, Ezra," he said. "For more than I can name. I love you."

Behind me, Mom cried—soft sniffling sobs that echoed in my mind.

My hands rose of their own power. In the next breath, I was hugging him back, so tightly he grunted, and he responded by squeezing me just as hard.

"I love you too, Dad."

RYDER'S CAT SPLAYED in my lap, purring furiously. I scratched the creature on autopilot.

"My dad is here. After nineteen years, he just hops on a plane and comes out here."

"He's here," Adam replied.

Two weeks had passed since the initiation and my father's surprise visit. The first semester was finally over and winter break had begun.

The two of us were in the living room. Adam sat at his little kid table, munching on reindeer Rice Krispie Treats. Val was going all out for the holiday. Four weeks at home and the first Christmas all of us were spending together. She gave Caroline the bug and, as a result, the house looked like Santa's workshop threw up in here.

Christmas trees in every room, lights strung through the corridors, mistletoe over the entrances, and a Christmassy theme to all of our food. That morning I ate a bowl of porridge with strawberry Santas.

I loved that woman to death, but none of it was enough to distract me from the fact that the man who'd been seven thousand miles away from me my whole life was now less than five.

"He's at my mom's house, Adam. So apparently it wasn't impossible for him to get on a plane. There wasn't this impenetrable barrier preventing him from seeing his oldest son."

"No," Adam agreed.

"And he and Mom are so happy."

"Happy."

"It's messed up," I said. "What are they happy about? They broke up because she wouldn't give up her career and he wouldn't give up his home. How are they cool living in the same house all of a sudden, chuckling over my baby pictures? It's crazy."

"It's crazy."

"That's what I'm saying," I cried.

A snicker snapped my head around. Val leaned against a column, eyes shining with amusement.

"Ezra, leave that baby alone and let him watch his cartoons."

I grumbled under my breath. "But he's a good listener."

"I am too." She crooked a finger at me. "Come, my love. I'll have Maverick move his project in here. He can watch him while you and I talk."

"Can I bring the cat?"

"I thought you didn't like her?"

"I like cats that like me." I picked up the purr machine and settled her in the crook of my arm. "Maverick used to bring home a lot that didn't. I won't tell you how many times those mangy things scratched me."

Val went off to find the animal rescuer in question. Maverick was working on some techy programming thing that was in parts now but would soon be a Christmas present. He moved it to the living room to let Val and me snag a minute alone.

"Are you really not happy your father is here?" she asked as we curled up on the couch in our bedroom.

I blew out a breath. "I don't know how to feel. Our situation has always been complicated. Growing up he wasn't here but he also wasn't missing. Whenever I wanted to talk to him, I'd call and he'd answer the phone. We'd video chat and talk for hours about everything going on in our lives. Between that and Mom, it was rare that I felt like I was missing something."

"Rare," she said softly. "There were times that you did."

I nodded. "A phone call describing about my birthday party isn't the same as him being there, even a five-year-old knew that."

She stroked my cheek. "Did you ever tell him you had those feelings?"

"No."

"It makes sense, then, that he finally came to see you after all of this time."

My brows drew together. "How?"

"Your situation wasn't ideal, but as long as his son put on a smiling face, he could believe it was enough. Finally telling him how you felt and then cutting off contact must have scared him into taking this step. He doesn't want to lose you."

She pressed a kiss to my temple and then on my nose. I closed my eyes, sinking into the warmth and love that was Valentina.

"It's a lot to process after all of this time and it's okay if you want to take it slow."

I scrubbed my tired face. "I wish I knew what I wanted. Mom invited us over for Christmas Eve dinner. We're all going to sit around like one big happy family and—"

—and I haven't spoken to Brian yet.

"And what?" Val asked.

"And home is the one place I don't have to be the mannequin man. Pretending everything is fine is as wrong as ruining my first visit with my father."

"It doesn't have to be either or," she said. "You can have a good visit and a serious talk about your fight."

I cracked a smile. "You are wise and beautiful, Valentina Moon."

"Am I a better listener than Adam?" she teased.

"No."

"Hey."

I ducked her swat, startling Cara out of my lap. The cat beat it out of my room, which was good because our minute alone got pornographic after that.

That night, I trailed my finger along her sleeping form. My mind wouldn't quiet enough for sleep. A repeat of the night before, and the night before that, ever since my second trip to the basement.

I needed to speak with Brian, but Dad's visit and Val's wish for a normal, happy Christmas got to me. I wanted to enjoy this ignorant bliss through one more holiday and this holiday, with the four of us together for the first time, warranted the reprieve. Why let Aiden ruin it?

Aiden Connelly.

The name stirred familiar loathing on the millionth pass through my thoughts. Val and I agreed not to talk about the Sams or Sallys over the holiday. I jumped on it to save me from lying to her, but it didn't stop me going around in my head about how to deal with him.

Somehow, he discovered Maverick's digging and, excluding his father, Maverick was the best hacker I knew. I haven't begun to scratch the surface of Aiden Connelly and I couldn't try if what he said about Brian was true.

But he did something to Sawyer and most likely Teagan too. If I give up finding them, Aiden gets off free and clear to do it again.

I drew Val close, enticing a soft, sleepy moan from her lips.

"Sleep, baby," I shushed.

One of us should sleep. And I would be the one lying awake, wishing I knew what to do.

VALENTINA

"Are you sure you're okay?"

"I'm fine," Sofia said. I picked up on her eyeroll through the phone. "I swear you're more worried about me than for yourself."

"Because you're my best friend."

I picked up the watermelon and transferred it to the cutting board. The chef was officially on duty, but I was doing my best to lighten his load.

"I know." Her tone softened. "I love you too. But really, Val, I'm okay. Leighton's research didn't include the fact that Mom told me about selling the formula herself. She was in a bad place after Dad's heart attack and a lot came out. I was disappointed, but I forgave her weeks ago. To be honest, I got it easy. At least I didn't discover my father had a second family or... you know... statutory rape."

My sympathetic hiss was hard to hear over the thwack of the knife. "I wonder if our secrets will truly stay secret."

"Can I ask you something?"

"Go for it."

"Why did you agree to become a Sally after that night? When you walked out, I thought you were doing it for good."

I stilled. I stayed because I'm going to find out what Leighton knows about me, why she's fixated on me, and what happened to Teagan once and for all.

"I'll answer if you do too," I said.

"Deal."

"I became a Sally because I still want the same things," I said instead. "I want what we were before that night and if we can get back there again, we'll have the four years of normal and fun."

I did want those things, but if the Sallys could give it, I no longer knew. What I did know is I couldn't let Sofia find out what was written on that card.

"Do we still think the Sallys were behind Teagan going AWOL?" she asked.

"Ezra believes Aiden and his buddies in the basement are the villains in this story and we don't have proof saying otherwise," I admitted.

"In that case, I can say my reasons are yours. I want sisters."

"Am I not enough for you?"

She laughed. "I want *more* sisters. They won't come near your level, but they'll do."

"Just remember they won't come near my level."

"Merry Christmas, Val."

"Merry Christmas." I gave the watermelon another satisfying whack. "I'm coming by later with presents and Christmas tree watermelon salad. Festive and healthy."

"Daddy will love it. See you soon."

"Bye."

I tossed my phone on the counter and returned to my Christmas Eve offering. Ezra's mother invited us all to dinner that night and I was heavily focused on impressing her.

It was Christmas. Everything had to be perfect.

EZRA

"Ezra's dad in the flesh," Jaxson said. "Somebody pinch me."

"Everyone just be cool," I replied.

The six of us climbed the steps to the wreath-covered door.

"Don't say or do... anything," I finished.

Jaxson knocked my shoulder. "You don't trust us around your old man?"

"It's better I don't answer that."

Evan let us inside and we scattered in different directions. I went straight for Mom's bedroom.

I knocked once, then let myself inside.

"Mom?"

"In the closet, sweetie."

I stuck my head in her walk-in. Mom twirled in front of the mirror, eyeing her green satin dress from all angles.

"Is that a new dress?"

"What? No," she said. "Why would you think that?"

My brow crept up my forehead. "I think that because I've never seen it before. It's not your usual style either. You said once you're north of forty, your hemlines are south of your knees."

She pinked. "This is a perfectly appropriate hemline, and if you insinuate I'm over forty again, you're out of my will."

I laughed. "Either you are or you had Brian at ten years old."

"Stranger things have happened."

"Are you wearing that for our guest?" I asked point blank.

"Excuse— Just what are you accusing me of, Ezra?"

"I'm accusing you of buying a new dress."

She stalked toward me. "Honestly, the way you talk to your mother. Wait for me downstairs." She shut the door in my face.

I stared at the wood, sensing Mom primping inside.

This is a worrying development.

I left in search of Val. She was in the dining room setting out her creation among the magnificent spread.

Christmas music played on low and mingled with the wafting aroma of Cora's cooking. Beef tenderloin, creamy mashed potatoes, roasted sweet potatoes, mixed vegetables, soup, turkey, salad, and dessert. Between the nine of us, we wouldn't make a dent, but we'd have delicious leftovers for days.

Val took one look at me. "What's wrong?"

"My mom is wearing a new dress."

She stared at me. "And...?"

"And"—I dropped my voice—"you don't think... she and my dad...?"

Her eyes bugged. "I wouldn't know. Do *you* think she and your dad...?"

"Shit. I hope not. The guy is married with two other kids."

"I'm sure it's nothing," she said. "It's Christmas and her ex is visiting. It's enough of a reason to want to look your best."

I bobbed my head. "You're right, of course." My eyes drifted up in the direction of my mom's bedroom. "But I'll sit between them just in case."

An hour later, laughter and great conversation filled the room.

"Adam, how many toes do you have?" I asked.

He threw up both hands. "Ten!"

We clapped and cheered him. "All right. I knew we'd figure it out in the end."

"He is the most adorable little boy," said Mom. "Adam, don't leave without getting your present from under the tree."

"Yay, presents," he yelled.

Adam bolted out of the seat and took off.

"Wait, baby. Not yet." Valentina chased after him.

"Tavi is about his age," said Hakim. "He cannot wait to meet you. Dana as well."

"I want to meet them too," I replied.

"Soon. Very soon."

Mom leaned around me. "Did you try Cora's rosemary rolls, Hakim? She made them especially for you."

"How kind. I must try one."

Their hands grazed each other as she passed him the roll.

"How long are you staying, Dad?" I asked.

"I don't wish to overstay my welcome." His eyes drifted over my head. "But I am in no rush. I want to spend time with my son."

An idea popped in my head. "You could stay with us. There's plenty of room at the manor."

"Don't be silly, Ezra," Mom cut in. "Caroline has more than enough on her plate with all of you at home. I've got nothing but empty rooms here."

"But it'll be easier for us to spend time together if he's just down the hall."

Mom tossed my argument aside with the flick of her wrist. "You're just down the road, sweetie. It's hardly difficult now."

Dad patted my shoulder. "It's bad enough I've imposed on your mother. I could not do so to your friend's mother as well."

"You're not imposing, Hakim. I can't express how happy I am that you and Ezra are together after all of this time." She reached out. "Stay as long as you can."

I snagged her hand out of the air before he got there.

"Mom, I forgot to say earlier how beautiful you look in that dress. Definitely not a day over forty."

"A little silver-tongued devil." She popped a kiss on my cheek. "But you're not a liar."

She returned her hand to her lap.

"Wouldn't that mean she had me when she was ten?" Brian piped up.

I fell silent as everyone laughed.

Today is not the day for our talk. Not on Christmas.

My fists balled under the table.

But Christmas is the reason we need to have that talk.

My brother, who had to split his Christmases between parents, would not miss out on being there for his children unless he had a good reason.

With every passing day I knew, Aiden did not lie.

THE ROUND-EYED, LIGHT-up robot zoomed around on triangular wheels, chasing a squealing Adam through the living room.

Maverick's gift had been a big hit with the toddler. All around, this Christmas haul was the best by far.

We woke up that morning and went straight to the Christmas tree. Breakfast and changing out of our pajamas as we exchanged gifts and delighted in Adam's happy shriek at each unwrapped present.

Adam received a mountain of new toys, clothes, and shoes. My family hooked me up as well. Adam drew pictures of me and him that Val hung in our room. Jaxson passed on the secret unreleased album of Cosplay Meltdown. Maverick gifted me a brand-new laptop with upgraded protections. Ryder got me cat toys for Cara and laughed himself sick while I opened them. And Val presented me two tickets for a getaway cruise to the Cayman Islands.

"This is the best Christmas I've ever had," Val said. She stretched out on all four of our laps, content and happy as she watched Adam play. "The only thing that could have made it better is Mom being here."

"Next time she will be," Caroline said. She reclined on the chaise, bundled tightly in the blankets Ryder heaped on her. "And we'll mark the occasion properly with a big Christmas dinner and all the families together."

"That would be great. Maybe Ezra's dad could come again with the whole family." She beamed up at me. "Wouldn't you love that, guys? A big Christmas family reunion. All of us together. We have to tell them so they don't make other plans."

"Let's get through this Christmas first, Mom," said Ryder, the voice of reason. "In November, if you're feeling up to it, we can make plans."

"I'm feeling up to it right now, my love. Twelve hours to enjoy this Christmas and then we'll plan for the next."

Twelve hours. That's how long I have too.

THE NEXT MORNING, HAKIM let me into the house.

"Ezra, my son."

He had been doing that. Saying my name like it was the first time he heard it. Calling me son like it surprised him to say it. And looking at me like we just met. In many ways, we have.

"Are you staying for lunch?" he asked. "Cora is trying her hand at one of my favorite meals. I'd like you to experience a taste of my home."

Hakim put his arm around me and led me into the house. The wonder of him being close enough to touch hadn't faded. He was the man I knew since I was old enough for Mom to put the phone to my ear, and him in person was familiar and yet different.

Like me, he was classic, well-dressed and neatly trimmed. His clothes were understated to a casual eye and expensive to knowing ones. No reason they shouldn't be. The restaurant my mother wandered into on that faithful day was one of many he owned.

Smart, discerning, and ambitious. That was Hakim Asadi.

I favored my mother in appearance except for where Hakim's genes burned strong. Endless black pools where green eyes should be. Thick raven strands for her second son and light brown waves for her first.

Hakim was a part of me as much as Mom, and as we walked through the halls speaking in polite tones instead of what truly brought him all this way, I realized we shared more than features.

"Lunch would be great," I replied. "But I have to talk to Brian first. Where is he?"

"His bedroom, I believe. He mentioned calling his wife and the girls."

"Thanks, Dad."

I was walking off before I finished the sentence.

Brian opened his door on the fifth knock. The phone was stuck to his ear.

"Yeah, it's Ezra, Mina. Want to say hi? Put the girls on too." Brian shoved the phone on me.

"Hi, Ezra," said a warm voice. "How are you? Did you enjoy your Christmas?"

I fixed on my brother as I spoke.

"I did," I replied. "It was perfect having my whole family here. Plus, eating Christmas dinner with my father. The only thing that would have made it better was if you and the girls were here."

Brian looked away.

"I wish we could have been there too. We miss you both," said Amina. "Girls, say hi to Uncle Ezra."

"Uncle Ezra! Uncle Ezra!"

Excited shrieks and squeals rattled my eardrums. I stared at my brother the whole time.

"I love you guys," I said. "I'll see you soon. Bye."

Brian reached out. "Wait—"

I hung up.

"Sorry. You can call back in a minute and tell them when you'll be home." I cocked my head. "When is that, by the way? You've been here for months."

He laughed. "You trying to get rid of me, little brother? Want Mom all to yourself again?"

"I want to know why you haven't gone back to your job or your family."

"I'm taking time off from work." Brian went over to the bed. A pile of Christmas gifts sat on the comforter. He gave me his back as he removed tags and folded his new clothes. "I spent more time in the air than I did with my family. This is the longest I've been in Evergreen. The longest I've been with Mom and you. I thought you'd be pleased."

"I'm happy you're here as long as it's because you want to be with us," I said, "and not because you're hiding from the Sons of Slaughter."

He stilled.

"Your four-month visit has nothing to do with your gambling debts, right? It's not about you getting in too deep with a cartel?" My voice rose, feeding the power of the shots firing at his back. "It's not because you fucked up and got yourself into serious danger!"

The wool sweater slipped through his fingers and covered his feet. I barely recognized the faint, raspy croak that came from him as my brother's voice. "How... did you f-find out?"

"That's what you have to say to me?" The veneer broke. The fury, pain, and fear I'd been holding back for weeks gushed forth in a torrent that dragged me under. "You want to know who told me and I want to know why it wasn't you! Look at me!"

I jumped on him. Gripping his shoulder, I spun him to face me and Brian's feet tangled in the sweater.

"Ezra!"

We fell, collapsing at the foot of the bed. That didn't stop me.

"What the fuck happened, Brian?!" I climbed on top of him. "How much money do you owe?"

"Ezra, get off!" He tried to buck me.

I threw him down and pushed my forearm down on his neck. Not as hard as Aiden, but enough to get his attention.

"You're involved with a cartel?! How? Why?"

"K-keep your voice down."

"Mom doesn't know, does she?" Spittle flew from my mouth. "What are they going to do to you, Brian? What's going to happen?"

The first tear landed on his cheek and traveled down like one of his own. Eyes widening, he stopped struggling.

"Noth-thing," he forced out. "Nothing will happen."

He pried me off his neck and shoved me off. I fell on my back but scrabbled up to go after him again. He caught me and pinned me to his chest.

"It's all right, Ezra," he whispered. "Everything is going to be okay."

I pounded his stomach, furious tears running down my face. He grunted under the assault, but didn't try to stop me. "Why didn't you tell me?! I had to find out you were in trouble from that piece of shit!"

"I'll tell you now. I promise. Just calm down."

It took him repeating that several times. The mist slowly cleared and the strength it gave me fled.

Brian eased me against the footboard.

"Damn." He cringed as he clutched his stomach. "Don't tell anyone you kicked my ass."

My mind was on one thing. "How did this happen?"

He sighed. "Where do I start?"

"The beginning would be nice."

"The beginning," he repeated.

Brian sat next to me. We looked out across the messy expanse of his room, broken and disheveled on the floor.

"I'm a pilot," he began. "People envision a glamourous life jet-setting around the world when I tell them my job. What it really is are long hours sitting on my ass, going to the same places over and over again, and spending little time in any of them. You do this long enough and you begin looking for quick, cheap thrills to fill the short hours of a layover."

"How did you fill your hours?" I asked, though I knew the answer.

"For my buddies, it was booze and anonymous fucks. For me, it was poker."

"Does Amina know?"

"She does now," he replied. "For a long time, I didn't believe I had a problem. I make a good salary. All the money I lost, I made back by the next paycheck. There was nothing to worry about."

"Until you sat down at a poker table with guys who call themselves the Sons of Slaughter," I said. "How did that happen?"

"It didn't." He sighed. "Or at least not as easily as you're thinking. Roman and I had two days in New York, so we hit the tables."

"Roman?"

"A friend and my copilot."

I nodded. "So what happened?"

"The first night we hit our usual places. I won some and I lost some, but it wasn't too bad," he said. "The next night, Roman tells me about a game in Manhattan where they play for higher stakes. All legit and a chance to make some real money."

He gripped my arm. "You have to understand, Ezra. I didn't slink through some back alley into a smoke-filled drug den and then sit down with guys that had their kills tatted on their face. The game was in a hotel. A nice one. They wore suits and drank three-hundred-dollar scotch. I threw my money down without hesitation. By the end of the night, I owed over two hundred grand."

My jaw slackened. "Two hundred?" I breathed.

"It was a setup. Roman. The game. All of it. I realized it, and the men I was dealing with, way too late."

He scrubbed his face, and his exhaustion reflected as it did in his words.

"I asked for time to get the money. They gave me two weeks with an extra grand every day they had to wait," he said. "I was shitting myself, Ezra. There was no way I could get my hands on that kind of money in two weeks. I missed the deadline and the next day three guys came to my hotel room and beat the shit out of me. They pulled a gun and that's when Roman came in."

I couldn't speak for the tight band around my neck. My imagination took me to the darkest places as I waited to know the truth. This was worse.

"Roman pleaded with them. Asked for another way to pay off the debt."

My mind made the connections all too quick. "They'd let you pay it off by running product over the border."

He nodded. "Private pilots skirt the security checks. I was exactly what they needed and Roman offered me up without a thought."

"He's one of them?"

"No," he said. "Not by choice. Like me, he owed them money and he saved himself a bullet in the head by trafficking their coke."

Sighing, I dropped my head back against the board. "He's the one who called that day, screaming about flying stuff out."

"Yeah, that's him. I agreed to everything they wanted to get out of that room, but as soon as I got home, I packed up the girls, sent them to Amina's parents, and came here."

I waited for him to say more. He didn't.

"Came here to do what?" I pushed. "It's been four months. Have you told Mom? Are you going to tell Mom?"

Brian raised his head; his eyes were hard. "No and no."

"Why not? She'd give you the money in a heartbeat and—" A thought broke in. "How have you gone this long without them catching up to you? Wouldn't your mother's home be the first place Roman would send them to?"

"He would... if he knew Amelia Lennox was my mother."

My face crumpled in confusion. "I thought you said he was a friend? How could he not know who your mother is? Why doesn't he know?"

"Ezra, don't."

"Do you keep her a secret?" I shoved him. "Do you keep us a fucking secret?"

"Yes! And it's a good thing I did, or I'd be dead!" He seized my wrist, stopping another punch. "You may like random shits stalking you and pretending to like you to get close to your rich, famous mom, but I don't. I'm Brian Spencer and my mom is a local journalist. The end."

I ripped out of his hold. "Is that why you won't go to her for help? Your stupid fucking mommy complex!"

His lips twisted. "Of course not," he snarled. "I didn't go to her to *protect* her! Now will you stop interrupting!"

The reply was a dagger to my rage. "Protect her?"

"You know Mom. She's not going to pass an envelope containing three hundred grand across the dining table and go back to eating her crepes. I'd have to tell her everything and she'd go after them. She'd turn the spotlight and a hundred cameras on their operation, putting both of you in danger.

"Despite their name, they're not some unwashed street thugs working out of a seedy apartment. They're smart and organized. The cartel leaders live in houses as big as this and can afford to pay out thousand-dollar suites to lure dumbass pilots like me into their game."

He grabbed my shoulders. "I'm not a good son." His fingers dug painfully into me. "I'm an even worse older brother, but credit me with loving you two enough that I wouldn't drag you into this mess."

I swallowed hard around the lump in my throat. He was right. Mom wouldn't give him the money without an explanation, and once she had it, she'd go after the Sons of Slaughter with the full force of her empire, adding fiercer enemies to the growing list.

"I will end this," he said. "Amina is borrowing money from her parents. She's selling our things and then finally the house. It'll take time, but once I have the money, I'll clear my debt. I've lost my job, so I'm not much use to the cartel anyway."

I stared at him in disbelief. "Selling everything you own and living off your in-laws isn't a plan, Brian. You have children. And what about Amina's job? How long can she be away from the firm before you're both out of work?"

The hard set of his chin endured. "It'll be tough, but we'll survive. We have her family and mine. The girls will be okay."

"You do have family." I grabbed him in kind. "You have me. Let me help you. I have about fifty thousand in my account right now, and I can get more. Not right away, but still faster than you'll pull the money together."

"No."

"But, Bri—"

"No." His grip tightened. "Ezra, you're having nothing to do with this. You never should have found out." Brian's eyes narrowed. "How did you? Did you break into my phone?"

"Your stuff was broken into," I said, "but it wasn't by me. The oh-so-innocent guy everyone told me to back off of, dug up information on all the pledges and their families. Aiden Connelly knows every-thing and he threatened to tell the Sons of Slaughter where you are if I don't back off."

"Holy shit." Brian rocked back. "He wouldn't really do that, would he?"

The look I gave him held the answer. "Deep down, there's some-thing not right about that guy. I can feel it."

"I'm sorry, Ezra. Hit me if I ever doubt your instincts again."

"You see? I'm already involved, Brian. Let me help."

He shook his head. "I have a plan and I'm taking care of it. Just give me some more time. I'll pay them back and then you'll handle this Aiden bitch. I'll even help."

"Brian—"

"Don't say it. I will *not* take money from you." He got to his feet and reached out to help me up. "Promise me that you will stay out of it. Promise."

Anger held my tongue. I wanted to rage and scream at the stubbornness carved on his face.

But none of it will do you any good if he won't take the money. There's only one thing to say.

"I promise."

VALENTINA

"I wish the boys were here to help us."

Sofia zipped her suitcase and hauled it up. "We're two strong, capable women," she said. "We can move me into the Sally house on our own."

"We can," I mumbled, "but I don't want to."

"I heard that."

The end of winter vacation came all too quickly. The second semester of our first year of college began the next day, which gave us eighteen hours to pack up Sofia's life and unpack it across campus.

"I'm surprised you decided to live in the Sally house after everything," I said. "I can't believe you all did. Palmer looked ready to kill Leighton after our little initiation ceremony."

Sofia crossed the room and began taking down her plates. "The Zeta Rho Sigma rooms are nicer, cheaper, and bigger than what I'm living in now. Also, worse secrets were revealed in that room than mine. I'm not angry at Leighton anymore, but I will be if you are."

She looked at me. "I'm serious. There are things you don't do and making you speak about your rape is number one through ten on the list. I don't give her a pass for it, and if you're upset, so am I."

"I'm not, trust me." The real sentence on that card floated through my mind. "It could have been a lot worse. Leighton let me off easy."

"What do you mean?"

Shut up, dumbass. I can't talk about this—not even with Sofia.

"I mean she didn't make me name names," I said.

Sofia released a shuddering breath. "That would have been horrible. She didn't make any of us name names. I hope she's right and we can all go on like that night never happened."

"Do you think we can? I haven't heard from Palmer, Mai, or Keily and I texted them all over the break."

"I guess we'll find out."

A half an hour later, Palmer mumbled a hello at us on her way out of the door.

"Do you need help bringing your stuff in?" I called after her.

She pretended not to hear.

"That's a no to going on like it never happened," I said to Sofia.

Sofia transferred her box to the other hand and fished out her new key. "Give her a minute," she said. "We're bound to be weird around each other for a while, but we're still friends."

"Sofia. Val." Patricia burst out of the kitchen. "You're finally here. We're so pumped to start a new semester with our new"—she hooked her arms around us—"sisters."

Sofia and I shared a look over her head. Apparently, some of us were not feeling awkward.

"You don't have to lug Sofia's stuff just the two of you," she said. "Reagan and I will help."

"Thanks," said Sofia. "We'll grab you after we unpack these boxes."

Sofia's room was everything she said. Nicer, bigger, and cheaper. Alumni donations got the Sallys queen-sized beds, flat screens, throw rugs, and a couch I flung myself on.

"This place is going to be gorgeous when you're done with it," I told her. "You can put your photos on that wall and weave lights through the drapes."

"Oooh. Good idea."

"Hey, guys."

Keily stood in Sofia's entrance. The time off looked good on her. Keily's auburn waves sported a fresh cut and a new gold necklace nestled on her chest.

"Hi," I said. "It's good to see you. How was break?"

"It was fun. Snow, Christmas movies, and messing around with my little brothers. It doesn't get much better than that. And... uh..." She shifted from foot to foot. "I wanted you to know I broke up with Wesley and Giovanni."

"Okay," I said softly. "If that's what you wanted."

Her throat bobbed against her new necklace. "It was the right decision. Are we okay?"

"Of course we are," Sofia said.

The first smile appeared on her lips. "Okay, good. See you downstairs."

"Downstairs?"

She pointed over her shoulder. "Leighton wants us all in the dining room. She needs to talk to us about something."

That works out because I need to talk to her too.

We followed Keily downstairs.

Leighton stood at attention at the front of the dining room.

At attention. It's interesting that's the first phrase to come to mind, but it fits her perfectly. She's like a tiny little general.

"Take a seat, ladies," she said. "Get comfortable."

I snagged the chair next to Blair. She nodded at me but didn't say anything.

"We're going to be busy this week with new classes and schedules, so now is a good time to go over details for this semester,"

Leighton began. "First, we've almost got enough for the Sams, but some of you said you'd like to keep fundraising for a spring break trip of our own. Show of hands if you want to as well?"

Everyone raised their hands.

"Great," she said. "If that's the case, we should stick with the bake stand. It's turning a great profit, and with more sisters in the house, we've got a lot of hands to help with the baking. Our schedules are different this semester, so we'll work up another timeslot sheet today and get it back up and running by tomorrow."

"I can do the night shift again," Sofia said quickly. "Eight to ten. I want that slot."

"I don't think anyone is going to fight you. Eight to ten is yours. As for house rules, you should know them since you've got the Sally handbook memorized, but just in case, we don't..."

Leighton went through the items on her mental list. She finished with the fun stuff.

"Pledging is over, but we still do bonding activities." She gestured at her second-in-command. "Let Reagan and me know if you want to join us on our run. Also, we're having a movie night on Friday to celebrate surviving the first week. It's exclusively horror movies featuring coeds."

That earned a few chuckles.

"Can't handle the blood and gore, then join us on Saturday. We're taking over the Sam house pool and their grill."

Leighton looked at me. "You can bring anyone along. Adam is more than welcome."

"Oh... uh... thank you," I got out.

She smiled and then moved on.

Confusion rooted like a seed and spread deeper through my opinion of Leighton. The girl who dismissed the pledges sobbing on their knees was at odds with the one I laughed with on the road to the ranch. She was at odds with the one smiling warmly and making an effort to include my son.

Can she be both people?

Sofia nudged me. "Want to do the movie or the pool?"

I shook my head. "Horror movies aren't my thing and"—I lowered my voice—"I'm steering clear of Aiden Connelly."

"Can't blame you."

"All right, sisters," said Leighton. "Let's help these girls move the rest of their stuff in."

"Ready, Sofia?" Reagan asked.

"Yes, I'm ready."

"Go on ahead," I said. "I'll catch up."

The girls streamed out of the room. I hopped in the wake of one and followed her out. Leighton didn't notice me behind her on the staircase. I waited until she topped the landing.

"Leighton?"

"Yes?"

"Can I talk to you for a second?"

"Sure." She motioned to the double doors at the opposite end of the hall. "In my room."

I'd never seen Leighton's bedroom. Stepping inside, I knew why.

My eyes widened as far as they could go. "What is this magical place?" I breathed.

"You crack me up, Val," she said, laughing.

Leighton's bedroom was a decorator's dream. I think she told the interior designer to go wild and this is what they came up with. The draped ceiling sported metallic rings that glittered when she turned on the light. A beautiful feature but not nearly as impressive as the fish tank headboard hovering over her bed. Multicolored fish drifted lazily through the water, waiting for their chance to lull Leighton to sleep.

Across from her bed, a hammock chair suspended from the ceiling, loaded down with squashy pillows and blankets. I ran up to it and something caught my eye.

Light peeked out of the closet, revealing my find. My nosy self threw the door open.

I gasped. "Oh my gosh. You turned your closet into a library."

Shelves took up the space where clothes should be. On the floor were pillows and blankets for Leighton to get comfortable.

"I have more books than clothes, so it seemed to me they deserved the space."

"This room is incredible," I said. "Did you hide it from us so we wouldn't drop dead from envy?"

She chuckled. "I didn't hide. You just never asked to see it."

"Good point." I plopped down on the hammock chair. "It pays to be Madame President."

Leighton pulled out her desk chair and took a seat. "I didn't get this for being president. I paid for the upgrades myself. I'll also have to take them out when I leave."

"Really? How are you going to move the fish tank?"

She snorted. "By paying someone else to do it."

I laughed before I could stop myself. Something drew me to her—compelled me. But I did not like this woman. Why did I continually need that reminder?

She's got good taste if nothing else. But these upgrades couldn't have been cheap. I wonder what her family does.

I scanned the room again, looking for something specific.

"I don't see any photos of your family," I remarked. *I don't see photos at all.*

"That's right," Leighton said. "And is that what you wanted to talk to me about?"

"No, it's not." I grew serious quickly. "I want to talk about the initiation."

Leighton got out of her chair. "We agreed never to talk about it again."

"You agreed. I *want* to talk about it."

"No." She made for the door.

I intercepted her, plastering myself against the wood. "Yes."

She raised a brow. I couldn't be sure but the quirk of her lips seemed to say she was amused.

"Why did you write that on my card?" I demanded.

Leighton lifted her shoulders. "Why do you think?"

"How did you know? You couldn't have hacked me. Maverick made sure of that."

She said nothing and irritation strangled the bit of good feeling I had toward her.

"I'm not playing games with you," I said through gritted teeth. "This isn't some stupid sister blood pact. This is my life. Why do you think I killed someone?"

Leighton stood immovable. She didn't twitch, blink, or move her lips.

"Did you go to the prison?" I pressed.

"Why would I go to a prison?"

"Then what?"

She heaved a sigh. "Valentina, move out of the way, please. I said please."

"Why won't you talk to me?"

"I won't talk to you or anyone. How I get my information is a presidential secret." She winked. "If you want to know, you'll have to take over Zeta Rho Sigma."

Humming, I bobbed my head. "That sounds like a huge, steamy pile of shit."

Leighton barked a laugh. "It does, doesn't it? But there it is." She took a step forward like she meant to go through me.

"Tell me this," I said. "What did you mean when you said you wanted me from the beginning?"

"Are you serious? I told you that from the beginning too. You're everything the Sallys stand for." She grasped my arms. "All those girls downstairs try to be what you already are. A true Sally." The glint in her eye unnerved me. I stepped back and her grip tightened. "If a gunman threatened this campus, you'd do whatever it took to stop him."

I gently, but firmly, removed her hands. "You can't know that. Sally Hollenbeck was an incredibly brave young woman and honoring her with this house is the least the school could do. But we're not her and no one could predict what they'd do in that situation."

Leighton's expression did not change. "I know what you would do."

This conversation had taken such a turn, I wasn't certain what to say.

"You're strong, Valentina," she continued. "You'd have to be to survive what you have survived and to do the things that you've done."

I stiffened. She was hinting at something. *Why won't she just come out and say it?*

She flapped a hand. "That initiation never applied to you. If anyone understands loyalty, it's you. You're a Sally now, Val. Like you were meant to be." She took another step. "Have I answered your question?"

I nodded. Once.

Leighton flicked her wrist. "Out of my way."

I stepped to the side without a fight.

"Feel free to hang out in here," she said. "The hammock is like being rocked to sleep in your mother's arms. You'll pass out in minutes."

She smiled and there she was again—the Leighton I knew and liked. She shut the door, leaving me alone in her captivating palace, more confused than ever.

Chapter Nine

V*alentina*

"I have anthropology and statistics today," I said. "My last class gets out at six. Why?"

"Come over to the Sally house, have dinner with me, and then you can keep me company at the stand," said Sofia.

"Why?" I repeated.

"Because you've been weird since I caught you walking out of Leighton's room the other day. And you've been even weirder around her. Let's hang out tonight and talk. We'll have our privacy at the stand."

I slid the phone down to my chest. *I can't talk about what was on that card and I don't know where to begin with the conversation Leighton and I had after my failed interrogation. There's nothing I can say, Sofia.*

I put my cell back to my ear. "Okay. I'll come over after class."

"Go over where?" Jaxson peered at me from my lap. "What's up, baby?"

"I'm going to meet up with Sofia for dinner," I replied as I set my phone aside. "You can tell Chef not to make anything for me."

Thursday, and the near end of my first week of classes, arrived quickly. It saw me with two chapters worth of anthropology home-work and a day off for Jaxson. He picked Adam up early from school and I pushed my reading assignment onto the weekend to-do list. The three of us were in the sitting room spending time together.

The sitting room was smaller than our main living room, but had plenty of space to act as Adam's second playroom. The boys moved his robot, basketball hoop, fire engine, train set, and mini Mercedes Benz in here after Christmas.

Adam zipped around the couch thanks to Jaxson's expert handling of the car's remote. His giggles were as loud as the music blasting from the car's MP3 player.

A soft smile cracked my anxiety. "You guys know you spoil him rotten, right?"

"Says the lady who got him fifteen of his twenty-four Christmas presents."

"That's different."

"How?"

I poked his cheek. "Hush. It's different because I say it is."

He laughed. "How long do I have you?"

"Class is at three. I'm all yours for two more hours."

"We'll have to think of a way to pass the time," he replied, complete with waggling eyebrows.

"You mean by giving Adam his bath and putting him down for a nap?" I teased.

"I meant what comes *after* that."

"Oh. Yes, we can definitely pass the time with that activity."

Two and a half hours later, I was in class writing furiously as my professor zipped through the slides. My cell vibrated all through the lesson but I didn't dare check it and miss half the information that would be on my midterm. That's what Professor Stokes promised. The slides were basically our test.

After I got out, I unlocked my phone to a flood of messages from Sofia.

Sofia: I'm making dinner tonight. Me. All by myself.

Sofia: If you want to stop me, you have five seconds to speak up.

Sofia: Five

Sofia: Four

Sofia: Three

Sofia: Two

Sofia: One

Sofia: Too late! Get ready for garlic shrimp, mushroom pasta, and roasted veggies.

Sofia: Just so you know, I haven't learned how to cook any of this stuff.

I was stuck between laughing out loud and crying. A life of personal chefs did not prepare Sofia for cooking for herself. She had a few infamous disasters in the kitchen that she force-fed me. From then on, she was ordered not to make more than cereal until she got lessons.

Me: Why do you do these things to me? I'm supposed to be your best friend.

Her reply came back quickly.

Sofia: LOL. And as my best friend, you'll be my guinea pig. I'm moving up from sandwiches and making Daddy dinner Saturday night.

Me: And if I die from poisoning, you'll know to call it off.

Sofia: Exactly.

I rolled my eyes but marched to my fate all the same.

Sofia was in the kitchen when I arrived, standing over a smoking pot.

"What's that?" I asked.

"The pasta."

"Shouldn't it be boiling, not smoking?"

"Should it?"

I snatched the serving spoon off the counter and brandished it at her. "Step away from the stove now."

Howling, Sofia put up her hands and slowly stepped back. I took over the cooking. It was fun showing her how to prepare the food properly. Our aromas wafting out of the kitchen brought Keily, Blair, and Palmer in.

I smirked at them. "You don't have to ask. I made plenty."

Palmer kissed me on the cheek. "Valentina Moon, you're an angel descended from the heavens. Keily and I were two seconds away from eating the stale pizza from the back of the fridge."

The five of us talking and laughing around the dining table felt like our brunch dates. Awkwardness hung in the air, but with them I was more than happy not to speak of that night again.

After dinner, they helped us carry the stand and food to Sofia's spot.

"I'm glad we're still friends," Sofia said after they left. "Even Blair."

I chuckled. "Have you ever noticed we do that? Say 'even Blair' when we talk about them."

"I have noticed that, yes."

A chill permeated the January air. The Sallys chose their menu with warm thoughts and a block of chocolate in mind. We had Irish mocha brownies, hot chocolate, hot tea, fudge cookies, mini chocolate cakes, cheesecake, chocolate chip cookies, ginger cookies, and more.

Sofia and I sat back and waited for the money to pour in.

"Now that I have you to myself," Sofia began. "What happened with you and Leighton the other day?"

"She's just really intense, Sof. If you heard her going on about me being just like Sally Hollenbeck, you'd understand. I don't get what she wants from me."

"What could she want from you? We're college students trying to get through the next three and a half years. That's it."

I shrugged. "Let's change the subject. How is your dad doing?" A grin stole over my face. "Is his heart healthy enough for sex yet?"

"Go away," she deadpanned. "We're not friends anymore."

I laughed so hard, I cried. "Five years," I wheezed. "We had a good run."

Sofia eventually forgave me and we passed the first hour selling treats to almost everyone who passed by.

"It thins out after nine," Sofia said. "People are inside doing their homework and getting out of the cold."

"Then we can chill. Let's finish that movie we were watching."

Sofia pulled out her phone and we huddled together in front of her screen.

She was right. The next half an hour we only had two people walk by the stand. We watched our movie with hardly any other interruptions but me.

"But that doesn't make any sense," I said. "If he killed her, who got in the car and drove away?"

"He must have—"

"Excuse me?"

A guy in a black sweater and matching beanie waved at us. "You still open?"

"Yep," said Sofia. "What would you like?"

"The ginger cookies and hot chocolate, please."

Sofia put his cookies in a baggie while I poured the cocoa. He thanked us and pulled out a hundred-dollar bill.

He smiled sheepishly. "It's all I got. Do you have change?"

Sofia stuck her head under the table to peek at the cash box. "Yes, we've got change."

"Great."

They exchanged money and he walked off, waving bye with his cookie bag.

"Have a good night."

"You too," Sofia called.

"Do we have any change left?" I asked.

"Nope. None." She picked up the cash box. "I'll run to the Sally house and get more. Be right back."

"Okay."

Sofia disappeared down the path to the Sally house. I picked up her phone and went back to watching.

I'll fill Sof in on the rest. Besides, this isn't as good as I—

A hand clamped over my mouth.

The reflex to scream hadn't struck before more hands seized me and yanked me out of the chair. I kicked out and connected with the wood. The stand upended. It fell to the pavement in an ear-splitting crash. I hit the ground hard, pain reverberating in the base of my spine. Rough fingers tangled in my hair and wrenched me back.

I looked up into their eyes... and screamed.

Five black-masked figures surrounded me. Fear living and unending blotted out my mind.

The figures took hold of my limbs and hauled me up. They ran, carrying me away from the stand. My butt swept against the ground and collected dirt and leaves in the lining of my pants.

I thrashed—pulling and kicking in their hold. The hand over my face clamped down so hard my lips smashed into my teeth. I flailed and metallic liquid filled my mouth.

They suddenly stopped and I fought harder.

"Argh!" I shrieked. "Hmh hmm!"

Sofia! Where are you?!

A rattling noise I didn't understand clanged behind me. The next thing I knew, I was flying into darkness. I struck the floor and agony exploded in my skull. The pain dazed me. Lights danced before my vision.

"Close the door," a voice hissed. "If someone heard the crash, they'll come running."

"Keep her quiet."

The light intensified and I winced. It wasn't from the pain; it was from them. Their phone flashlights swept the space. Green, wooden slats revealed themselves. Hanging from the walls were metal items that glinted in the beams.

I squinted through the gloom. The figures beneath their black jackets and the muffled, gravelly voices told me they were men. This barely had a chance to register when a boot came down next to my head.

The guys grabbed my collar and forced me up. The fabric tore as he pinned me to his body and wrapped his arm around my head, covering my mouth. A stale, nauseating smell of pine and sweat invaded my nose. My hands flew up and pounded them. They clamped harder in punishment. I forced my jaw apart and bit down.

"Argh!"

My captor wrenched me to the side and my face struck a hard, unforgiving surface. My jaw slackened in a haze of pain.

"Careful!" one of them shouted.

"Get her hands."

Grips like iron bound my wrists and pulled them away from my silent captor.

"What do we do with her?" one of them asked. I couldn't tell whose mouth moved through the masks and dim light. "We were supposed to grab the other one. Richards."

Icy terror ran through my veins. That one word ricocheted in my screaming mind.

Sofia. Sofia! No! Please, no!

"We do her too," replied a deeper voice. "Quick. And then we grab Richards."

No sooner had the order left his mouth than a hand flashed out and grabbed my necklace. They tore it from my throat.

Tears soaked my face. They ran down the arm penning in my screams and splashed down my chest. I wailed my throat raw as the earrings were torn from my head and the bracelet from my wrist. I fought harder, jerking until my limbs ached.

Muggers. Filthy, disgusting, fucking muggers and they're after Sofia! I have to do something.

They found my phone and flung it at the wall. It shattered into pieces that struck me.

"Hurry up and take the pictures."

One of them unzipped my jacket. I knew what he was going to do.

Horrid visions of nightmare and reality fueled my panic. I drew my leg up, found his head, and kicked with all my might.

His neck snapped around as he went flying, releasing me.

"I said hold her down!"

Two of them grabbed my legs. They forced them to the floor and sat on them.

The one I kicked righted himself and reached for me again. He forced my zipper down and sought the rip in my collar. My shirt fell in tattered pieces on either side of me. Then he reached for the bra's clasp.

My screams were hoarse, smothered cries that did not reach help—or them.

The two not holding me down turned their flashlights on my bare breasts. Frigid air chilled the sweat dripping down my body. I shivered in cold and disgust.

The man holding my head in a vise held out his phone. The other guy took it and pointed it at me. I didn't understand why until the first flash went off.

Click.

Click.

Click.

"Get her pants off."

I bucked and twisted under them. The captors on my legs put more of their weight on me. My bones crunched under the pressure and I cried out in more than fear as one of them worked my pants down to my knees.

Click. Click. Click.

"That's enough. We're here for Richards. If she comes back and sees the mess, she'll freak."

One of the guys on my legs spoke up. "Someone has to stay with this one until we get her."

A hand snaked over me and squeezed my breast.

I jerked away. "Hmm!"

"What the fuck are you doing?" The guy standing on my left sprang forward and slapped his hand off. "Don't touch her! That's not what we're here for!"

He clasped my bra and tugged my pants up to punctuate his point.

"Just keep her here and quiet. We'll grab Sofia."

My eyes widened.

That voice... I know that voice...

The guy on my right ripped my shirt completely off and used the strips to bind my wrists and ankles. When he was done, the weight on my legs vanished.

A band of light fell on me as they opened the door. I saw my surroundings clearly... and I watched the four of them leave to attack my best friend, abandoning me with their quiet, violent partner.

He moved the moment the door shut. He grasped my head with both hands—clamping one firmly on my mouth—and dropped me to the floor.

He ripped open my bra, breaking the clasp. Freely, he pawed me.

Trashing side to side, I tried to escape him. I threw my head back and freed my mouth for one blessed moment.

"Help! Help me!"

He scrambled to cover me again. I snapped and trapped the tip of his finger between my teeth.

"Argh!"

Pain exploded in my face. He slapped me, and in the shock, I released him.

The sound of a zipper being drawn down echoed in the air.

Nightmare and reality took hold, and the only safe place was neither.

I retreated. The thing on my mind as I sank was Sofia.

Light flooded the space. My eyes bugged as a man burst into the shed. My attacker fumbled to stuff his dick in his pants as the man grabbed a tool and swung.

The shovel connected with his neck. He smashed against the riding lawnmower, clutching his throat.

The man raised the shovel over his head.

Gasping, the attacker shot to his feet and raced out of the door. The man didn't chase him.

He dropped to his knees next to me.

"Fucking hell," he raged as he freed my legs. "Are you okay? Fuck! Of course you're not okay."

A thick, British accent poured from his mouth. As the shock cleared, I saw him properly. Thick, brownish-blond hair clung to his forehead. The adrenaline impacted him. Beads of sweat collected over his stormy blue eyes and his hands shook as he freed my wrists.

I clapped my hands over my body and he instantly pulled off his sweater.

He put it on me and then helped me into my jacket.

"You're safe now," he soothed. "My phone is charging in the other building. We'll go and call the police. That bastard won't get far. What's your name?"

My jaw worked. The rasp forced itself out of my raw, aching throat.

"H-Hudson."

His brows snapped together. "I'm sorry. Do I know you?"

I tried again. "S-Sofia."

Hudson's eyes sharpened. "Sofia?"

"Sofia," I croaked. "She's in d-danger. They're after her. We have to go now. Sally house."

Hudson moved faster than I'd ever seen. He scooped me up and ran out into the night.

The wind beat and tore at us, powerful as the heart thundering against my ear. Hudson didn't stop or slow down. We saw no one as he tore up the familiar path.

Please be safe, Sofia. Please be safe.

Greek Row loomed ahead of us. Hudson sprinted to the end of the street and bounded up the porch.

"Hello? Hello, Sofia! Open the door! We need help! Hel—"

It flew open. Leighton stood at the threshold, eyes wide. "What the hell is going on?"

"Sofia," I croaked.

"We need help. She was attacked." Hudson brushed past her and carried me inside. "She said they were after Sofia Richards too. We have to find her right now!"

Leighton put up her hands. "Whoa. Slow down. I can tell you that Sofia Richards is safe. She's upstairs."

"Are you sure?" I cried. "Tell me she's here!"

She looked at me steadily. "She is, Val. I walked past her myself only five minutes ago. She's safe."

I went boneless with relief. Then the floodgates opened. I sobbed loud, wrenching cries that shuddered my body.

I felt a hand on my forehead. "Bring her in here," Leighton said softly.

Hudson carried me into the living room. Paisley and Reagan sprang up and he set me down in their place.

"She was attacked," Hudson explained. "Assaulted. The guy got away, but I hurt him."

His voice was gruff, but his hands were gentle as he rested my head on a pillow and draped the throw blanket over me.

"Call the police. I'll give as much of a description as I can." He peered into my eyes as he said, "They'll find him."

"Sofia," I sobbed.

"I will check on her right now," he promised. "Everything will be okay."

"Thank you," said Leighton. "Thank you for saving her and for bringing her here."

"I could have done nothing else." Hudson tucked me in like a father putting a child to bed. "Rest now. You're safe. I'm going to Sofia."

Reagan put her arms around him and guided him out. "She's upstairs. Third door on your left." She shut the door behind him.

"Val." Leighton knelt beside me. "Do you feel up to telling me what happened?"

"The police," I whispered.

"Reagan will call." She addressed her. "And a washcloth and something for Val to drink."

"Yes, Leighton."

Reagan swept out, leaving the three of us alone. Leighton sought my hand under the blanket and laced our fingers together.

"Whenever you're ready," she said.

I was ready. I was more than fucking ready.

"They mugged me." My wretched throat made my hiss low and menacing. "Five guys in black masks stole my jewelry and my money. T-they stripped me and took pictures. After that, four of them left and I was alone with the o-one Hudson h-ad to save me from." My semblance of calm was cracking.

"Did he try to...?" Leighton did not have to finish the sentence.

I nodded.

Patricia clapped her hands over her mouth, her eyes huge with horror.

"They had a plan," I continued, "and it was to take Sofia."

"Why Sofia?"

Wetness washed down my cheeks. "She's usually there alone, tucked away in a different spot while she waited for Hudson."

"Shit." Leighton punched the floor. "I should have had you girls man the stall in pairs!"

I shook my head. "It's not your fault. Two of us were out there tonight." The blanket balled in my fist. "And I don't think it's a coincidence a guy came up with a hundred-dollar bill, forcing one of us to leave to get change."

Leighton's gaze sharpened. "You can identify one of them?"

A sob escaped my lips. "Not just one. The guy who tried to rape me. I know who he is."

She shot to her feet. "Who?"

"I can't be sure," I added reluctantly. "He didn't speak and I never saw his face."

The hard set of her jaw was fixed. "Then I'll make certain." Leighton marched to the door and stuck her head out. "Reagan, get my stuff."

"What?" I fought my way out of the blanket to sit up. "What are you talking about?"

"That guy said your attacker was injured."

"Yes," I said slowly, understanding dawning. "Hudson hit him in the neck with a shovel. There will be a bruise he can't hide."

"What's his name and do you know where he lives? I'll find him and if there's so much as a hickey on his fucking neck, I'll have the cops there in minutes."

I threw the blanket off. "I'm coming with you."

"No, Val. You should stay, get cleaned up, and—"

"I'm coming with you!" The scream shocked even me, but once I started, I couldn't stop. "He hit me, touched me, and tried to hurt my best friend! *I* will find him and *I* will see him put in cuffs!"

Pat stepped forward. "Val, just let me..." Pat trailed off as Leighton raised her hand.

"Okay," Leighton said. "Can we come with you? We want to help."

"Yes. I might... need help getting there."

Patricia and Leighton immediately encircled me under the arms and lifted me up. I leaned heavily on them as we made for the door. Reagan reappeared in the hallway, holding a bag.

I pulled to the right. "I have to check on Sofia first."

"After," said Leighton. "If they're making a run for it or destroying evidence, we're giving them too much time to do it."

"I need to make sure—"

"You need to make sure the people who tried to hurt her pay for it. That's what your best friend needs right now."

The words pierced through me. She was right. Their plan didn't go the way they thought. I got away. There was a witness. The stand was all over the ground. And they didn't get Sofia. As a result, they might be running or retreating to plot a second attempt.

"Let's go. Hurry."

The girls carried me to the door and I passed the hall mirror. My reflection stared grimly back. A knot the size of a fist purpled on my forehead. My lip was cut and swelling. The redness on my cheek sharply brought his slap to memory.

Tears collected in my eyes, but I did not let them fall.

No more crying. It's his turn.

"Let's go."

Four of us slipped out into the night.

"It's not just the one Hudson hit," I said. "I think I could identify another one, but I'm not sure and I won't be sure until we speak to the guy who assaulted me."

"Just tell us where to go," Leighton said.

I did.

We were a silent group marching across campus. Though I didn't speak, my mind spun with a thousand different endings to tonight.

What if it's who I think it is? What if it isn't? How do I tell Sofia? What do I tell the boys?

I physically jerked as the thought punched the air from my lungs.

When they find out, Jaxson, Maverick, Ezra, and Ryder will kill them. No exaggeration. No hesitation. They will kill those men with their bare hands.

I'll deal with this, another voice broke in. *I'll find them and have them arrested. Leighton was right. I have to bring the police on them now before my boys get there first.*

Reagan got out in front of us and pulled open the door. It wasn't late enough for the dorm to be quiet. Music, laughter, and television poured out of the gaps beneath the doors.

"What floor?" Leighton asked.

"Second."

We bypassed the elevator without giving it a look. I had to keep moving.

The hallway we stepped out on was no quieter than the first. What sounded like a party raged three doors down from the one I focused on.

"That's it."

They helped me to the door. My heart pounded loudly in my ears, matching my sharp raps on the wood.

"Coming," a voice shouted from within.

My nails drove deeper into Pat's forearm. She didn't utter a sound.

The door flew open. A billow of steam and fresh, piney scent seeped out.

Logan blinked at us over the threshold. His damp hair dripped water onto the towel around his neck.

"Hey, can I help—" He looked at me and his eyes bugged. "Val? Are you okay?"

My muscles bounded tighter. The arm crushing my head. Rough, groping fingers in the dark. The sound of the zipper. It all roared through my mind.

"What happened to you?" he cried. "I—"

"Take off the towel," I croaked.

He frowned. "What?"

"Take it off."

"I'm not—"

"Excuse me." Leighton sprang forward. She ripped the towel off so violently his head snapped to the side and smacked the doorframe.

My knees gave out.

Patricia strained to hold me up as I gazed at the red, angry bruise on his neck.

"It was you," I rasped.

Logan clapped his hand to the wound, but it was far too late. "What are you talking about?"

"We're not playing this game, fucker," Leighton snarled.

She shoved him. Logan staggered back and she went with him into the room. Patricia and Reagan helped me through and then shut us in.

"What the hell is your problem?" Logan snapped.

"You attacked me," I said. "You and your friends."

I straightened and pushed the girls away. Looking him in the eyes, I said, "The police are on their way."

Logan swung his head around, gaping at us. He was the picture of confusion. "On their way to do what? I didn't *attack* you, Val. How could you even think that?"

He advanced on me and jerked back.

Leighton and Reagan jumped in his path.

"Don't go near her," snarled Leighton.

"Whoa." He threw up his hands. "Okay, that's enough. I want all of you out of here right now."

"Playing innocent is not going to work," said Reagan. "Val identified you. The guy who rescued her whacked your rapist ass with a shovel and that mark on your neck is telling the rest of the story."

"Rapist?" he repeated, eyes bugged. "You're insane! I didn't rape anyone! I *fell* in the shower!"

I pressed my lips together, body shaking. Who knew he was such a good actor? But then, he would have to be.

"I was here all night studying." He gestured at the pile of notes and textbooks on his desk. "I didn't leave my room once."

I lit on something partially buried beneath his papers and my eyes flared.

"Leighton, that's it! That's the phone!"

No sooner had the words left my mouth than they both darted for the desk. Leighton closed over the cell.

"Get off!"

Logan seized her by the back of the head and shoved her face-first into the wall.

I ran to help. Patricia and Reagan were faster.

Reagan hooked him around the neck. He fought for breath as they pulled him off and wrestled him into the desk chair. He thrashed in her chokehold, gasping as she wrapped tighter still. His eyes bulged and desperately he kicked out at Patricia who held his arms to the chair. Logan was going nowhere.

"Easy." Leighton straightened and dusted herself off. She appeared completely relaxed for someone who had just been attacked. "Let him breathe."

Reagan eased up. He gasped, sucking in deep lungfuls.

"I'm going to guess by your reaction that there are some incriminating photos on this phone." Leighton handed it to me. "I'm sure the police will be very interested in seeing them."

"Wrong, bitch!" Logan's pleasant, faultless mask was nowhere to be seen. "There's nothing on that phone! You can see for yourself. One, nine, eight, seven."

Dread weakened my spine. *No. We can't be too late.*

I typed the password in and hurriedly flipped through the gallery.

"Nothing," I said, laced with disbelief. "There's nothing here."

"Are you sure?"

I let Leighton take the phone.

Harsh, grating laughter filled the room. "Look all you want. You won't find anything. I was here all night and I got this from falling in the shower. When *I* call the police about this, that's exactly what I'll tell them."

"I see." Leighton let the phone drop on the floor. "You and your friends attacked her. You mugged her, stripped her, photographed her, and then, you tried to rape her. You terrorized Val and I could see from the ridiculous act you pulled, that you pretended to be her friend."

Leighton's deadened tone didn't match the emotions swirling in me as she laid out each horrible crime.

"After everything you've done," she whispered. "You have the balls to sit there with a smile on your face and pretend like you're the victim?"

"I *am* the victim," he snapped. "You guys came after me for no reason."

She raised her chin. "You have one more chance to admit what you've done, name the others, and apologize to her. The next thing out of your mouth better be the truth."

"I didn't do anything!"

Leighton didn't reply. She walked over to Reagan and rifled through her bag.

I focused on Logan. "You can deny it all you want but I have you. The guy who came to the stand must have been a part of it. Plus, there's what your buddy said that brought me to you in the first place."

I closed the distance between me and the glowering piece of shit. Strength surged in me with each step.

His bleats of innocence won't work. I have him.

"The jewelry you ripped from my ears didn't give you a clue? I have the money to hire the most ruthless lawyers in the state. A whole fucking army of them. They'll rip your 'I was in my room all night' alibi to shreds and then Hudson will testify that he hit you right where that bruise is conveniently located."

A sickly pallor tainted his cheeks. It gave him away though the mocking smile hung on his lips.

"You're scared, but not half as much as I was," I taunted. "Not yet."

"Reagan, step aside, please," Leighton said.

Reagan released him just like that. Logan surged forward. "Bitch—"

Grabbing him by the hair, Leighton wrenched his head back. She raised a gloved hand and the steel glinted in the light.

Time slowed. My scream echoed in my ears as Leighton put the knife to his throat and slashed. Logan's eyes popped. Surprise overcame the fury etched into his face.

He gazed at me—through me—as hot, red blood gushed from the wound.

"Val!"

Reality crashed in with the force of her shout.

"Stop screaming," Leighton said. "Do you want someone to call the police?"

"What did you do?" I shrieked. "What did you *do*?"

Leighton released him and his head lolled forward. Her placid expression was a mirrored image of Patricia's and Reagan's.

"I did what I had to do," she said. "You heard him. He was going to deny everything."

"He wouldn't have gotten away with it. I was—"

"Going to hire a bunch of lawyers, parade your witness, and say your statement with a stiff upper lip," she rattled off, derision obvious in her tone. "That was supposed to work against masked attackers and no confession? With our trash justice system?"

"Yes! The police would have interrogated them. They would collect evidence and prove they were lying."

She shook her head. "Even if that happened, he wouldn't have received the punishment he deserved. This is the way it had to be."

I couldn't breathe. The band around my chest constricted tighter as my mind rebelled against the scene.

Logan was dead. Leighton killed him. The bloody knife dangled from her fingertips while she looked at me like she was disappointed.

Staggering back, I hit the dresser and slid down. "Why would you do this? I didn't want this."

"Val, I told you. It had to be done." She crouched down, meeting me at eye level. That smile lit her face. "After the shock wears off, you'll see that. A guy like that can't be fixed. He can't be rehabilitated. If he ever made it to a prison, it wouldn't have done him any good. Now he'll never hurt you, another woman, or *Sofia* again."

She flung her name like a weapon and it solidly hit the target.

"You can't identify all of them," she said. "While you were rounding up lawyers, he and his friends could have tried to hurt Sofia again."

"Don't," I forced through clenched teeth. "Don't use Sofia to justify what you've done. This wasn't self-defense. It was murder."

Leighton's smile faded. "I'm surprised you feel that way," she said evenly. "I was sure you, of all people, would understand killing a monster to save innocent people."

"What I understand doesn't matter. When the police get here, I'm telling them the truth and..." I trailed off as the smile returned.

Leighton laughed. "The police aren't on their way, Val. Reagan never called anyone. Just in case we had to take care of this ourselves."

The hard lines of Reagan's face reflected the truth.

"Your sisters are here for you," said Leighton.

I pushed myself up. "You're not my sisters," I snarled. "And if you won't call the police, I will."

"Reagan. Patricia."

The two ran at me as if they were waiting for the command.

Screaming, I raced to the door. I gripped the knob just as they grabbed me. Reagan clamped her hand over my mouth. They dragged me around, both of them held my wrists securely.

"I said to stop that screaming," Leighton scolded. She crossed over to us. "First of all, let me apologize. Manhandling you after what you went through tonight is horrible, but you've left us no choice."

She raised the knife.

No!

I flung myself back, screaming through her fingers. Burning, naked fear overwhelmed my senses.

"Whoa, whoa, whoa," Leighton cried. She instantly dropped the knife. "Valentina, calm down. No one is going to hurt you. I just need insurance."

Insurance?

"Patricia."

Once again, only one word and the girl sprang into action.

Patricia pried my fingers apart. She kept my hand immobile as Leighton pressed the hilt to my palm. She closed it tightly and the textured surface bit into my flesh.

"There." Leighton retrieved the knife and stepped back. "You're new and you don't understand how it works." She pointed over her shoulder. "He is no longer a concern of yours. We have friends who will dispose of the body and make it so Logan never existed."

What? How—

My mind stalled. It couldn't conceive of what she was telling me.

"But that doesn't work if you go shouting about this to the police," she continued. "We don't need any more complications this year, so this is how it goes: if you tell anyone what happened here, his body will suddenly reappear with a murder weapon covered in *your* fingerprints.

"And I mean anyone. You don't speak about this to Sofia, or your boyfriends, or even to your priest. Don't think for a moment I won't find out if you do. You know I have ways of digging up what I need to know. So, do we understand each other?"

She nodded at Reagan and she dropped her hand from my mouth. "Do we?"

I strained to pull moisture in my throat. "We do," I rasped. "I won't tell anyone."

"Good. Let her go, sisters," she said to Reagan and Patricia. "She won't run."

They dropped their hands. I swayed on my feet, but didn't move. Leighton was correct. I couldn't run.

"All right, there's just one more thing," Leighton said. "The pictures. We couldn't find them but he flipped out when I touched his cell. At the very least we can use it to go through his contacts and—"

"No." To my surprise, the denial came from me.

Leighton frowned. "No?"

"Yes, no. There is no we." I straightened my back. "If there is something on that phone, I'll find it myself."

"Why? Because you're afraid of what I'll do to the others once I find them?" She cocked her head. "Are you intending to show them mercy?"

"I was attacked, not you. I've never needed someone else to take care of my problems and I'm not starting now." My resolve hardened with every word. "I will find the rest of them and I will give them the punishments I see fit. But you can be sure, I *will* punish them."

Leighton considered me for a long time. What went on behind her copper eyes, I had no clue. It was clear to me that I never did.

"You're right."

I didn't let the shock show on my face. *She's agreeing with me?*

"This was done to you, and it's not our place to take over." She bent and picked up the phone. Leighton put it in my hand without a fight. "Tell us if you need our help."

Patricia slipped her hand into mine. "We're here for you, Valentina. Whatever you need."

"Whatever we have to do," echoed Reagan.

Leighton smiled. "It's what sisters are for."

Chapter Ten

Valentina

I eyed the three women strolling down the path. They chattered about their new classes like nothing happened.

Cult.

That had to be it. The strange pledging process, the barbaric initiation, their obsession with sisterhood and... tonight.

Ezra, Sofia, and I stumbled into a cult.

My gaze drifted down to Leighton's bag and the bloody knife concealed within.

A very dangerous cult.

I didn't speak the entire walk to the Sally house, and Leighton, Reagan, and Patricia didn't pay me any mind.

They went inside and headed into the living room. I burst into a run as soon as the door shut.

"Sofia? Sofia!"

"Val?"

We collided at the top of the landing. Sofia squeezed me so hard my sore body protested.

"Where did you go?" Her voice was thick with unshed tears. "Hudson told me everything, but when I came down, you were gone."

I squeezed my eyes shut. "Leighton and the girls took me to the emergency room to check me out."

That much was true. They insisted on it and I didn't know what would happen if I refused.

The nurses checked me for a concussion and then gave me an ice pack and pain pills for the lumps on my head. We didn't make it back until three in the morning.

"Have you been up worrying all night?" I asked softly. "I told Reagan to text you that I was okay."

"I couldn't believe it until I saw y-you." Her voice broke on a sob. "I'm so sorry, Val. It's all my fault."

"What? How can you say that?"

I led her down the hall to her bedroom. Together we sat on the bed, arms securely around each other.

"You wouldn't have been there if it wasn't for me," she said. "I knew Hudson was working tonight and I wanted to finally introduce you. When I came back for the money, I noticed I got frosting on my clothes and got held up changing. If only I had been there! I never should have left you alone."

"Hey, look at me." I cupped her chin. "You have no idea how grateful I am that you weren't there. I couldn't stand it if anything happened to you. All that matters is you're safe."

And I'm going to keep you safe.

"Hudson said they knocked over the stand and then... took you into the shed." She pressed the heel of her palms to her eyes, attempting to slow her tears. "He said they were after me too."

"You're the one at the stand at that time," I said. "I was terrified they'd catch up to you walking back."

"It's my fault."

"Please don't say that." I stroked her hair. "The people responsible are the bastards who attacked me."

"I'm so happy Hudson found you. I hope that fucker he hit crawled into a hole and died!"

My stomach heaved. Thoughts of Logan, the knife, and the gushing red choker flooded my mind. I shoved them down and locked them away.

"For the record, I really like Hudson."

"I really like him too." She pressed our foreheads together. "Even more now."

"Lock that one down. The accent is reason enough."

"Don't make me laugh right now," she said. "It's been a long, awful night. Just let me hug you for the next twenty minutes and then I'll drive you home."

"No." It came out louder than I meant.

"No?"

"Sof, the guys can't see me like this. Once they find out what happened, you know what they'll do."

She nodded. "They'll find the fucker in the hole and kill him again."

"And that's if they're feeling merciful."

"What do you want to do?"

"Can I stay here? Just until I figure it out."

She hugged me. "You know you don't have to ask. I have clothes and a toothbrush for you. Stay as long as you need."

"Thank you."

I took what I needed to the bathroom and turned on the shower. Only when I was beneath the spray did I start crying.

I SKIPPED ALL OF MY Friday classes and hid out in Sofia's room. That was an easy choice. What wasn't easy was fending off the men I loved.

The four of them called me six separate times. Hudson rescued my sim card from the janitor shed and Sofia let me borrow one of her old phones. I was able to answer their calls, but I refused to. I couldn't risk them picking up something in my voice.

Ezra: Why didn't you come home last night?

Me: I slept over at Sofia's.

Ezra: One of these days I'm going to get the note that you two ran away together.

In the midst of everything, I smiled.

Me: I could say the same about you and Cora.

Ezra: She keeps turning me down.

Me: Same for Sofia.

Ezra: Guess we're stuck with each other. Good thing I love you.

Ezra: I'll see you tonight. My dad is coming over for dinner. Chef is making something special.

My heart squeezed as I typed my reply.

Me: I won't be there. The Sallys are throwing a movie night and tomorrow there is a barbeque. I'm going to do the sister-bonding thing this weekend.

Ezra: Why?

Me: It'll be fun. I love you. Bye.

I threw the phone across Sofia's bed.

"Everything okay?"

Sofia reclined on her couch, reading a book. I also made her skip classes and hide out in her room. She had no problem saying yes.

No, I'm not okay. Four of the guys who attacked me because I got in the way of their assault against you are still out there. What if they're planning to go after you again? I believe I can identify two of them, but how do I find the others? I can't trust that you're safe until they're gone.

"Everything is fine," I replied. "Just hungry."

"I'll bring you some food." She winked. "I promise not to cook it."

I dropped my smile after she left the room.

What if I go to the police?

And tell them you were attacked by four men? another voice asked. *If they mention Logan under interrogation, the police are bound to search for him. Leighton was very clear on how she'd feel about that.*

But everyone else thinks the police are handling this—even Sofia. I could convince her to hire bodyguards to watch her back.

I tossed my head.

They would be trailing her forever until I solved the real problem. I had to find the men who did this and make sure they never think to touch her again. I know where to start. I just need backup. I can't take the boys, and Leighton's offer of help would never be cashed in.

All of a sudden it dawned on me. I snatched up my phone.

He didn't answer on the first try, so I called again.

"Hello, Miss Moon?"

"Jacob," I began. "I have to speak to you about something important. Can you come to the Zeta Rho Sigma house tomorrow? Don't tell anyone."

THE THUMPING BASS REACHED me across the lawn. The Zeta Rho Sigma pool party sounded like a hit, and by the buff shirtless men wandering around, they had a few party crashers.

I watched them from Sofia's bay window. I couldn't pick her out in the crowd, but I knew she was down there with Hudson. He came by to see how I was doing and I wheedled both of them into going by saying I could use some space.

Hudson didn't want to go to a pool party at all. They argued about it while I hid a smile behind my book. But when Sofia came out in her bikini, he had a change of heart.

This is what I want for her. Pool parties, boyfriends, study groups, and normal. I'll take care of this, so she can have everything she wants.

I thought of that while I waited for Caroline's bodyguard/companion to arrive.

A knock sounded on my door at two p.m. on the dot. I set my book down to let him in.

"Miss Moon, how—" Jacob took one look at my split lip and bandaged forehead. His hand flew to his holster. "Who did that to you?"

He pushed past me and swept the space.

"They're not in the room," I said.

It didn't stop him from ducking into the closet and bathroom.

"Jacob, please sit." I sat on the window seat and motioned for him to do the same.

He planted himself in the middle of the room instead.

"What happened, Miss Moon?"

I told him. I shared the entire awful story, leaving out the part where Leighton, Patricia, Reagan, and I paid Logan a visit. I left Logan's name out completely.

Jacob was infamous for his stoicism. He stood by Caroline's side silent, devoted, and expressionless. This didn't change. He listened to me without uttering a sound or so much as moving.

Jacob didn't speak until I finished. "Did you contact the police?"

"No. I want to handle this myself."

He didn't ask how or why.

"What do you need from me?" Jacob asked.

"You're always with Caroline, but I know there is a whole team of you," I replied. "How does that work? Are you from a firm? Do I have to hire you guys?"

He shook his head. "We work for Shea Industries and the Shea family exclusively. Our services extend to you."

I released the breath I'd been holding for more than a day. "That's perfect, Jacob. It's exactly what I need."

"For us to track down the men who attacked you."

"For you to protect Sofia and find the men who attacked me." I pushed aside my book and rescued the paper hiding under it. "I want at least three guards on her at all times. Can you spare that many?"

He nodded.

"Good." I continued down my list. "I'll tell her they're guarding her, but I want them protecting her even if she disagrees. If that happens, they have to hang back and blend in, but she's never to be alone except when she's home. She's safe with her parents.

"I told you I suspected the hundred-dollar-bill guy of being a part of it. He wore black like the others and they attacked me immediately after she left for smaller bills. I wrote down what he looked like," I said. "There's him and then... Shawn."

I spat the name like it burned. "I didn't recognize him until he said Sofia, instead of Richards. We met him once and he belted out her name like a jackass. I noticed then that he pronounced it SOH-fia, and not So-FI-a like most people."

And once I realized he was involved, I made the connection to the smell of my attacker and Logan who always smelled of musk and pine.

"Do you have a last name?" he asked.

"Yes, I looked him up on Facebook." I tapped the name written on my sheet. "Shawn Dimov. Physics major. Between the two of them, I'll get the name of the others."

"You want us to interrogate them," he stated.

"I'm not asking anyone to do anything illegal, but having armed guards at my back while I speak to them should loosen their tongues."

"What exactly do you intend to do once you've identified them all?"

I met his gaze steadily. "It doesn't matter. That part comes after and no one else will be involved."

He inclined his head, acknowledging the terms.

"As for Sofia," I continued. "She's going out with Hudson tonight and she's safe. I expect she'll get back late—if not tomorrow morning. While she's out is the perfect time to find Dimov. Can the men meet me tonight to track him down?"

"They certainly can meet you tonight, Miss Moon. I already have the men in mind. What time would you like them to be here?"

"Nine o'clock."

"Nine it is."

A wash of gratitude propelled me out of my seat. I hugged him. "Thank you so much, Jacob."

The guard didn't return my embrace, but he didn't pull away either. "The men who harmed you will be found, Miss Moon. I can assure you."

I gave him another squeeze and then stepped back. "One more thing," I said. "Promise me you won't tell Ryder, Jaxson, Ezra, Maverick, or Caroline about this."

"I promise."

"I will tell them myself, but after I've dealt with it." I gripped his forearms. This was the most I've touched or spoken to this man in years. "This is to protect them. I won't have them do something they can't come back from."

He gently removed my hands. "I promise, Miss Moon. This will stay between you, me, and the guards I assign. May I have the name and descriptions?"

I placed it on his palm.

"I must get back to Caroline," he said. "Will you be safe here? I can have someone posted outside in thirty minutes."

"I'm safe. I'm not planning on leaving this room anytime soon and I'm surrounded by women who are... not to be messed with," I finished.

He nodded. "Thank you for coming to me with this."

"No, thank you, Jacob."

I felt lighter after he walked out the door. The horror of that night clung to my skin like film. It crawled under the torment of phantom fingers and hungry gazes. As awful as Logan's wide, shocked eyes seeking me in my nightmares.

That night would plague me forever, but with Jacob's help, I could move forward and right the wrongs done to me.

I passed the hours in Sofia's room reading, watching TV, and texting Caroline about Adam. My baby was safe, comfortable, and asking for me.

Me: I'll be home soon. I promise.

"Val, are you sure?" Sofia plopped on top of me, dragging my attention away from my phone. "I can stay. I *want* to stay. Hudson and I can go out anytime. You need me more."

"It's been nice having time and quiet to deal with what happened." I poked her side. "I want you to go and have fun. If I need you, I'll call."

"Promise?"

"Yes."

It took some more cajoling, but at eight thirty I finally got her out of the room. I climbed back in her bed to wait.

Punctual as ever, Jacob texted me at eight fifty-nine.

Jacob: They are downstairs.

Me: On my way.

I jumped out of bed and hurried downstairs.

First, we'll go over Sofia's protection. Then we'll speak to Shawn. If he gives up his friends and the photos without a problem, I won't have to call my hacker. My best friend will be safe while I make them pay one by one.

"Coming," I called at the door. I jogged past the girls watching a movie in the living room and threw it open. "Thanks..."

My greeting died on my lips. Ryder, Maverick, Ezra, and Jaxson loomed over me, the expressions on their faces ones I never wanted to see.

Quickly, I covered my mouth.

Ryder's hand flashed out and pulled it away. His silver eyes flashed like lightning within his thunderous face, and it burned through to my core.

"They're dead."

The harsh, frightening hiss loosened my tongue. "Why are you here?" I croaked. "Jacob promised me—"

"Jacob works for the Shea family. He keeps our secrets. He doesn't keep secrets from us," Ryder said. "He knows he'd be fucking dead too if he didn't tell me."

Tears sprung unbidden to my eyes. Of course he told them. I was stupid to think he wouldn't. "I don't want you to do anything," I cried. "I—"

Ezra held up the paper I gave Jacob. "It's too late for that. Shawn Dimov is getting a visit from us tonight. Maverick already found his dorm."

My eyes snapped between the four of them, reading their intent so clearly my stomach twisted. I didn't give a fuck about Shawn Dimov. I wouldn't shed a tear if he was run over by a flaming truck twice. But I did not want my boys driving that truck.

Leighton killed a man for me and it was a lash on my soul that would never disappear. My loves being driven to it would destroy me.

"What are you going to do?" I whispered.

"I haven't decided yet. Every new punishment I come up with is more inventive than the last. I'm waiting until the right one hits me."

"I'll come with you," I tried. "To make sure it doesn't get out of hand."

They didn't bother voicing their denial. In unison, all four silently shook their heads.

What could I do? They knew his name. They knew where to find him and I couldn't hold back all four of them. And in that acceptance, the fight went out of me.

"I'm sorry," I whispered. "You must be so angry with me."

"No, Val," said Maverick.

Ryder tugged my wrist. I stumbled into his chest. Surprise stopped my tears as he held me. "You have nothing to apologize for," he said gruffly. "We're sorry you didn't feel like you could come to us. But we're here now, Val, and we're going to take care of you."

Something in me broke. The pain, fear, trauma, and loneliness of the past three days surged out.

I cried loud, stomach-clenching wails as my boys surrounded me.

Behind me, footsteps signaled my cries attracted an audience.

"Valentina? What's wrong?" Blair asked.

"She'll be okay," Ezra replied. "We're here now."

EZRA

We took Valentina home. She cried the entire drive, curled up against Maverick's chest as he whispered sweet, soothing things in her ear.

A feeling I couldn't name swelled inside of me as her sobs filled the car. When Jacob relayed everything Valentina told him, I thought at that moment that I might be capable of anything. As I listened to her cry, I knew I was.

Jaxson carried her inside and up to his room. We washed and dressed her in soft, warm pajamas. After, we brought her to the one person who could comfort her as well as we could: Adam.

We placed her next to the sleeping child and drew the covers to her chin. Her hand shot out and grabbed me as I moved away. I read in her eyes that she wanted us to stay. It was the hardest thing I ever had to do to place her hand back on the pillow and walk out of the room.

Ryder shut the door softly behind us.

"Which dorm?" I asked Maverick.

"McAshton. Room 3112."

I reached for the paper. "And the other guy Val described?"

"Too many guys fit that description. Dimov's friends on social media hardly narrowed it down."

Jaxson pushed through us. "Then let's ask Dimov for the name. I'm sure we can get him into a sharing mood."

"Agreed"

We marched out. The ride back to campus was made in silence. There was nothing we had to say to each other that hadn't already been said during the hours we waited for nine o'clock. For ten minutes, the biggest shock of my day was Jacob away from Caroline's side and speaking to me. Then he brought me to the living room where Maverick, Jaxson, and Ryder waited and told the news Valentina brought to him, not us.

We went back and forth—raging, shouting, breaking every expensive thing in the room. We made up our minds to storm the Sally house. Caroline stopped us in the front hall.

"Val will be waiting for you at nine o'clock," she said. "Get yourselves under control by then. What she needs is love, support, and for you to know she kept this from you to protect you. Even now she puts you four first. Show her it's okay for her to need you."

It was as close to impossible as an act could be, but we waited... and we planned.

Ryder killed the engine near McAshton House. We got out, walked across the empty lawn, and let ourselves inside. The ride up the elevator was charged with rising emotion. The sooner we got to him, the more I shook.

It opened, letting us out directly in front of 3112. We fanned out in front of the door and Ryder knocked.

We heard movement inside, and then the door flew open. Shawn Dimov took one look at us and his jaw stuck half open. He paled.

"Good," I said. "You know who we are."

Maverick punched him dead in the face. His neck snapped all the way around and he hit the ground—out cold.

We stepped over his body and streamed inside. The click of the lock was a clanging bell, signaling a line would be crossed to which none of us could return.

Jaxson took hold of him and propped him against the dresser. While he did so, I gazed around the room of the man who dared to touch Valentina.

It was a mess. Dirty laundry, crumpled paper, and food crumbs littered the floor. The stench permeating the air pointed to how long it'd been since he washed those clothes. On the walls, half-naked women smiled and smirked at me. It was a typical guy's room, but there was nothing typical about Shawn Dimov or what he and his friends chose to do to Val, and wanted to do to Sofia.

But it will be the last mistake he ever makes.

"Laptop," I said, arriving at the desk.

Maverick went over and turned it on. "If he has the pictures on his computer..." He stopped. The muscles in his jaw ticked. Jacob didn't get through telling us about the photos before Maverick flipped over the television.

"I'll find them," he continued.

The three of us watched in silence as Maverick did what he did. If his computer was clean and Maverick found proof he went to a movie that night or something, we had an apology to give. But Val was certain he was one of the men, and that was enough for us.

"Anything?" Jaxson burst out.

"I think so," Maverick replied. "I found a file hidden on the hard drive but I haven't gotten it open yet. He's smarter than we thought."

"Can you get in?" Ryder asked.

Maverick leveled us with a look. "I'll get in."

The tapping of keys were the only sounds in the room for a solid ten minutes. None of us would interrupt him. What he found on that computer would determine the course of the night.

"I'm in."

We surged forward. Ryder, Jaxson, and I leaned over Maverick as he clicked on the untitled folder. A string of items with no icons greeted us.

He chose the first one.

Maverick shot out of the chair. It would have toppled into me if I wasn't already across the room, towering over Dimov.

"Wake him up," I hissed.

Ryder chose to do that by banging his head once, twice, three times against the dresser. Shawn came to groaning. He peeled his eyes open, finding us standing above him. His lips twisted.

"What the fuck do you think you're doing?" he shouted. "You can't—"

Jaxson socked him across the jaw. "Don't speak," he said dispassionately. "Just listen." He flexed his knuckles. "And don't make me have to tell you again."

Blood trickled from the corner of Shawn's mouth. The false bravado vanished and fear flickered in his eyes.

Good.

I crouched down in front of him. "This is how it's going to go," I began. "I am going to ask you questions, and you're going to answer those questions with nothing but the truth. If you lie or try to justify what you've done, you will regret it. Do you understand me?"

His tongue darted out to lick his dry lips. "I haven't done anything. You're making a mistake."

"Ryder," I said.

Ryder buried his fist in Shawn's gut. He doubled over and Jaxson yanked him back up by the neck.

"I told you not to lie to me. We found the pictures."

Blood and spittle flew from his mouth as he sucked in ragged breaths. "Stop!"

Jaxson raised his fist again.

"No, I'll answer!"

"Excellent." An icy calm gripped me. I never felt more secure in what I needed to do. "First question, what hand did you use to touch our girlfriend? Which one held her down? Which one *violated* her?"

He stared at me, eyes wide. "I-I don't—"

"Do you need a reminder of what happens when you don't answer?" I asked.

Slowly, Shawn raised his right hand. Jaxson seized it.

"What are you doing?" he shouted.

Jaxson forced his hand onto his knee, palm down.

"Next question," I continued. "What are the names of the other men who attacked her?"

"Names?"

I balled my fist. "I'm going to add another rule about making me repeat myself. Last chance. Give us their names."

Shawn's eyes rolled in his head, darting between the four of us. If he was looking for mercy, he found none. He finally landed on me.

"I-I know you," he said. "I know who your mother is." Shawn straightened. "If you think I'm going to give a big confession for you to blast all over MMBC, you're a fucking idiot."

I listened expressionlessly.

"You think you got me because you found some pictures?" Shawn spat, gathering steam. "I downloaded those off a porn site and you can't even see the girl's face. What's the sentence for that?" He barked a laugh. "You want to beat me up? Do it. And get me in the face because it'll look great to a judge when I get all of you for assault!"

He smirked in my face. "Oops. I broke one of your precious rules." Shawn raised his chin. "Go ahead. Get me in the nose this time. I—"

I grasped his index finger and wrenched it back until I heard the snap.

Ryder was quick. He stuffed a dirty t-shirt in Shawn's mouth as he howled.

The boy threw himself back, screaming as tears leaked from his eyes. Ryder and Maverick clamped down and held him still, preventing him from ripping out of Jaxson's grasp.

"I should have explained," I said evenly. "The cost of further pissing me off isn't a few punches or kicks. It's the breaking of every finger you put on Valentina." I tapped each one in turn. "If you haven't learned by then, I move to the next hand."

Shawn whipped his head side to side, pleading through the white of his eyes.

"If after I've broken all of your fingers, you still haven't answered my questions, I'll break the arms that held her down. I'll break the legs that ran after Sofia—one of the sweetest, kindest people I've ever known." I leaned in close. "And then I'll break your ribs... for fun."

Shawn tossed his head wildly, his muffled shouts getting louder.

The beast in me woke. It shook off sleep, uncoiled its body, and spread through me, filling the deepest corners of my being. I wasn't Ezra Lennox. I wasn't the mannequin man. I was new. Forged in the flames of trauma, nursed by resentment and rage, held down by shackles of civility, and then ignited by love. I was now what Valentina Moon needed me to be.

Ruthless.

"You're right, Shawn," I said. "After all of that, you'll appear incredibly sympathetic to a judge, but then the question is, how much pain can you withstand?" I clapped my hands. "I'm eager to find out. What about you boys?"

"Oh, yeah," said Jaxson.

"Definitely," Maverick threw in.

"Let's take turns," Ryder said.

"I'm going to try this again," I said. "What are their names?" I pulled the shirt out of his mouth.

The words poured out of him in a rush. "King Paxton, Brandon Kollie, Finn Joseph."

"And?" I prompted when he didn't say more. "There were five of you."

Shawn dropped his head. "The fifth guy was Chance Smith."

My eyes narrowed. "You just lied to me, didn't you?"

"No," he cried. "No, I didn't."

"Avoiding eye contact. Using the most common last name in the country for your fake one. The Media Maven herself taught me what to look for in an interview, Dimov." I tsked, shaking my head. "I warned you what would happen if you lie."

"No! N—"

Maverick stuffed the shirt back in. The crunch of his middle finger echoed through the room.

"We're going to try this again," I said to him.

Dimov's bright red cheeks ballooned as he tried to suck air in through the fabric. Tears, snot, and blood ran down his face, soaking the shirt. His cocky-shit act was over.

"Tell me the name of the fifth person, and keep this in mind, we'll be paying King, Brandon, and Finn a visit tonight too. I have a feeling they're going to be very forthcoming. If the name they give us doesn't match yours, we'll be coming back here for another chat. Nod if you understand."

He bobbed his head so hard he smacked it against the dresser.

I signaled for Ryder to remove the gag. "What's his name?"

"Logan Bilius," he sobbed. "I swear, I'm not lying. Don't do it again—"

My eyes narrowed. "Logan? You mean the cupcake bitch? Val and Sof's friend?!" The first hint of my rage broke through. "Why would he do this? Was it his idea? And why"—I fisted his collar—"would you try to protect him?"

"Because he's my cousin!"

The boys and I exchanged a look. The picture was only getting murkier. Val said that Logan was a friend and that he had a crush on Sofia. Why would he and his cousin do this? Was it their plan the whole time?

"Why did you target Sofia and attack Val?" I asked.

"We did it for the money! We know how fucking rich Sofia Richards is and we knew where she was almost every night, all alone. We were going to grab her, snatch her money and jewelry, take some naked pictures of her, and then let her go. I swear!"

"Why the pictures?"

Shawn threw his head back. "Please," he begged. "Please, let me go."

I reached for his ring finger.

"No! No, okay! We took the pictures to blackmail her parents."

"What? Her parents?"

He nodded hard. "We were going to send them the pictures and demand two hundred grand to keep them from getting out. Forty thousand for each of us. Sofia was supposed to be alone. We tried to get the other girl out of there, but Sofia left instead."

Shawn slumped in on himself. Maverick and Ryder held him up as another sobbing fit wracked his body.

"We c-couldn't wait," Shawn said. "We were running out of time. There was no one around, so we decided to grab your girlfriend and just keep her out of the way. We figured Sofia would come back and think she went to the bathroom or something."

As he spoke, I heard what Valentina did and the different way he pronounced Sofia.

Good job, baby. You got us here. Now we'll get you justice.

"But then she kicked over the stand and everything went wrong. While we had her, I thought why not get some money for her pictures too? Then we could grab Sofia walking back." He swung around to Ryder. "That's it. That's the truth, I promise. Make him stop!"

Ryder laughed. It was a harsh, chilling sound. "Don't look at me, Dimov. Ezra is the nice one. You should have heard what I wanted to do to you."

"You know, I don't think that is it," I said as he started crying again. "Why would Logan want to do this to Sofia in the first place? And why did you say you were running out of time?"

Shawn's jaw worked. It took him a minute to reply. "Logan's parents cut him off. They'd been fighting all semester, but when he got home, it blew up. They said they weren't paying for Somerset. Tuition, housing, nothing. Then they threw him out.

"He wanted to stay with me, but my mom took her sister's side and closed the door in his face. He was desperate. Logan killed himself for four years to get into Somerset University. He needed to get his hands on twenty thousand dollars by the tuition deadline, and he asked me to help."

"By attacking Sofia and blackmailing her mom and sick dad," Maverick said. "Why? Because he knew she had money?"

"Because she was a stuck-up bitch!" he cried. "Lording her money over everyone. She gets herself a fancy dorm and fills it with big screens, silk sheets, and Persian rugs while her mansion sits twenty minutes—"

Searing fury swarmed my senses. I dove for his finger.

"Wait, no," he screamed. "That's what Logan said, not me. I didn't even know her. It's what he said."

"What else did he say?" I forced through my teeth.

He yanked at Jaxson's hold. "Don't break it, please!"

I raised my hands and indicated for him to speak.

"He said that she led him on," he continued after a minute. "She made him nip at her heels like a puppy, but she was never going to date him because he wasn't rich or famous enough. His words," Shawn stressed. "Logan said her parents would pay whatever we wanted to protect their princess. After they coughed up the money, we'd sell the pictures online for even more.

"There are sick freaks out there willing to pay serious money for rape porn, and I mean the real thing. But I wasn't going to let it go that far." He peered into my eyes. "I told them we'd just strip her and take pics of her tied up and held down. That's it."

I bared my teeth. "You think that makes you some kind of hero?" I hissed. "Because you drew the line at rape? But one of you did attempt to rape Valentina. Hudson caught him on top of her with his dick out."

I encircled his ring and pinky finger. "Which one of you was it?"

"He attempted to...?" The blood drained from his face. "That's not true. We left Logan with your girlfriend and he's not *that*. He would never."

I bent his fingers back inch by inch. "Are you calling Valentina a liar?"

"No," he said quickly. "I just— I— He's my fucking cousin. I know him. He wouldn't—"

I laughed mirthlessly. "You know him? Did you know he would lose his shit over being rejected? Did you know he'd try to solve his problems by assaulting innocent women? Did you know he was a sociopathic piece of garbage? If you did, you can't be surprised to hear he took it further."

Shawn's weak chin quivered under the force on his fingers. I hadn't broken them, but I wanted to.

"I don't understand why you went along with him, Dimov," I said. "It seems like you're all sick freaks. Who would do this to a woman for some money?"

"It wasn't for the money. I was giving Logan my cut." A tear dripped on my hand. "I did it because he's family. He needed my help and I didn't see another way. Logan was going to end up on the street. Lose everything he worked for, while trust-fund princesses and manicured douchebags skated through Somerset and then were handed careers by their parents.

"I knew it was wrong, but you do what you have to do to protect your f-family." His voice cracked on a sob. "I'm sorry. I'm so sorry."

Something stirred in me as he sniveled. I gazed at Shawn Dimov—broken, bruised, soul in shreds—and I finally realized what I needed to do.

"Shut up," Jaxson snapped. "Let's finish this. Tell us what you did with the pictures."

I looked at Maverick and he immediately went to the computer. He'd delete every trace of their existence.

"Nothing," Shawn said. He looked from me to Maverick. "The whole plan was fucked. We left to get Sofia and then Logan called me and said Valentina got away. He told me the police wouldn't be far behind and we needed to get back to our dorms. He sent me the pictures and ordered me to wait until after he saw Valentina and Sofia again and made sure they didn't suspect us."

"For your life," Ryder said, "you better not have sold them."

"I didn't," he rushed out. "I didn't do anything with them. I just hid them on my computer. Logan left, so I did—"

"Whoa." I held up a hand. "What do you mean he left?"

"The day after, he texted me saying it was all too much and he was dropping out of school." He sniffed. "I haven't seen or spoke to him since."

"If you're lying—"

"Check my phone," he yelled. "I've been calling and texting and he hasn't answered. Check!"

I rose and walked over to the bedside table. I typed in the password Shawn recited and opened his messages.

Logan: I can't do this anymore. I'm dropping out. Don't look for me. I want to start over.

Shawn: You're dropping out after everything? Why?

Shawn: Logan, call me back.

Shawn: I just want to know you're okay. You don't have money or a place to live. Do you want me to sell the stuff? I'll send you the cash.

I didn't have to ask what "the stuff" was.

Shawn: Logan?

There were more messages, but none came from Logan.

"It looks like Logan ran," I told the guys.

"We'll find him," said Ryder.

"That we will," I agreed. I crouched before Dimov and tossed the phone in his lap. "Listen very carefully because this is what happens now," I began. "You don't go to school here anymore. Tomorrow, you're going to pack your shit, get in your car, and drive as far as you can get until you hit ocean, and then keep driving."

I leaned in, getting so close his bulging, terrified eyes filled my vision. "If I ever see you again, I'll kill you." I grasped his jaw and pulled him closer still. "Now, I'm going to repeat that just in case you thought it was an exaggeration or an idle threat. Look into my eyes and understand... I will kill you."

Trembling in my hold, Shawn didn't speak.

"Fuck," Jaxson suddenly cursed.

I glanced down. A dark, growing stain spread through his pants. Releasing him, I got to my feet. "Maverick, it is done?"

"The pictures are gone. It's done."

"Then let's go. There are a few more guys we have to visit."

Chapter Eleven

E*zra*

Valentina was beautiful always, but there was something about her in sleep. Her growing chestnut hair fell over her cheek and tickled her lips. I ached to brush it back, but I didn't want to wake her. None of us did.

Maverick, Jaxson, Ryder, and I stood over Adam's bed, watching them both sleep. The sight of them cuddled tightly and Adam's arm splayed over Val's neck soothed us. It had been a long night. So long, it was nearly morning. Orange-purplish light peeked through the superhero curtains, reminding us time relentlessly marched on.

We paid King Paxton, Brandon Kollie, and Finn Joseph a visit. We left them with broken bones, bloody faces, and an order to be gone in twenty-four hours, but they were alive.

"From now on, Val has guards with her whenever she leaves the house," I whispered.

"Already done," Ryder replied.

"And give Jacob a raise."

He cracked a smile. "Already done."

"Good." I gazed at Valentina and said, "There's only one thing left to do… and I need your help."

"Anything," they said at once.

"Let's go outside."

After the door shut behind us, I spoke. "Brian owes money to a drug cartel."

Jaxson's jaw dropped. "What the fuck?"

I told them everything. I started with the initiation and ended on my conversation with Brian.

"He wants me to stay out of it," I said, "but he's basically in hiding. He's cut off from his family, lying to Mom, out of a job, and watching his life flush down the toilet. I can't sit by when I know I can help him. We're family and it's what you do. Not that psycho, twisted loyalty shit that Dimov spouted, but the real thing." My gaze drifted to Adam's door. "Honest, selfless sacrifice for the people you care about."

I looked at the guys. "You know I wouldn't ask this if—"

"You know you don't have to ask," Ryder cut in. "Tell us what to do."

I might've hugged the guy if that was our thing. I might do it anyway.

"I have fifty thousand in my account. With what Brian lost at the table and *interest*, he owes over three hundred grand. I need to pull the rest of the money together before the guy sells his house and everything he owns."

"I've got about sixty thousand," Maverick chimed in. "There's more in my trust fund, but I'm assuming we're not telling anyone about this."

I shook my head. "Not until it's done."

"I have seventy-five in my personal account," Ryder said.

"Guys, stop," said Jaxson. "You think our parents won't notice if we zero out our balances? This won't work."

"We don't have a choice," I said.

"Yes, we do. I'll sell the Ferrari."

"What? You can't," I said automatically.

He snorted. "Yes, I can. A one-point-four-million-dollar car selling with a million knocked off. It'll go fast. I'll just tell Dad I wrecked it." Jaxson strode off. "I'll start looking for a buyer," he called over his shoulder.

I was speechless. There were the brothers we were given and the brothers we chose. I chose well.

"Thank you, Jaxson. You can have my car until I buy you another one."

He waved as he disappeared into his room.

"All right, Maverick," I continued. "We need to contact the Sons of Slaughter to tell them I have their money and where to get it. My brother's proven he's hackable, so look for someone named Roman. He was Brian's copilot and the one who got him in bed with the SOS."

"Got it."

Ryder clapped my shoulder. "We're going to handle this, Ezra. It's what we do."

THAT NIGHT, VAL AND I gazed at each other across the pillow.

"You promise?"

"I promise, Val," I said. "We roughed them up a little and strongly impressed upon them that they should change schools. In a couple weeks, the police are going to get a tip about a few things we planted on their computers. They'll be the sick fucks who paid for photos they shouldn't have. Those men will go to jail, Val. They won't hurt Sofia or anyone else again." I brushed the hair from her cheek. "Did we do good?"

A soft smile graced her lips. "Good is relative in this situation, but yes. Thank you."

"There is just one more," I continued. "Logan. It's only a matter of time before we track him down."

"Let's talk about something else," she said. "What did you and Adam get up to while I was at the Sally house? Also, how was dinner with your dad?"

He blew out a breath. "Dinner was weird. Mom and Dad insisted on sitting next to each other and every time I looked away, their heads were together and they were laughing about something. Adam and I had a long talk about it after they left."

"Ezra, you have to stop using our son as a therapist," she said, giggling.

I stilled. "Did you just say…?"

"Our son." She flashed me a teasing smile. "Yes, I did. Got a problem with it?"

"No, I don't." I captured her lips in a sweet, slow kiss. Our tongues entangled, drawing soft moans from us both.

"I love you," I whispered. "I love our son. And our family. I would do anything for you guys."

She caressed my cheek. "And we would do anything for you."

THE TWO WEEKS I WAITED for Jaxson to sell his car were the longest of my life. He was right about it being snapped up quickly. The problem was the buyer rode in on a mix of elated and suspicious about the great deal. He insisted on checking, re-checking, and then checking the car again. Then he called cops to make sure it wasn't stolen.

"My dad almost picked up that call from the police," Jaxson griped. The four of us were in Ryder's room gathered in his sitting area. "But we're good. The money transferred into my account this morning."

"And I found the SOS," said Maverick. "Roman's not stupid. He covered his tracks pretty well. In the end, I had to get in by cloning Brian's phone number and tricking him into clicking a link in the text. It got the spy program into his phone, emails, social media, all of it." He shrugged. "I figured Brian's ignoring calls from him, so Roman can't out us."

I leaned forward in my seat. "What did you get?"

"Like I said, he's smart. He doesn't directly mention drugs or anything illegal, but there was one thing that was suspicious." Maverick turned his computer around. "He regularly texts this person named Dax and their messages are odd. 'I'm on my way to Belize. I'll bring you back a mug' or 'I couldn't find the chocolates you like. I'll get them the next time I'm in Costa Rica.'"

"What's odd about that?" I asked.

He motioned at the screen. "It's all they talk about. Hundreds of messages about souvenirs and what country he's flying in or out of."

"That's their code for the drugs."

"Gotta be. Dax is one of the SOS and this is his number. He's who we'll contact to arrange the meet."

"With this." Ryder reached into his pocket and took out a cellphone. "Jacob got it for me, but he doesn't know why I need it. The phone's completely untraceable. Obviously, we can't let them know you're the son of a billionaire investigative reporter."

"I got this, guys. Don't worry."

"We," Jaxson said. "Get that through your head, playboy. You're not meeting this guy alone."

I put my hands up in surrender. "Trust me, I'm not interested in being alone in a dark alley with a guy who calls himself a son of slaughter. I'll take the backup."

"No darkness or alleys," Maverick said. "Have him meet you between classes on campus. There'll be too many people around to risk trying anything."

"There's also campus security," Ryder added. "We can't have my security team there since they report to Mom, but at least there'll be someone out patrolling."

"We've got our bases covered, gentlemen," I said. "All that's left is to arrange the meet."

"Not quite," said Maverick. "What about Val?"

"She's dealing with a lot right now," I said. "She only goes to campus for class and she hasn't been by the Sally house in weeks. I won't have her worrying about me on top of it. After it's taken care of, I'll tell her everything."

"She's going to be pissed," Jaxson stated. "Our girl's about to tear you three new assholes."

"I'll take my punishment. We're focused on her and what she needs. We save my brother's ass, then it's all about Valentina." I held out my hand. "Let's do this."

Ryder handed it over. I'd been going over for weeks what I would say to a dangerous cartel member to get them to travel from wherever they are to meet a random person. In the end, I kept it simple.

Me: I have the money to clear Brian Spencer's debt. I can put it in your hands this Friday.

"Do you think they'll respond?" asked Jaxson.

"I just offered to give them over a quarter of a million dollars in five days. They'll respond."

Apparently, they wouldn't respond quickly.

The four of us hung around Ryder's room waiting until Valentina poked her head in to see what we were doing. I occupied the rest of the day checking the phone every five seconds and driving Adam around the house in his mini Benz.

Near lunchtime, I drove him into the kitchen for some food. The borrowed phone buzzed as I settled him in his chair. I ripped it out so fast I almost dropped it.

Dax: Who the fuck is this? How did u get this #?

I replied immediately.

Me: I got it off Roman. I also have the money to clear Brian Spencer's debt. You want it or not?

Dax: Who is this?

Me: Cas Wells

Or the name I would have gotten if Dad had chosen and the last name of my mom's favorite journalist. Mom's fifth rule, anchor a fake identity with true personal details that you'll never forget. I wonder if Mom knew how transferrable her lessons were to issues outside of journalism.

Dax: U got the wrong # Cas Wells.

Me: Give me the right one. Unless your bosses aren't interested in over three hundred grand sliding into their pockets.

Dax: This is Spencer. We've been looking for u.

Me: No, I'm Cas, and I know why you've been looking for him. We're taking the first option and paying off the debt. It's a good deal. You can buy yourself another pilot and a plane with the money. Do you want it or not?

Dax didn't reply. An hour slipped into two. Sunday became Monday, then Tuesday, and then Wednesday. Still nothing.

I had the phone on me at all times. The temptation to text him demanding an answer was overwhelming, but that was another lesson from Mom. Never show eagerness in a negotiation, you immediately give the other party the upper hand.

Wednesday afternoon, I returned home after class and dumped my backpack on my bed. I heard a buzz from the depths and left it a minute to use the bathroom. I came out, shedding my clothes as I went, and picked it up. There was nothing on the screen. It wasn't my phone. It was the other one.

Dax: Roman's never heard of u. Do u know who ur fucking with?

Me: I said I got the number off of him. Not from him. Of course that shit doesn't know who I am. I'm not connected to this or any of you. It's my job to arrange the handoff. I've got 350,000 dollars to clear Brian Spencer's debt and end his association with the SOS. You'll take the money and you never bother him again.

If we have a deal, come to Somerset University, Parking Lot D, on Friday at 2pm. I'll have a blue and silver backpack.

Dax: No. We pick the place.

Dax: U come to Jimmy's Bar. Brooklyn. Fri at 11pm.

Me: Not a chance. If you want the money, you'll be at Somerset on Friday. If you miss the meetup, there will not be another one.

I hit send on the last message, and then I blocked his number. A lesson I got from life was to always maintain a position of power. Otherwise trash like Aiden, Roman, and Dax put you on your knees.

I tossed the phone on the bed and reached for mine. I sent a text to the boys.

Me: Friday afternoon. It's on.

FRIDAY MORNING, I CAREFULLY placed the blue and silver backpack in my trunk. The phone was nestled inside. I fished it out, unblocked Dax's number, and stuffed it in my main pack. I'd need to know his car or what he looked like.

I didn't have a reply confirming he'd come but I knew he would. I was offering him too much money to do otherwise.

This is it. We end this today.

I closed the trunk and found Valentina standing in front of me.

I jumped. "Val? What's up?"

"Want to give me a ride to campus? Sofia and I are meeting up for bagels."

"Love to."

We got in the car and set off for Somerset. Despite my confidence in the plan, my grip tightened on the wheel the closer we got to school.

"Do you want me to go with you to brunch?" I asked.

"No need," she replied. "The bodyguards you've got on me will keep us company."

Shit.

"Did you think I wouldn't notice?" she asked.

"They were supposed to be discreet."

"Three women who definitely don't look like college students suddenly popping up everywhere I am and four extremely protective boyfriends." I sensed her eyeroll without seeing it. "It wasn't hard to put it together."

"Are you going to ask me to call them off?"

She placed her hand on my thigh. "No, I'm going to ask you—all of you—to talk to me about these kinds of decisions. Just because you think I won't approve of something, doesn't mean you do it behind my back."

My stomach heaved. Her reprimand struck harder than she intended.

"We're in a serious, committed relationship, Ezra, and we discuss our issues."

"You're right." I took a deep breath. "Tonight, we will talk and get it all out in the open."

"Thank you."

I drove into campus and chose a parking lot as far away from Parking Lot D as possible.

Val kissed me goodbye through the window. "Tonight, Lennox. It's a date."

"It's a date," I agreed. "Now walk away, so I can watch."

She flung her head back, sighing. "Can never behave yourself," she mumbled. All the same, Val did a little wiggle as she walked off.

I chuckled. *Damn, I love that woman.*

A ringtone went off and my laugh died an abrupt death. That wasn't Cosplay Meltdown.

I put the untraceable cell to my ear. "Hello?"

"We're here. Parking Lot D. The blue Rolls-Royce."

I blinked. I didn't know what I expected of Dax's voice. I couldn't even be sure this was Dax's voice. However, the smooth, mellow tone coming from the other end was a surprise.

"You're here?" I glanced at the clock. "It's eleven. I told you two."

"The only flight out of this fucking town today is at twelve forty-five, and I'm going to be on it. If you're not here in ten minutes with our money, it's off, and then you can tell Spencer he won't be buying his way out of the bullet I'll put in his head."

"If—"

He hung up.

The phone slipped out of my hand. Panic rose like bile in my throat.

Ten minutes? Jaxson's still at work. Ryder is in class and I don't know where the fuck Maverick is. How are they going to get to their spots in time? What do I do?

Nine minutes.

"He won't buy his way out of the bullet I'll put in his head."

Jamming the key in the ignition, I tore out of the parking space. I knew what to do. I would save my brother.

I dialed as I pulled onto the street.

"Hello?"

"Jaxson," I cried. "It's now. The meet is happening now."

"What? It's supposed to be at two."

"He just called and said I have"—I checked the time—"eight minutes to get there or he's leaving. I'm almost there."

"Ezra, no," he yelled. "You can't meet him alone. We agreed."

"I won't be alone," I reasoned. "There are students all over the place. I'll put the backpack in his hands and walk away."

"Ezra, don't go without us!"

The nearest parking lot to D loomed ahead. I wouldn't risk driving into the same one and chancing them seeing my license plate. I veered sharply into the right lane, eliciting a few honks.

"Listen," I said. "Call the guys and send them if you can. Blue Rolls-Royce. I can't be on my phone when I approach them."

"Ezra—"

I ended the call. Jaxson called me back, but I ignored it.

Seven minutes.

Pulling into a space, I willed my heart to slow. I couldn't show up rattled.

Just give them the money, make them say they'll leave Brian alone, and then get out of there. It's simple.

I climbed out, grabbed the backpack from the trunk, and set a brisk pace to the meeting spot.

It was an unseasonably warm day and students took advantage of it. People strolled around in light sweaters, tossed the football around, and returned to the open-air food stalls to sip coffee and study notes.

I bounded up a grassy mound and cut through Taki's Tacos' space. A girl stepped into my path carrying her food, but I veered around her without breaking pace. The parking lot was in my sights.

Four minutes.

"Ezra? Hey, Ezra."

I whipped my head around.

Austin and a Sally girl occupied one of the taco tables. He said something to her and then jumped to follow me.

"Wait up," he called.

"I can't talk right now."

Austin jogged faster. "It's about the Sams. I don't like how things went down last semester. I joined but it wasn't because I was okay with what Aiden did. I hope we're cool."

There.

In the parking lot, idling between a Jeep and an overgrown sequoia tree, was the blue Rolls-Royce. It was unmistakable.

Three minutes.

I stopped dead, pulling Austin up short.

"You and I are good, Austin. You weren't responsible for what
happened in that basement." I gripped his arm. "I have to go. See you
around."

"Okay, I—"

I took off. Thankfully, he didn't follow me.

As I approached, the driver's side window rolled down. I made
out another figure next to him. It wasn't surprising since Dax did say
"we."

Two minutes.

I stopped just before the sequoia and looked at... myself. His mirrored shades reflected my blank expression as I looked him up and
down. From behind his glasses, I sensed him doing the same.

"Are you Dax?" I asked.

He nodded. "You Cas?"

"That's me."

Dax was both what I was expecting and nothing like what I en-
visioned at the same time. The multiple ear piercings and the neck
tattoos of flames, wings, and the letters SOS didn't shock me. It was
the full pink lips, strong jaw, and golden-brown hair styled closely to
mine that knocked me back. He looked like he modeled for the SOS
instead of running dirty pilots for them.

My eyes slid to the man sitting next to him. He was shorter and
skinnier than Dax. His gray, buttoned-up shirt was rumpled and his
dark brown hair begged to be combed.

"Roman," said Dax.

I kept the surprise off of my face. This is the guy that set my
brother up?

Dax jerked his head at me. "Recognize him?"

"No, Dax. Never seen him before."

"You sure?"

"Yes."

Dax removed his sunglasses. Brilliant green eyes continued their cold assessment of me.

"You a cop, Cas?"

"No." I slid the backpack off my shoulder and held it out. "I'm here to deliver the money. That's it."

Dax made no move to take it. "So, Spencer hired you." He smirked. "Is he too afraid to meet us himself?"

"He wants to make sure this is done right," I said simply. "Three hundred and fifty thousand to pay off the debt and then everyone can go back to their lives."

Dax sucked his teeth. "Three hundred and fifty is more than he owes."

"Then use the rest to buy yourself something nice."

He laughed and the harsh, cruel sound revealed not all of him was deceptively pleasant.

"I think I'll do that." Dax finally reached for the backpack.

"That's the end of it," I stated. "You've got your money. Brian Spencer is done with the Sons of Slaughter."

It didn't seem like he heard. Dax handed the bag to Roman who rifled through it.

"It's all there," I said.

"It is," Roman agreed. "And no dye packs or trackers."

"Then we're done," Dax said. "Spencer can consider his debt paid."

I needed to be sure. "We're good? You'll leave him and his family alone?"

Dax nodded.

It's over. Relief nearly made me smile. *Brian's going to be pissed when he finds out, but I won't let fuckers like these mess with my family. All that's left is Logan Bilius.*

"There's just one more thing, Cas."

I pulled out of my thoughts. "What?"

The green-eyed, tattooed drug runner smiled at me, displaying a row of stained, crooked teeth. "Will you deliver a message to Spencer for me?"

"What message?"

Dax raised his hand.

I looked into the barrel of the gun. My mind screamed at me to run and then a piercing noise blew it away.

Air pressed in and solidified around me, holding me upright as Dax peeled out of the parking space and tore off in a haze of smoke and squealing tires.

I pressed my hand to my chest. Slowly, it came away with blood.

The peaceful college scene was broken. Students ran screaming in every direction, tossing aside things and people in their haste to get away, and I was the reason.

I've been shot.

"Ezra?! Ezra!"

Legs giving out, I landed hard on my knees. The world blurred as a thought entered my mind.

Always maintain a position of power. Otherwise trash like Aiden, Roman, and Dax put you on your knees.

If only I'd known that was a warning.

"Ezra!"

Hands caught me before I fell.

"Au—"

"Don't try to talk." Austin eased me onto the ground. "You're going to be okay, Ezra. Just breathe and— Ezra, don't close your eyes! Look at me. Look—"

Darkness closed in, swallowing me whole.

Chapter Twelve

Valentina

"Leighton's been asking for you." Sofia cut her muffin in half and offered me a piece. We were taking up a corner booth in a cute café near my Developmental Psych class. "You've missed all of our events for the last few weeks and you haven't been by the house."

I bit off a big chunk of chocolate chip muffin to spare me time to answer.

I can't be around her. Watching her smile and laugh and joke while the picture of her standing over his body with a dripping knife is burned in my vision.

But I knew my reprieve was coming to an end. She was reaching out through Sofia. Soon, she'd bring her demands to me.

I swallowed. "Sofia, do you trust me?"

She paused with the food between her teeth. "Do I trust you? Why do you have to ask? You know I do."

"I'm going to ask you to do something and I need you to do it without asking questions. Just trust that I have a very good reason."

"Val, you're scaring me. What's going on?"

Taking a deep breath, I replied, "Remember at the start of the year we said we wanted normal. Normal classes, normal friends, normal relationships, and a normal life."

"Yes," she said slowly.

"Well, Zeta Rho Sigma will give us none of those things. Sof, I want you to drop out of the sorority."

I thought about this for days. I knew Leighton wanted me, but she wouldn't have Sofia too. Whatever was really going on in that house, couldn't change Sofia or who she was, but she didn't have to be around it either.

"Drop out of the sorority," she repeated.

I waited for her to say more. She didn't.

Sofia studied me for a long spell as the muffin dangled from her fingers.

"Let me ask this," she began. "Do you want me to drop out because Ezra was right all along?"

I nodded rather than speak.

"I'll write the resignation letter tonight."

I reached for her hands. "Thank you, Sof. Besides, you can still hang out with Keily, Palmer, and the girls. You're kicking butt in class and you snagged yourself a dashing, British boyfriend. You don't need the Sallys."

Sofia flushed. "He's not my boyfriend."

"Yet," I finished.

She sighed like I was the most frustrating person she ever met. "Anyway, you're right. The sorority was a fun thing for us to do together, but we never needed that place. We'll do something else. Join a club or devote more time to eating at every restaurant on this campus. Next week, we do the sushi place."

A weight lifted off my shoulders. What was I worried about? Of course, Sofia trusted me.

"I heard they have an amazing tempura chicken roll," I said. "Blair said if we try it once, the place will drain our bank account for the rest of our lives."

She scoffed. "Is that supposed to put us off? We'll go tomorrow."

My phone went off in the middle of me cracking up. I fished it out of my bag.

"One sec, it's Ezra." I hit accept. "Hey, how—"

"Valentina? Is this Valentina?"

I frowned. "Yes. Who is this?" An odd wailing sounded in the background. "What's that noise?"

"It's Austin from the Sam house. Valentina, you need to get to Mount Evergreen Hospital right away. Ezra's been shot."

A buzzing went off in my ear. I heard someone speak from far away. "What did you just say?"

"Someone shot him. He's on his way to the hospital now."

The phone clattered to the table. "Sofia, we have to go now."

"What?"

I snatched up my things and seized her wrist. "Right now!"

We ran the whole way to her car.

On the way to the hospital, the flood of calls came in from Maverick, Jaxson, Ryder, Caroline, and Amelia. It was a chaos of shouts, tears, confusion, and figuring out who would get to him first.

"I'm almost there," said Jaxson. "Five minutes."

"How did this happen?" I cried. "I just saw him. He took me to campus. I thought he was going to class."

"Baby, I... know where he went."

"What are you talking about?"

"There's something I need to tell you..."

EZRA

"...stupid..."

"...come to me..."

"I was trying to protect you guys."

"Your brother is in a hospital bed, Brian. How well did that work for you?"

I peeled my eyes open. No point in trying to sleep when they were at it again.

"And don't get me started on you three."

Ryder, Maverick, and Jaxson shrank into the couch.

"You should have come to me immediately," Mom snapped.

"I asked them not to."

Mom spun at my voice. "Oh, I'm sorry, sweetie. I didn't mean to wake you. Go back to sleep."

"There's no point. I'm being discharged today, right?"

I'd been in the hospital for over a week. Fate smiled on me that day and the bullet didn't hit any major organs. Even so, there was a long road ahead.

"Yes, you are, and you're coming home to recover. I won't hear any argument about it."

I did not dare argue with her. Mom was furious with everyone except for me and that was only because lying in a hospital bed with a gunshot wound plucked too many maternal feelings for her to yell at me. Brian and the boys were not stirring the same emotions.

"I told Ezra I was handling it," said Brian. "I didn't know he'd try to handle it himself."

Brian came over to my side. "Thank you for what you tried to do for me, but I'll never forgive myself for this. It's my job to save you. Next time, let me be the big brother." He smiled. "I promise I'll be a much better one from now on." Brian snaked an arm around Mom. "And a better son. I'm excited for me, Amina, and the girls to move into the manor."

"Me too." Mom kissed his cheek. "Having you all close by and safe while the police chase down the SOS will help me sleep better at night."

"At least they caught the shooter."

That was an "at least" I was pleased about. Dax made it all the way back to Brooklyn before Roman's conscience won out. It turned out he did recognize me from an old photo in Brian's house. Getting his younger brother shot was apparently where he drew the line on fucking up my brother's life, but putting one vicious piece of shit in jail wasn't enough to end an organization.

"They caught him and recovered the money, but the last I heard from the NYPD is that *Dax* isn't talking," said Mom. "I've dispatched my best to New York to begin digging into the SOS. I'll join them myself in a few weeks." She stroked my cheek. "After Ezra gets on his feet."

"You're leaving?" I asked.

"Yes, but your father will be here with you."

I turned my head to Hakim. He was sitting next to my bed where he'd been all week.

"What about your family?"

"You are my family, Ezra." He smiled. "They can spare me at home for a few more weeks. Besides, my wife and I were just speaking about the three of them coming to see you. It's past time you met your brother and sister."

"Hey, guys." I shifted to address Mom, Brian, and the boys. "Can you give us a second?"

One by one they filed out of the room, leaving us alone.

"Is something wrong?" he asked.

"Dad, there's something I've been meaning to talk to you about for a while," I began. "And after an experience like this, I've realized I may not have as much time to do that as I thought, so it's better to say it while I have the chance."

"I see." Hakim sighed as he straightened. He looked like a man preparing to face a firing squad. "I've been expecting this for a while, my son, and I'm ready. Everything you have to say, I deserve to hear. Don't feel you must hold back."

I collected all the anger, frustration, and disappointment brewing for the last nineteen years and finally said what I needed to say.

"I forgive you, Dad."

"You... forgive me?"

"You had a choice back then. You picked your home and your fi-ancée before you knew about me. I won't lie and say that growing up I didn't wish you made another one. It was hard knowing you could have hopped on a plane any time but chose not to."

Hakim dropped his head. "Oh, Ezra."

"We wasted nineteen years of my life being polite strangers to each other and I don't want to waste any more." I squeezed his shoul-der. "I forgive you, Dad. Let's start over."

Hakim placed his hand over mine. "I would like that very much, Ezra, and I want you to know that choice wasn't easy for me. If you can believe it, I thought I was doing what was best for you. I see now, much too late, that wasn't good for you or me. I will not let another nineteen years or nineteen months go without seeing you again."

I smiled. "I'm going to hold you to that."

"Ezra, sweetie?" Mom pushed open the door. "Can we come in? We have to finish packing your things to go home."

I looked from Mom to Hakim. "One more thing," I said to him. "Are you and Mom having an affair?"

Mom tripped into the room. "Ezra James Lennox!"

"We are not—"

"How could you suggest—"

"Asking your father such a question!"

Mom's face was beet red. "I'm so sorry, Hakim. I swear I raised our son with some *manners*!"

I grinned. "She did, but I've been shot, so I get to be blunt."

"You most certainly do not. Keep that fresh mouth quiet and let's go home." She bent over and kissed my forehead. "Cora made you something special."

"Oh, Cora. I missed her most of all."

VALENTINA

I moved the daisies across the room and set the peonies on the bedside table. I stepped back to admire my handiwork.

"What do you think, Adam? Will the flowers brighten up the room and make Daddy Ezra think of springtime?"

"Yes, Mommy. Flowers are pretty."

The four-year-old crossed the carpet and carefully placed Ezra's clothes in the dresser. Adam and I were happy to go ahead and prepare Ezra's room for his homecoming.

I picked up the baby on his way back and snuggled him to my chest. "You and I are going to stay over for a few days to take care of him. Would you like that?"

"Yes," he said, waving his little pudgy hands.

"Knock, knock," a voice called. "Val, it's lovely in here. Thank you so much."

Amelia came in and held open the door. Ezra followed, pushed in his wheelchair by Hakim. The boys were on their heels.

"Thank you, Val and Adam." Ezra pointed at the open box on the bed. "Couldn't resist helping yourself to my chocolates, though."

"Those are my chocolates actually," I said. "Austin gave them to me. He sent you the DVDs. He's a really nice guy, Ezra, and I'll admit I like him a hundred times more now."

Amelia smoothed back her son's hair. "He ran to help you while everyone else ran away. I'd say that earns him coming over for dinner."

"That's why I invited him over this weekend," he said. "We're going to watch some of those movies too."

"Hold up," Jaxson said. "Are you telling me Ezra made a friend other than us? Can he do that?"

Ezra busted out laughing and immediately regretted it. He clutched his chest, wincing. I rushed to his side while Amelia chased the others from the room.

"Want a snack, Adam?" she asked. "Cora made you cookies."

My son didn't need to be asked twice.

Everyone stepped out, allowing us time alone.

"Can I help you to the bed?" I asked.

"Only if you're going to join me."

I pecked his lips. "That comes later. There's something I have to talk to you about."

"What is it?"

"The day that you—" I tried again. "That day we promised to sit down and be honest with each other. It's time I did that, Ezra."

No more secrets. No more lies. I almost lost the man I loved with a thousand confessions on my lips. I don't care what Leighton does to me, I'm telling the truth.

"It's about the night I was attacked," I began. "It wasn't just Dimov I recognized. It was Logan too."

The light behind his eyes went out. "Val?"

I forced myself to keep going. "Hudson rescued me and brought me to the Sallys. Afterward, Leighton, Reagan, Patricia, and I went to his dorm."

I told Ezra the whole story—the murder, the blackmail, and the promise that her "friends" would take care of everything.

"Friends?" he hissed. "What the fuck is that? What kind of friends dispose of dead bodies for you?"

I met his gaze. "The same friends who kidnap people off the street and fake reasons for why they're gone."

"Sawyer," he said, his expression grim.

"You were right all along, Ezra. There is something very wrong going on behind the walls of those perfect houses."

He cupped my face. "Why didn't you tell me sooner?"

"The truth?" I whispered. "I was afraid of what would happen if you guys rushed in to save me. Leighton is unpredictable. She's dangerous. She knows things she shouldn't know, and she's fixated on me." My eyes swam with tears. "I can't stand for anyone else to get hurt, Ezra. There's been so much blood, death, and pain around me my whole life. I just wanted it to stop."

"It's okay." He gently brushed the wetness from my cheek. "I understand. You were scared, traumatized, and being blackmailed. You did what you had to do."

"No, I didn't, and it hit me while I sat next to your hospital bed. If I want this stuff out of our lives, I have to do something about it. No one is looking for Teagan or Sawyer, and Leighton is hanging a murder she committed over my head. Something has to be done."

"What are you going to do?"

I dried my tears and rose to my feet. "I'm turning her in. Leighton, Reagan, and Patricia. I'll tell the police about Logan and their *friends*. I'll deal with whatever happens after that."

"You won't do it alone, Val. You have us and we won't let Leighton carry out her threats."

I smiled. "I know you won't." I held my hands out to him. "Let's get you in bed. We can talk and get everything else out."

"I love you, Val."

"I love you too."

I PARKED IN FRONT OF the Sally house and shut off the engine. For a while, I stared at the pristine façade. I couldn't begin to understand what was going on. If they were a cult, they were hiding in plain sight because I doubt Mai, Keily, Palmer, or my other friends had a clue. No one on this campus had a clue that Leighton and Aiden were more than they appeared.

My talk with Ezra included the truth of the Sams' initiation ceremony. Aiden's cryptic taunt about Sawyer being in a better place solidified that I was doing the right thing.

I made the climb up the steps, holding that thought in my mind.

I'll give her one last chance to confess, and then I'm calling the police.

I walked inside and made it two steps before a sound stopped me. In the living room, three girls were huddled together crying.

"Palmer? What's wrong?"

"Val." She ran over and gave me a tight hug. "I'm glad you're here."

"What happened?"

She sniffled in my ear. "It's awful. We didn't want to tell you while you were with Ezra, but... Leighton's dead."

I went rigid. "Excuse me?"

"She's dead, Val. She went to visit her parents last weekend and got into a car accident on the way there."

Her parents?

My eyes rose to the ceiling and the bedroom above that didn't contain a single photo of family.

"Did anyone ever meet her parents?" I whispered.

"What?"

"Nothing." I hugged her back. "It's awful. I'm sorry you guys have been going through this."

"We're planning a memorial for her now. It'll be small, but it's something we can do."

"Who is in charge now?" I asked. "Reagan?"

I felt her shake her head. "Reagan left, Val. Her and Patricia. Leighton was their best friend and they couldn't face staying."

"They're gone?" Disbelief rooted me to the spot. All three of them gone in less than a week? "Did they tell you they were leaving?" I asked.

"No. They didn't want a sad goodbye, so they left during the night. They texted us after saying they loved us and good luck." Palmer let me go and pointed up the stairs. "Reagan did leave you something. We were going to bring it to you. It's in Leighton's old bedroom."

"Thanks." I gave her one last hug and headed upstairs.

Leighton's room was stripped bare. The fish tank headboard was gone. The draped ceiling was removed. All that was left of the hanging chair was the lone hook in the ceiling and a peek into the closet revealed neither clothes nor books. The only thing to see was the single wrapped present lying on top of the mattress.

I tore the paper, tossed it to the side, and lifted the cover.

Lying on top of the tissue paper was a bloody knife wrapped in plastic.

As I stared at the gruesome gift, I knew with certainty, Leighton was not dead.

"DEAD?"

"That's right," I said into the phone. "Apparently, she went to visit her parents and got into an accident. Just like Sawyer's supposed sister got in a car accident. They're all gone, Ezra."

"So what now?"

"I don't have Leighton. I don't have a body. And the murder weapon incriminates me. Our plan is ruined. If we're ever going to discover the truth about Sawyer, Teagan, the Sallys, and the Sams, I have to stick around and find more proof," I said. "Aiden or someone may slip up."

"I don't like this, Val. You said you were going to drop out."

"I can't now. We're the only ones who know something is wrong and you can't go near the Sams. Anyway, it's safer for me now. I have the knife."

"What will you do with it?"

"On my way to take care of it now."

Through the windows, dense forest surrounded me. Soon it would give way to miles of sandy beach and a teeming ocean. Few people lived out here and those that did were wealthy and obsessed with privacy. The only cars on this stretch of road for the last several miles were mine and a white car puttering behind me.

"I'm going to Jaxson's beach house to throw the thing in the ocean. No one will notice me and they won't care if they do," I said.

"Just be careful."

"I will. Love you. Bye."

I made good on my promise. I drove the hour to the beach house and flung the knife into the waves with all of my might.

Done. Now I'm going home to curl up with my son and my man. I'll figure the rest out tomorrow.

I got in the car and set off for home. Twenty minutes in, I squinted at the rearview mirror.

"Is that...?"

I picked up my phone and called Jaxson.

"Hey, baby. What—"

"Jaxson, I think I'm being followed." My eyes darted to the mirror and the same white car. "They were behind me on the way to your beach house and now they're following me back."

His tone sharpened. "Do you recognize them?" he asked. "Dad? Dad! Call the police."

"No, I— Hold on. They're getting closer."

The glare off the windshield made it nearly impossible to see. As the distance closed between us, I made out a green hood and white hands clutching the wheel.

"I'm not sure who it is," I admitted.

"It could be one of your security team."

"No, I told them not to follow me. I had to do something in private and—"

Suddenly, the car accelerated.

"Jaxson!"

They rammed my bumper. The force sent me and my phone flying. The seat belt snapped, biting into my neck, and I gasped from shock and pain.

"Val," I heard. "Val, what happened?"

"They hit me," I screamed. "They hit me on purpose."

The car came for me again.

The impact knocked me sideways and the car veered off the road. My screams tore the silence as I sped off the embankment headed for the trees. The last thing I saw before the impact was a squirrel scurrying out of the way.

Wicked

Valentina

I don't know the secrets that lurk within my sorority, and apparently neither does anyone else.

My search for the truth behind the disappearances meets with blank stares and pleas of innocence.

But someone knows.

They're watching. They're waiting. They're hiding. They're attacking the man I love.

The only way to put an end to it is to bend the Sallys to my will.

I'm taking over and hunting the kidnappers down.

Before the next person to disappear is me.

Jaxson

Valentina and I share a lot of things: a love of music, dancing, and the feeling that someone is out to get me.

A year of playing servant to the wealthy, demanding, and talented is what I expected.

But I wasn't ready for sabotage, malicious whispers, and an unknown enemy following me wherever I go.

Wicked is the one who promises with their lips but lies with their eyes.

When the unthinkable happens and Valentina is taken, I make a promise of my own.

I will save the woman I love... and destroy anyone who gets in my way.

Keep In Touch

Join Ruby's Mailing list for news, teasers, and more:
https://www.subscribepage.com/rubyvincentpage

ABOUT THE AUTHOR

Ruby Vincent is a published author with many novels under her belt but now she's taking a fun foray into contemporary romance. She loves saucy heroines, bold alpha males, and weaving a tale where both get their happy ever after.